Books by Peter De Vries

Let Me Count the Ways

Let Me Count the Ways

by Peter De Vries

Little, Brown and Company · Boston · Toronto

Published simultaneously in Canada
by Little, Brown & Company (Canada) Limited

PRINTED IN THE UNITED STATES OF AMERICA

Contents

STAN

one

MAN IS VILE, I know, but people are wonderful. Within a couple blocks where I lived as a child there was a woman who wore blotters in her shoes to absorb the unhealthy vapors that arise from the ground she said, and another who carried a chihuahua in a leather handbag zipped just far enough shut so its head could protrude from the top. We boasted a contractor who built a house on the wrong lot, and one of them cranks now largely disappearing from the American scene, who drive cars with signs on them reading, "This lemon was sold to me by the So-and-so Motor Agency." This bird also paid bills he considered exessive in inconvenient sackfuls of pennies. One of them utterly standard but in their way always refreshing crackpots. And let's see. There was a family named Muchbetter, who didn't seem to mind. They took it in stride. Our neighborhood hero was a bedridden man, Mr. Hadley, who played the trumpet flat on his back. In summers he would lie on the screened sleeping porch where he would keep we kids enthrawled blowing the saliva from a special valve in his instrument, slightly less so with his renditions of "Blue Moon" and "By the Waters of Minnetonka."

Most of those personalities have gone, and those of us who were kids then have grown up to take their place. One or two of us still live there on Sparrow Street, which exept for television aerials is still the same old neighborhood, rows of frame cottages so close together you can hear your neighbors quarrel and sometimes even snore, the back yards divided by fences over which our wives gossip and our bushes grow, so that we smell each others roses and eat each others razzberries. I married a woman from the Polish section of town farther down by the river. Elsie was a Wishnotski before she become Mrs. Stanley Waltz.

My wife is one of my favorite people. One day a few years after we were married I see a letter she wrote to one of them health commentators she listened to on the radio. It went: "Dear Mr. Emmett, Can you recommend a good book on personal hygiene? I think I've got it." At such times I just shut my eyes and imagine she's Hawaiian. Or that my senses are deceiving me and I didn't actually see or hear what I think. We all have to overlook things in one another, and what we overlook somehow adds in the end to the love, even when we are shaking our head over the other party. I could let such things roll off my back and come home after a day on the moving van and walk up to the stove where she's cooking dinner and with a friendly slap on the peach halfs say, "Well old girl, what are we suffering from today, acute diagnosis?" and no harm done. But there are limits to what a man can adjust to, the punches he can roll with. One blow fell that I was absolutely not prepared for. That threatened to finish us. She got saved.

Anybody who has ever been up against that sort of thing (I don't mean intellectual converts to Catholicism or cetera, I

4

mean being plain lowdown, cornball, meat-and-potatoes Jesus *Saves* saved) knows that such people are beyond redemption. When I heard Elsie singing hymns in the tub and saying grace over the food while it was still on the stove so it would include my portion too, I knew she was hopeless. She spent her spare time at the Gospel Mission where she first seen the light, or testifying on street corners and handing out religious tracks. Once when the piano crew I was working on that day came out of a diner where we had stopped for coffee-and, lo and behold there was my wife on the sidewalk handing out leaflets. Smilingly she hands one to McGurk, to Art Salerno — and to me! Her husband. I ask you to close your eyes a minute and imagine having your wife distribute you a pamphlet on the public street corner. What would you do? I said to her through my teeth when I got home: "Don't ever do that again."

"It's my duty to do everything I can to save your immortal soul."

"I haven't got any. Neither do you. How many times do I have to tell you? All right, where did Cain get his wife?"

"We're not going through all that again."

"The hell we aren't." I grabbed her by the wrist and swung her around from the icebox where she was. I had been drinking, as what husband wouldn't who wakes up and finds he's married to the bride of Christ. I pinned her arm behind her back and repeated, "Where did Cain get his wife? I won't let you go till you answer. Who must he of married, if we take the rational approach?"

"He married his sister," she said at last, and I let go, to let her rub her arm.

"All right. So incest. The whole human race is the product

5

of incest, some crown of creation, if your hodgepodge of ancient documents is true and the Blue Book I gave you to read on evolution is not." I sat down at the kitchen table with a bottle of beer. I brooded, wishing again she was a Catholic, a highly sophisticated sect where even the priests are educated enough not to know a damn thing about the Old Testament.

"I wish you wouldn't eat in your undershirt," she said. "It's so common. Nobody does that."

This sent me into a rage. "Then in that case it's not common, it's rare!" I said, rising, and, as luck would have it, belted her one.

"You ought to be ashamed of yourself," she would always say later, after this kind of extreme, and I would tell her, "I am! What kind of person do you take me for? This kind of thing is harder on me than it is on you. I got higher standards. That's why I wish you wouldn't rile me the way you do." We keep forgetting that people are a lot better and a lot worse than we sometimes think.

Insisting you're wrong and admitting it are two different things. Now I wanted to apologize to her. But one trouble. I have to be oiled just exactly right for that sort of thing. Its one of the most wearing things in human relations, worse than a pitched battle. I always need a few to get me into the mood — but that mood is a very narrow waveband and very short lasting. One too few and I'm not mellowed enough. One too many and *psshht*, I'm over the line and on the warpath again. Especially when one of your favorite people turns out to be this stranger, bringing your life to such a pass.

So the next day I am trying to limit my after-work intake to get into this pleasant simmer without boiling over. Then Elsie joins me in the parlor with a glass of vegetable juice left over from the health fad days and begins to lecture on the dangers of alcohol — which calls for a drink in itself. "It helps us bear things," I said, looking at a stack of pamphlets on the table. One or two were on booze. Yes, added to the evils now raising their heads in the house — faith, innocence, absolute honesty — was now temperance. She was after me to take the pledge put out by some Temperance Union she had joined under the influence of a woman she met at the mission, whose friendship was evidently important to her. This woman tells her, "People who drink have nothing within themselves."

I remedied that with another stiff double, and says, "You've got to *drink* to be temperant," bringing my fist down on the table in a way that awgured ill for any meeting of minds. "Temperance means moderation. You can only *take* something in moderation, not leave it alone. You're intemperant."

"I have never raised my voice to you in public or private."

"Well raise it. It'd be better than this patient longsuffering aimed at making you a martyr and me an I don't know what."

"I have never tried to make you out any such thing. You do it yourself. You say you're an atheist, and that's intellectual, but you behave on a completely physical plane the most of the time. And you don't realize what a spectacle you make of yourself, especially when you're strutting your stuff."

"When do I strut my stuff? Name some times. A few examples please. I'm all ears."

"You're doing it now. You do it on the truck when you get your back under a piano with a woman watching. This beautiful mass of muscle. You can't even go out and cut the grass or clip the hedge without an audience. A regular peecock."

"Drink is a better escape than church going or temperance unions or health fads. Isn't life hard enough without all these

7

damn solutions!" I said, sweeping the pamphlets to the floor. "Audience? Peecock? What are you talking about? Who is this stranger you're describing? Explanation please. Some enlightenment."

She took a sip of the vegetable juice, some cocktail hour together, some relaxation at the end of the day's weary toil.

"Have you ever noticed how you always manage to be out there when the college girls are out of their summer classes and going down to the river for a swim? You seem to time it, or spot them coming down the street in their shorts and halters, and instead of eyeing them, that would be human, you throw out your *own* chest and start showing off your beautiful brown muscles. Clipping the hedge naked to the waist, a splendid specimen of manhood."

"So this is Christianity. This is what Christ died for. This is how we practise it, his followers. What ever happened to the ignorant, delightful girl I married?"

"A regular Adonis furniture mover. Well that was all right years ago maybe, but you're older now, and yes fatter too. You could use for Pete's sake a halter yourself!"

That was when I hauled off and *psshht*, belted her another. People use to say they liked to visit the Waltzes but they'd hate to live there.

Naturally I worried about the effect of all this on our ten-year-old son, Tom. Was it already too late? A mother's influence can louse up a child emotionally at a very early age, psychologists tell us. They've shed some alarming new light on that. Unstable characters and the havoc they keep wroughting can definitely be traced to early maternal influences. The hand that rules the cradle rocks the world! I can remember my mother taking my hand when she thought she was dying and making me promise to go to church. She attended St. Michael's where most of the local Polaks went. I promised of course, with the fingers of the other hand crossed. What else can you do? I'm outside the pail, but I do have principles. St. Michael's was the church I wished Elsie had gone to. She wouldn't now be a convert to this godawful Gospel Mission in a rented store downtown, that she was trying to drag the kid to, this corny revivalism typical of the Bible Belt — which still exists you know, don't you forget it, and which runs through the entire country, not just the Middle West. Though what we're talking about here happens to be the Middle West. We live in a town called Slow Rapids, Indiana, really a small city of about 40,000 nestled in a bend of the Wayne River by a rather tame waterfall, as the name implies. Three miles upstream is a really boiling cataract from which the current abruply eases, broadening toward this gentle falls which even the unadventurous like to take in canoes.

All those years Elsie was harboring under the delusion that I was a potential convert too. The bitterness of my hostility proved that I was wrestling with God. Once she seen me dozing over a copy of *Awake!*, that Bible Society magazine I'm sure you've had thrust into your hand at one time or another too, and mistook it for open-mindedness. I made it clear that my mind was made up. I was not in the market. "Some sort of overall Intelligence I'll accept, yes," I said. "Farther than that I will not go." In time I abandoned even that position and became an out and out atheist. No doubt encouraged to that conclusion by the example set for the other position in my own house.

I got far more intellectual companionship from a friend of ours named Lena Salerno. Her husband worked for me at the

9

time. I own a small moving and storage business which I built up from scratch after a few years on the van for somebody else. Art Salerno wasn't the best furniture mover in Slow Rapids, being on the slight side, in fact he was called the hatbox man, which is movers slang for somebody who can't really lug his weight, but he could crate like a house afire. He did nearly all my packing and crating for long distance, but occasionally you had to send him out on the truck, sometimes even on the piano crew, where you just hoped he wouldn't strain his milk and wind up at the doctor's with another hernia. The Salernos and we were neighbors as well as friends, and stepped out as a foursome once a week or so to dinner or a movie, sometimes for a spin to Chicago, thirty miles away. There were times when I simply had to get the taste of provincialism out of my mouth and up to old Chi.

One night when we had a dinner date with the Salernos I hightailed it home early, leaving the office in charge of a girl who worked for me, with Art still crating on a job that had to go out to Denver first thing in the morning. I was bucking for a beer with Lena before our respective spice arrived. I needed somebody sympathetic to unload my head of steam on or I'd be a foul ball the whole evening. I dressed while waging the usual battle with my wife over the big crisis — how to raise the kid. "You want to raise him as a believer," I says in the bathroom doorway drying my back after a shower, "I want to raise him as an atheist. O.K. we'll compromise. We'll bring him up an agnostic. That's my last offer. That'll be middle ground, from where he can make up his own mind later." Elsie said, "That logic is a little like your argument when we were going together, remember? You said, 'You want to get married, I don't. We'll compromise — we'll live together.' " "That was a joke," I shouted, "for Christ's sake!" "I hope so, Stan," she said, and giving me a serious look added softly, "for Christ's sake." I pretended she was Hawaiian and got dressed.

I once read something in a magazine I'll never forget. It was a quotation from a writer whose name I can't recall. Maybe it was somebody named Swift. He said: "You can't reason a person out of a position he hasn't been reasoned into." Check, but away we reason — to stone walls. What got my cork was Elsie's refusal to be ruffled any more than she could be budged. All my rantings, which finally become blasphemous, were met with the same meek longsuffering: she was witnessing for the truth while men reviled her. Not being able to get a rise out of her was like the frustration of trying to slam a door with one of them suction stops on it — which was the case with the screen door I tried to huff out of. It just sprang back at me with a Christian sigh. I had more luck with the alley gate out of which I turned to walk the half block to the Salernos.

So to wake up and find your married to somebody who isn't an intellectual companion can be one of the worst things on earth. I don't mean I'm a brain, or anything much more than just another Polak piano mover who worked up his own business, a lot more than most people get to achieve, let's not forget that, but I do try to use what gray matter God gave me. Oops, there isn't any. I do try to read my way out of the ignorance and superstition I was born into. Ingersoll, Tom Paine and Clarence Darrow are my heroes. Well the main thing is that Tom must have a college education and climb out altogether, and on that Elsie is at least agreed. She has got law on her mind for him, I don't know why. Probably because the only relative she has who made it is a lawyer, a shirttail cousin in Chi who got into Polak ward politics there, she claimed, and worked his way up to persecuting attorney (sick). I don't care what profession Tom chooses but profession he shall have as long as his father can hump furniture.

I hoped Lena Salerno would be ready when I got there.

two

LENA WAS SETTING out nuts and potato chips on the terrace where we were to have our drinks. She is a horse, but at forty still firm in outline, beautifully rounded muscle, not fat. No, not by a long shot yet. We should have her carrying keyboard on the piano crew instead of Art! That was what I often thought working the heavy corner beside Art as we came downstairs under a soggy Chickering upright, most of the weight on my hump.

Lena is one of them Earth Mothers they call them, a burst of sheer Life Force that kills everything in its path. Flattens all oppositions in a scorched earth policy. A childless Earth Mother has to work off this creative energy in some form, and hers was disseminating birth control information for some society fighting the population explosion, endeavoring to educate people to the evils of overcrowding the planet and one thing and another. So she hands out tracks too but what a difference! "Don't fill hungry bellies with more babies," was a typical title. When she wasn't distributing tracks she was meeting with reasonable Catholics who are trying to get the church to liberalize its stand.

There was no want of subjects for missionary work right here on Sparrow Street. Next door to the Salernos was a family named Gromulka with five, six, finally now eight kids, and the usual nother one on the way, no need to go to India with the pamphlets. Mrs. Gromulka, the neighborhood blimp, resented the pamphlets Lena was always trying to hand her, and finally refused to accept no more. So Lena would fling them over the high stockade fence that separated their back yards, calling out, "Read this through please, Mrs. Gromulka. See what you're *doing* to the world. We must stop breeding from the bottom!" And back Mrs. Gromulka would holler in even shriller tones, "I'll breed any way I damn please! What we do is none of your business," and back the pamphlet would come over the top of the fence, fluttering like a dead bird at Lena's feet.

There had been just such a low scene when I turned in at the alley gate I could tell. The tail-end of Mrs. Gromulka's diatribe could be heard as Lena set out the snacks. I could tell she was boiling, her complexion having that mottled look it takes on when angry. The screen door over there banged shut on the wail of some child being dragged into the house.

"Mrs. G. sounds fit to be tied," I says.

"She *should* be tied." That's our Lena — funny as a crutch and twice as perceptive. Her humor is bitter. "There ought to be a law demanding it — or sterilizing the husband. Serious thinkers are beginning to urge it. That when a man who already has more children than he can support has another one, he should be sterilized. It's a simple operation that in no way interferes with sexual pleasure."

I changed the subject by giving her a pat on the peach halfs and complimenting her on how she looked. She wore a watermelon red linen dress with a high neckline cut straight across the shoulders, a beltless thing under which her body, tanned the coppery red of tiger lilies, moved with animal ease. Lena is a proxide blonde.

She paused at the door, after taking my order for a beer, and said with one of them pregnant pauses that are the extent of her fertility, "I can't ask you in, Stan. Art isn't home yet."

I hadn't made a move to follow her in, but it was her way of indicating that there was Something Between Us. No minority report from me. She built it up by constantly denying it. The first inkling I had of it was the statement that it couldn't be. We had been walking by the river one night, Art and Elsie up ahead and we behind, when she stumbled over a root or stone or so and I caught her hand. She withdrew it slowly with a significant look and said, "We better leave it the way it is, Stan." There hadn't been anything to leave the way it was, but now there was. I had no doubt she told Art out of a clear sky, "There's nothing between Stan and me — absolutely nothing," thereby putting the bee in his bonnet too. Lena don't need no chastity belt but she needs a good belt across the chops three, four times a year. Oh, I suppose it's all the human need to inject a little drama into our drab lives, or to use one of the phrases Lena is always stealing from writers she reads or plays she sees, "to recover a little of the lost poetry from the prose of existence." Sometimes its fresh snow on the whatsis. Slush of disenchantment. Shenanigans with Lena would of involved all your waking hours, but there was another objection. The endless intellectualizing you'd have to pay for it with. You would have to get around to it by long discussions about the changing sexual morays of our time, the need to purge the Puritan ethic from the American conscience, et cetera. It just seemed too much red tape to go through to unknot a halter that when you got it unknotted you would have 2, 3 lbs. of potato salad. Still there were times when just to look at Lena made me feel like my blood was carbonated.

Now, standing out there in the back yard while she waited with the screen door in her hand for some sort of reply, I just said, "Stan Waltz has decided to take unto himself a wife but he hasn't decided yet whose," and thrun a peanut at her.

Waiting for my beer, I admired again what Lena had done with the yard. It was the dinky 25 by 50 ft. we all had on Sparrow Street, but she had laid it out beautifully in a single big cross of gravel walk with a bird bath in the center and four triangles of flower beds around it. The gravel was pink — a Japanese idea I think. "They do their decorations with such economy," she said the evening we had initiated the new yard with an outdoor barbecue. "They have to, they don't have no money," said Art from the charcoal grill, and Lena said, "I'm talking about artistic economy. It's *space* they don't have." Though I had thought what Art thought she meant too, I returned her look with an understanding smile, which was like copping a feel. I sometimes despair of ever meeting my standards. Still in all my faith in this human stuff was restored again as I thought how much we all meant to each other, taking in the garden there in the cool of the evening, how much we manage to do on our modest incomes while the wicked flourish like the green bay tree. Beyond the tracks was the vulgar element.

"Hey I want to talk to you before Els and Art get here," I called into the kitchen. Just then she kicked the screen door open and came out with a tray with two drinks in tall glasses of plastic silver with foliage on top. Beer was never served with a sprig of mint to the best of my knowledge. "I thought you might like a Pimm's Cup first," she said. "You can have all the beer you want later." It's another one of her drinks with a cough remedy base, but I put it loyally down as I sit across from Lena getting her viewpoint on the crisis she knows all about and wants to hear the latest on.

"I'm living with a different person. I'm a different person," I told her. "My life isn't the same. It certainly isn't my life. I no longer recognize my existence. Her faith is something she's 'got,' like the personal hygiene. What am I going to do?"

Lena sits on the glider thinking. She crosses and uncrosses her legs, sprawls back, leans forward for potato chips and nuts, spanks the salt from her hands. She goes on thinking, the springs of the glider groaning under the strain, her face screwed up in a variety of expressions.

At last all at once the fruit of this deliberation: "I can't communicate with Art."

This deal I am familiar with — whole marriages are based on it — but it hardly answers my question. I don't begrudge Lena her style of living, the dramatic airs, but how about me for a change? Besides a wife, I have a child.

"How should I handle it?"

"What?"

"Elsie. What am I going to do about this situation? That obtains?"

"I know exactly how you feel. Oh don't I just! He needs a little more lemon in him! That's his main trouble. If he'd only get up on his hind legs once and tell somebody something *back* . . ."

She rises and begins to pace, breathing smoke and wagging a cigarette holder the size of a clarinet. I take in the nutbrown legs, the thighs that churn you to butter. How would it be if I had married her instead of Elsie? She was always the intellectual of the crowd, not being able to communicate and so on, even in the old days when we were young. A copy of *Redbook* or *Cosmopolitan* always under the arm, always leading the boys in the drugstore from the soda fountain to the paperbacks. Always the one to stop on the way out of the movie and complain to the manager, "Why don't you show some foreign films once in a while?" (Answer: "They're in another language.") Lena was always a big *zaftig* girl, dominating the group even without speaking. What would *she* do if Art reared back on his hind legs and started telling people where to get off at? It might start at home, this identity stuff, like charity. I open my mouth, but it is little use for the moment exept to eat another potato chip washed down with Pimm's Cup.

"A little more starch! In everything, all walks of life. That's what he needs. Starch." She stops as though making a mental note to have him pick some up from the store on his way home from work. "Why for instance does he let you tell him to stay overtime and finish a crating job after he's been out on the truck all day? Why doesn't he tell you to hire him for one thing or the other? If you want him to crate, let him crate full time and you hire another helper for the truck."

"We have an average of two, two and half days furniture to crate a week, Lena. We're a one-horse outfit. Only two trucks."

"He's meek with waiters. Such a mollycoddle! He never tells them to take it back to the kitchen when they bring him the wrong thing and get them what he ordered, or the right thing but it's burned. To a crisp! Or even when they bring me the wrong thing, his wife. When somebody bumps into him, *he* says excuse me. He apologizes to tables and chairs. A regular Casper Milktoast."

I remember Lena's admiration when I took the plunge and went into business on my own, mortgaging my kidneys to buy a truck, then her bewilderment when I can't stand being cooped up in the office I aspired to and have to go out on the truck again to get the feel of a loaded dresser on my back or my shoulder under a piano — that weight a man can feel in his marbles. If I was her husband, would I have to take lip for this public forfit of social standing I had worked so hard to get? Would we be always clanging the status cymbals?

Lena sits down again, and in the silence that I haven't taken advantage of, being sunk in these thoughts of my own, she continues but in a quieter, more brooding vane.

"So he has this sense of weakness that he has to make up for in little ways. He'll deliberately leave his beer bottle in the living room after dinner when is it any trouble to take it to the sink on retiring? A gesture of independence, that makes me subservient. He'll leave his socks where he drops them, and his underwear, for me to pick up and throw in the laundry — to assert his masculinity a minute. Then there'll be little digs, things will start coming out, especially after a few drinks. You wouldn't expect it from Art, would you? All this is a revelation. This is a total surprise to you, the quiet little lamb of a guy who wouldn't hurt a fly. And he *is*, and he *wouldn't*, exept with a little Dutch courage under his belt and the universal human habit of taking things out on those closest to us. They're the only ones available at the time."

A longer silence falls. I run the tip of my finger around the rim of my drink. An unexpected intimacy has sprung up between us. First Art's socks, then his underwear, and now sly digs at her. A door closes somewhere, a car starts up in the alley and drives off, a tinkle of voices and laughter — the symphony of the summer night. Lena looks away, sitting against the side of the glider with her arm along its back. She drums the pad with her fingers.

"Did you know that he could belch whole sentences?"

"What do you mean?"

"It's a trick. He started in to do it with a buddy in the war. They were drinking beer in a bar in Germany, fooling around, getting kind of high and crazy, and they began to *talk* in belch after a drink. That was what they called it. Then some other American soldiers at another table joined them, and they had a contest to see who could belch the longest sentence. One of the officers was educated and got this experiment really going. Have you ever heard of a writer named Oscar Wilde?"

"No."

"Well, he defined all German poetry as attenuated beer belching, according to the officer, a Rhodes scholar. They began to belch the German classics. 'Ich Weiss Nicht Was Soll Es Bedeuten Dass Ich so Traurig Bin.' That's that song we use to sing in school, remember, the 'Lorelei,' but it was originally a poem by Hiney. I don't think this promotes international understanding, but they were going along with the gag like a bunch of kids. Kids do this you know. Anyhow Art got pretty proficient at it, and came home with that ability. Now when he's horsing around the house he'll start it, partly because he knows it annoys me — just exactly somewhat like kids doing something they know annoys their elders. He has to have a few drinks in him. Once he belched the entire Pledge of Allegiance. If he hadn't done his share in the war I'd have reported him to the FBI. When he got to the 'under God' that Eisenhower stuck in, that he feels the same way about as you, it came out with such a roar that it was simply appalling. At such times he can be an absolute *chlop*."

"The entire Pledge of Allegiance in one belch?" I said. Not that I asked out of anything but normal curiosity. I didn't want any more information about this house. This would be quite enough, thank you. "In one running broad-jump?"

"No, no. You stop after a string of words to fuel up for air. What prompts a person to behave in such a manner? A person who's had every opportunity, a fine marriage. What sense of satisfaction can there possibly be in it for them, what feeling of achievement? I honestly ask you that. You've been through eighth grade."

I honestly couldn't answer. It wasn't for me to say. We're complex creatures, infinitely mysterious is the human spirit. Why is everything so mixed in with its opposite? Nobility with moral squaller, love with hate, the sublime with the ridiculous. Once in a diner booth I seen a deaf and dumb couple, and they were *quarreling*. There they were blurting out things with their fingers they'd later regret. Should you laugh or cry? I remember it as a fantasy. The scene here was fantastic enough, because watch. See what happens next. Here I had come to wonder out loud, air, why I was married to Elsie, and staying to wonder what Lena was doing united to Art. Still you have to be careful about judging marriages from the outside. Anything ridiculous on the surface may have all the more value to it underneath. I have a rule. When I see something that makes absolutely no sense whatever, I figure there must be a damn good reason for it.

"Oh, God!" Lena suddenly exclaimed, swatting the table. "The things that go on! With what life does to all of us, how can people do the things they do to each other! Oh, God!"

"Oh, shut up!" came a voice from the next yard. "Can't we ever have any peace and quiet around here?" It was Mrs. Gromulka probably listening at the stockade fence, thinking she was getting an earful of a marital squabble. Her way of lashing back no doubt. So again — where does reality leave off and fantasy begin?

"Oh, shut up yourself!" Lena called back without turning her head. "Go on back to your love life. There's only two billion of us on the planet, half of them starving, so go on replenish it some more. Go on with the copulation explosion. We can hear you half the time. We lie there listening to you, like beasts. Of the field! What do I care? Where were we?"

"How Art has no gumption and is always tyrannizing over you with — "

At this point the screen door squeaked open and the object of this discussion himself came out — Art Salerno.

He couldn't of been a nicer dark-complected guy with horn-rim glasses and a ready smile. Exept that the smile was kind of sly, coming at you around the corner, as though he knew something to your disadvantage. It was only out of the goodness of his heart that he wasn't blabbing it around. Well neither did I blab it around that he left a lot to be desired on the keyboard, which is the least important position on a piano crew.

"Hello, *paisan*."

"Hello, *chlop*," I says, returning it in Polish. "Els is still waiting for the sitter, so I thought I'd mosey over and have a quick one with you all. Did you get the job finished?"

"Just — with the last nail in the keg. Remember to order some of the six-penny. And we're nearly out of one-by-fours."

I don't know whether he kissed his wife when he came home or not as a general rule, but probably not judging from the clumsy production made of it now for my benefit. First he went around the table, kicking its leg and mumbling some apology to it as he went by, then he leaned down over the glider with one hand on the back rail of it, so that the glider swung back and made him lose his balance and miss Lena as he bent over her. She steadied it and helped him complete the ritual, rolling an eye at me as she raised her well-lipsticked mouth. "You smell like Naphthalene," she said, the moth flakes we strew furniture that's going into storage with. "Not that I don't rather like it. I think some of the most wonderful smells are those you'd least expect. Coffee is another."

"And gasoline," I said. "I like gasoline fumes."

We all looked at Art to see if he had some favorite fume to contribute to the discussion, and after a minute he says, "Tar."

"Tar has a certain nostalgic quality to it," Lena said.

"Not only that, it takes you back. To when you were kids. My whole past won't go by me no faster when I drown than when I get a whiff of tar," Art said. "Remember the smell of streets being paved, Stan? I can still remember that summer when they paved the street in front of the fireworks factory. The whole summer is in one whiff of tar. Vacations, going barefoot. We use to chew the stuff. It's suppose to be good for your teeth."

When Art went in to wash I sat on the glider beside Lena to show we had nothing to hide. "Where the hell is Elsie?" I said, glaring at my wristwatch. A few minutes later the gate opened and she came into the yard, her hair combed in a bun, in the shiny blue dress that sent up detrimental highlights.

Lena was always trying to give her pointers on how to dress and make up. She begged her to stay away from shiny "ribbon counter fabrics" she called them, which tended to drain out the little color she has in her face. Elsie has a clear but very pale skin, lily-like, and the exeptionally high cheekbones of the Wishnotski tribe sometimes make her cheeks look hollow, even sunken, when she isn't careful about dresses and cosmetics. "Strive for soft fabrics and gentle colors that won't wash out your skin and your pale blue eyes," Lena said. Elsie never paid much attention, and now that she had her mind on eternal things and not the material aspects of this life that don't matter, she didn't pay any at all. I was surprised to see Tom traipsing after her through the gate, reading a comic as he walked.

"Do you mind if he has a Coke with us?" she said. "The Kovacs girl can't sit tonight because her folks are going out and she has to stay home with their pack. But it's perfectly all right to drop Tom off by Kovacs and leave him there."

"Of course!" said Lena, zeroing in on the kid with a hearty smack. "Cokes I'm out of, but I just got a lot of Seven-Up to put in the Pimm's Cups. Pimm's Cup O.K. for you, Els?"

"Anything will do, Lena," said Elsie with her freedom from all mundane matters. "It makes no difference."

Tom wiped the lipstick from his cheek and sat on the glider with the comic. He hadn't raised his eyes from it since com-

23

ing in the yard, reading it with a steady grin on his fox face. He has a pointed nose that seems to grow sharper as his smile broadens.

"Why don't you read a book once in a while, Tom?" I said, watching him. "Do you want to be a Polak all your life?"

"Paderewski was one, as I recall," said Elsie.

I closed my eyes, thinking hard. "Paderooski," I said, imitating her pronunciation. "I don't believe I ever heard the name. Though there was a Paderevski some years ago who was a great concert pianist."

Elsie's Christian humility has an arrogant streak in it (like Christ's). I'm not condeming or defending, only pointing out another example of opposites going together. Abraham Lincoln was suppose to've had this arrogant streak. Elsie's came out in this pretending to be Americanized and so superior to the first and second generation Poles. But (here we go again with paradox) it took the form of not pronouncing Polish names the way the hunkies beneath her and the Americans above her would — that is correctly. So it was out of giving herself airs that she made mistakes, and out of the vow to make Tom educated that I tried to make him sound like the great-grandparents and other neighborhood oldtimers I wanted him to be as unlike as possible. Let him even learn some Polish, a second language. Human relations can become so screwy you can't make head or tail of them. There was another skirmish in the war over religion.

"They've got books by the Kovacs," Elsie said, "and they've certainly got a Bible. He can go on with the Old Testament stories. You've agreed about that."

"As stories yes. I have no objection to that. As stories, some real, some myth, of an ancient people with their own particu-

lar tribal deity named Jehovah. How far have you got, Tom?"
I asked him pleasantly.

Without raising his eyes from Toots and Casper he said,
"Samson," turning a page. "The part where he kills the lion
with his bare hands."

"Those are all exciting stories," Elsie said. "The Bible is
exciting — it doesn't have to be dull. Far, far from it. But it's
important for a person to read it all the way through from
beginning to end. Too many educated people are completely
ignorant of spiritual matters."

"What's spiritual about tearing a lion in half with your two
hands? Or rain coming down for forty days and forty nights,
or living in a whale's belly for a while? Let's not use words like
that too loosely."

"What's spiritual about it? Incidentally the Bible doesn't
say whale, it says a big fish. But let that pass. The length of
time Jonah was in it was three days, thereby symbolizing
Christ's death and resurrection after three days. The Old
Testament is a preparation for the New. It foreshadows the
events in it."

"Correction, foreshadows what some people think are
events, others myths. What about this resurrection? Who
said he arose? Where's the witnesses? Affidavits please?"

Lena came out in the thick of this and said, "At it again?
I'm not sure it's good for two parents to make a debating society out of a marriage in front of the kids."

"Why not?" I said, taking the beer which she now had the
decency to hand me. "It gives the child both sides to the
question *and* shows him his parents give him credit for enough
intelligence to make up his own mind. Later of course, when
all the votes are in, when all the precincts have been heard

25

from. Let them hear from all the precincts, they can take it. Eh, Tom? Tom!"

The kid's seeming indifference to the subject Els and I took to be just that, but Lena said it was a defense mechanism — there is a lot of that going around, to judge by the reports — concealing deep wounds resulting from the family division.

"Anyway, he doesn't want to be a minister or a lawyer or anything like that," I said, throwing a peanut at him. "He wants to quit school and work in the fireworks factory all his life. Or spend it humping pianos. Eh, Tomasko?" I reached over and rumpled his head, shaking an extra grin out of him. "And I'll pay you ten cents an hour for washing your face."

We dropped him at the Kovacs and drove in my car to a steak house by the river, where our eye was caught by an outdoor art exhibit. Or Lena's was, and nothing would do but we see it before eating. For me this was one of those unexpected turns in the road that life takes us on without any warning and without our in the least dreaming what lies in store for us around the bend.

There were about ten or a dozen local artists with their paintings standing on easels and nailed to fences and even hung on bushes, the usual mixture of schools. Our foursome began to break up like an ice flow as generally happens when each follows his fancy, and so at one point I found myself standing before an oil of a horse that I figured was probably a self-portrait judging from the general execution, when someone appeared at my side who accepted responsibility for it.

She was a woman of about forty, so much like Lena in size and even appearance that I thought at first it was her, and checked a remark just in time. She explained it was an early effort of the kind she had outgrown for abstracts, to several of which she now led me. They weren't bad. I know a lot of fun is poked of these things, but I'm usually able to enjoy a picture — or not — entirely irregardless of its type. Take it on its own terms, what's all the sweat? A mass (or even mess) of color and lines for their own sake can give you a sort of kick. And as for those conglomerations of stuff with newspaper headlines, whiskey labels and chicken bones stuck in them, why not? What is life but a conglomeration of newspaper headlines, whiskey labels and chicken bones for each of us to make his own head nor tail out of? The colors in the oils the woman now showed me were laid on in thick layers in a kind of painting called antipasto painting or something like that I believe. Green-eyed and blonde, she made herself up in the same technique. She had a mouth like a shrimp cocktail like Lena. Her pictures had a zing to them, and I told her as much in so many words. One was a bitter commentary on the futility of trying to strive for the kind of beauty they did in olden times, when it was all a fraud and a delusion anyway but nobody knew it. This consisted of an old-fashioned gilt frame that the canvas was put *around*, in a hollow square, typifying she said a frank recognition that the artist no longer has anything to say.

"I'll buy that," I said.

"Oh, wonderful. Do you want to take it with you or leave it till the end of the show? A small deposit will hold it. I have a price of fifty dollars on it."

"No, I don't mean I want to buy the painting. I just mean

27

that I agree with what you're trying to say in it. I see eye to eye with you."

"Oh," she said rather sadly. I felt so embarrassed that I stood there letting her point out some of the painting's merits I might otherwise of overlooked in a spiel lasting ten, fifteen minutes, while my party vanished completely from view. The use of a nasal spray to get a rippled effect on the paint for a finishing touch was honest despair, she said, not bad faith or intellectual perversity.

"I like it quite well, but I like that one even better, I think," I said, pointing to another, just to give me something else to seem to be wavering between, and thus ease myself off the hook. "Oh, I like all these much better over here."

"I'll tell Bruno Hoffman," she said. "His start over there."

This was really a hell of a note. I couldn't go and I couldn't go till I had patched this booboo up somehow. This woman might be going through menopause, a nervous breakdown or what not. I caught a glimpse of my party way down at the other end of the exhibit, looking for me. But I couldn't leave till I had smoothed this over, which meant hanging around to admire her work a little more in as casual a way as possible. It was a hot night. I had left my coat in the car, and I had on one of those Harry Truman sport shirts with the palm trees that are plenty representational and short sleeves. I stood in profile to the woman with my gut sucked in and a thumb hooked in my belt so as to show off the muscle of my right arm, the majority of which is covered with tattoos.

At last the woman came over.

"Have you ever posed?" she asked.

"No ma'am, I never have."

"You have a magnificent build. What do you do, may I ask?"

"I'm a furniture mover."

"Ah. Well I could use one of those too. I've got a piano I can't get rid of." She laughed. "Have you ever tried to *discard* a piano? It's a sort of monstrosity my mother's had in the apartment, that's just cluttering the place up. But nobody wants it. The Salvation Army doesn't want it, the settlement house doesn't want it, even the town disposal won't take it. Nor a private trash man I called about it. He said it isn't 'reasonable refuse.' " The woman laughed again. "It's one of those crazy no-way-out Samuel Beckett situations."

"He that new cartage outfit in town?"

"No, no, this is the theatre of the absurd, where there's no solution to anything. Do you see any solution to it? I mean you must have situations like this, where somebody doesn't want a piano moved *to* anywhere, just *out*. Where do old pianos go when they die? They must go somewhere."

"To charity places, other people. Somebody who might want one for a rumpus room or something."

"Nobody wants this. Don't think I haven't tried to unload it! So now what do I do? Chop it up and slip it piecemeal into the garbage? Pour kerosene on it in the back yard and burn it up? Or what?"

I stood there thinking, enjoying the smell of perfume and the rise and fall of a bosom in a green silk blouse while I turned over the crisis vexing their owner — who watched me through horn-rim glasses. I had seen a comedian eat a pair just like it on television the night before. His were props without lenses of course, probably carmel or taffy he could stuff into his mouth and chew up for a finish to a skit where he was distracted by lust. A state of mind I appreciated. Suddenly I had an inspiration. "Just a minute," I said.

I turned and by dint of wigwagging like a lunatic got the attention of the other three and then got them to come back. When they did I asked Elsie, "Would the Gospel Mission like a piano? You have nothing but that portable organ you take out on the street don't you? This lady has one she'll very kindly give you."

"Oh, that's very charitable of you," Elsie said to her, "but I think a family is donating us one. What kind do you have?"

"It's an old Mendenhall upright." I winced but said nothing. That's a piece of antideluvian artillery that hasn't been made since around 1920. I only saw two in my life, and I would rather move the truck up and down stairs.

We left it that Elsie would find out for sure about it and I would call the woman, who scribbled her name and number on a piece of paper in return for one of my business cards, which I always carried in my wallet. Elsie contributed to the exchange by handing the woman one of the leaflets she carried in her bag. "I don't know whether you're saved or not, but I'd like you to take this home and read it. It may change your life." The woman saw what it was and quickly put it in the pocket of her skirt, not before I saw it was the one entitled "Where will you spend eternity?" with a picture showing heaven like a magnificent hotel and the line "You can make your reservations now. Simply call Jesus." The woman's name was Ona Mervin I saw as we walked away, and I lagged a step behind to make sure the telephone number on the slip of paper was elegible before tucking it into my billfold.

The incident made me a foul ball at dinner. We went to a

fish house with outside tables where you could smell the cooking from a Chinese restaurant across the street. Parading within view of us was one of those religious nuts that it's a mistake to think are limited to cartoons. I have seen them on the streets of New York and Chicago as well as here, ranting away and waving their Bible. This one didn't preach. He carried a placard predicting the end of the world, besides handing out leaflets in which he specified the exact date of the Second Coming as worked out by his interpretation of Revelation — Monday, June 11. Two weeks from now.

"Let's all remember to put it down on our appointment calendar," I said.

Elsie was reading a leaflet she took from him when he passed us. She knew him from the mission, and had exchanged a few words with him. "I don't think it's right trying to prophesy the exact day," she said, "but the end is coming some time, and he may be correct. Who knows? It says in Isaiah the heavens will be rolled together as a scroll. Have you ever thought what an atomic explosion looks like? Just like a scroll. Mock all you want, but you're trifling with your immortal soul."

I had drunk three whiskies by the time our fish came and now poured out some beer from my bottle. Art poked his trout with his fork, as though making sure it wasn't still alive before tackling it. I said, "Did you know I could belch the entire Ten Commandments?" Lena laid a hand on my arm across the table and said, "Everything is relative. With the Persians it's a sign of courtesy to your host. That you enjoyed the meal." See, with Lena always the obscure fact, the little-known detail.

When we squared up I made sure again I had the slip with

the woman's name and phone number on it. But that wasn't necessary. Two days later she telephoned me at the office to check whether the mission could use the piano, and I had to report that they already had one.

"Oh, dear. That leaves the last resort — the city dump. How much would you charge to take it there?"

"It's twelve dollars an hour for three men, and five dollars for the first flight of stairs and three dollars for each additional flight. What floor are you on?"

"Third, at 21 Poplar Street. Just off the river."

"It'll come to over twenty dollars. I'll make it twenty."

"Lordy. That's a lot of money just to throw something away. You couldn't use a nice oil, could you? That blue and gold one with the leaves that you admired? I had a price of sixty dollars on it."

"Oh, I couldn't do that to you, lady. I know you artists need the money."

three

ONE LOOK AT that stairway and I knew the piano would have to go out the window by block and tackle — another twenty dollars. Even getting a little apartment spinnet under them low headers and around them corkscrew turns into the light of day would be like giving birth to something, and the Mendenhall upright staring us in the face was twice the size and weight. We had McGurk with us to top it, but my regular keyboard man, Bill Bascomb, was on a long haul to Detroit, and so Art Salerno was working keyboard today.

In view of all this I was relieved we had to swing the dinosaur, but nervous about breaking the news to the woman, who wasn't going to like the extra twenty smackers. We were all up in her studio waiting for her to get off the phone so we could tell her. McGurk sat on the floor snoozing with his back to the wall, like a Mexican taking a siesta, which is what he makes out of any delay, while Art Salerno walked around rubbering at the pictures. I avoided them, not wanting to be seen admiring something and having it shoved on me as payment at this junkture. After all I appreciated the woman's point — we were only taking the fiddle out to the dump. Out of the tail of my eye I looked for the leaf study I was suppose to be mad about, without success.

She was chattering away about the prize awards with somebody who had also been hung in the show, and between them I gathered they differed violently with the jury's selections. She was dressed in spattered white garageman's overalls with a smock over them, and the horn-rim glasses were shoved up onto her forehead. She sat on a low stool with her back to us, so I figured it was safe to go on a cautious tour of the paintings, at least those behind her.

Stepping over McGurk, I saw several that I recognized from the exhibition, both the representational and the non. Then suddenly there were several canvasses in a whole nother vane. Either she was living with somebody who also painted or she was going through more periods than you could shake a stick at. These were vague dreamy landscapes of moonlit woods and misty rivers you could hardly make out they were executed with such feeling. Nocturnes I guess you'd call them. Even the scenes that weren't nighttime had this vague poetic feeling — like nocturnes during the day. Why

33

had I missed these at the outdoor show, if they were there?

Art Salerno, working his way from the other direction, bumped into me in front of a seascape. Together we viewed it.

"Jesus," he said under his breath.

"Oh, I don't know." I must admit now that he gravels me, so that I can hardly agree with him even when he expresses an opinion I share. "I rather like it," I lied.

"If she could only make up her mind."

"She's been going through different periods."

"She was going through one when she painted this thing."

I ignored the vulgarity of the remark. It's the kind of joke you might think of but wouldn't say. I could increasingly appreciate Lena's beefs about this man. At the same time I was glad he deserved them. It justified my cause with Lena, or would if I ever got to have one. Lena made me think of the woman and I turned to her thinking, "Christ lady, do you want to cauliflower your ear with that damn telephone?" Then I thought of my wife, and in a fit of rage at the sheer difference I looked at the woman and said mentally, "I'd like to pin you to the mattress, baby, I'd like to split you in two like a broiler." I prodded McGurk with the toe of my foot. He smiled up at me like a child awakened from sleep, shoving his cap off his dirty face. Strong as an ox and twice as bright, I like McGurk. No complications. The best piano topper in the business and no complications. He jerked his head toward the woman, who was rattling away about something in the show that had a certain macobber charm. It was costing her twelve bucks an hour for three men talking about macobber charm. "Nice big window anyway," McGurk said lazily, then settled down to resume his nap, leaving the diplomatic crisis

34

to me. But just then the woman suddenly wound up the conversation and he snapped to his feet.

The woman swung around on the stool and smiled brightly at us. "Well so!" she said, as though to ask why wasn't the fiddle on the truck and on its way to the dump. I took a step forward.

"Lady," I said, "that piano won't go down them stairs. I'm afraid we're going to have to swing it. You know — lower it out through the window with block and tackle. That's twenty dollars extra."

With the dying smile, like a fire blown out in a high wind, she took me in from head to foot. She twitched the glasses down to her nose to size me up as a specimen. "Oh but it came up the stairs. Why not down?"

I glanced at McGurk, who turned away, rubbing his nose. This is the wheeze you are prepared for when the customer's pocketbook is threatened with a swing job — the piano came up the stairs, why can't it go down? The trick now is to jog their memory just a little as an alternative to calling them a liar. I made a concerted effort to be polite.

"Are you sure?"

"Yes."

"May I ask the name of the crew that performed that miracle?" The piano crew is considered the aristocrats of furniture movers, and ours was regarded as one of the best in Indiana, that is with Bascomb on keyboard. You would have to go to Chi to find the beat, and even there I understand they are beginning to follow the eastern custom of using four men on a crew instead of the classic three — which I don't regard as legitimate.

The woman turned to a table for a cigarette and a holder,

and by the time she turned around waving a match out and breathing smoke from her nose, the resemblance to Lena was uncanny. "Well, the piano was moved here from South Bend a long, long time ago, and I wasn't actually here at the time, but my mother was."

"Ah."

She appealed to McGurk. "Don't you think it can go down the stairs either?"

"I don't get paid to think, lady. It's all up to Mr. Waltz here. He's the boss. What he says goes — out the window or through the door it makes no never mind to me."

"Lady," I said, "what anybody else can do we can do. We don't shirk no just claims on our brawn. But backs are broken and hernias sprung by taking pianos down stairs people said they came up, only they didn't when checked into a little. Could we get in touch with your mother?" I held my breath, hoping the old lady wasn't dead. But it was nearly that bad.

"My mother happens to be in a sanitarium," the woman said, breathing smoke.

"I'm sorry to hear that. Nervous or physical?"

"But I'll try to call her if that seems to be necessary. In order to throw a piano away." Hers was a deep and belligerent melancholy now, and she sat down on the stool with the same kind of force you'll smack a table with to emphasize a point. She was built like a Mendenhall. "Maybe they can wheel her to the telephone."

"Aw, lady."

McGurk sat down on the floor for another snooze while Art resumed his tour of the pictures, leaving the doghouse to me exclusively. Seeing the woman shuffle through the directory

I sauntered over. "Where is your poor dear mother stopping? At what sanitarium?"

"Nestle Down."

"A very good place. Highly spoken of. Not no snake pit. We move lots of furniture in there, including pianos. They let old people have their own belongings now days, it makes them feel more at home. I hope your mother is — isn't too ill?"

"My mother," the woman said over her shoulder, "is completely helpless. Not an organ in her body functions properly. She has to be fed."

She dialed the number while I said "Aw" again and then asked either to talk to her mother — Mrs. Tinsdale was the name, so this woman was either married or divorced or both — or have a message taken to her while she held the wire for the answer.

"I don't like to quibble about money," the woman harped away while we waited, "but it does seem a little ridiculous to pay all that just to throw something away. Forty dollars is more than the piano is worth."

"It's like you said the other day — the theatre of the absurd."

I strolled out to the hallway for another gander down the stairs. No, there wasn't room enough for two to tango in the squeezes, which meant that as heavy corner man at the bottom I wouldn't even have Art to carry any keyboard to speak of, but would be carrying most of it myself on the turns. Since the turns were sharp as well as narrow, you would have to turn just a little in advance of the piano, as it were, which meant you would be carrying it out in front of you, like a pie. That's when you feel weight. That's when you can feel it in your marbles, when you're carrying it out in front of you. That's what puts backs out and springs hernias. It's frankly why I don't like to top a piano. I'd much rather be down there under it.

I went back into the studio to see what the old lady had to say. I remember thinking it was a pity the daughter wasn't one of them wire and metal sculptures who utilize junk. The piano would give her materials for years to come.

The woman was just hanging up, slowly, after saying "Thank you" to somebody on the other end. She turned slowly toward me on the stool. "My mother is dead," she said. "She just passed away."

"Well in that case," I said, "I guess we can take that piano down those stairs. It's the least we can do."

We tried to buck the woman up by this offer after letting her show a little emotion. Get the first shock out of her system. We insisted she have a stiff drink of whiskey, in which we all joined her. It was amazing the way the mood in that room changed from self-centered whining to mature cooperation. There was the feeling of friendship and human solidarity the news of death always inspires among the survivors. The woman told us something of her mother's past, her life as a young woman in South Bend and her heroic efforts to keep a wayside refreshment stand going after her husband had been knocked down and killed by a truck that always stopped there for hotdogs and pop. She spoke of her mother's suffering after she came to live with the daughter, now mercifully over. All arrangements had been made beforehand by the sanitarium, who were already proceeding with the undertaker of the family's choice which the woman had given three, four months ago, when the old lady started to fail.

There was nothing for the daughter to do now but try and distract herself by throwing herself into her work with redoubled zest. Life simply must reassert itself.

"I've been commissioned to do a mural for a new office building downtown," she told us, "in which I'm expected to depict the usual things like Capital and Labor and so on. The conventional sort of thing you can't avoid in dealing with official committees. You know how it is." McGurk nodded from the floor, whiskey glass in hand. Twelve dollars an hour for three men. "Well it's just struck me like a flash from heaven that I could do worse than get a few camera shots of you men in action now that I've got you here performing this sort of Herculean task. I mean what more perfect models could anybody dream of for Labor? What better specimens?" Art looked modestly at the floor. I hoped he was wearing his truss today. The woman walked the floor with her palms together, in an absolute tizzy they call them. Inspirations were striking her at a rate that none of us would survive. "And what better theme than furniture movers to symbolize the mobile society of our time."

"You do them sculptures too lady?" McGurk asked.

"No, no, I don't mean mobile in that sense. I mean our culture with its lack of roots and sense of place, its absence of home identity and family feeling. In some things it's impossible to work from live models, but photographs are a good substitute. So if you don't mind while I load my Leica . . ."

Because of a bad turn in the inside vestibule we had to dolly the piano on end to the hallway. There we took her down three, kicked her back to McGurk and carried her down the first flight, just barely clearing the header. It was like working in a cave. On the first landing we set her on end on the dolly again and wheeled her around into position for the next flight, which had the really nasty bend in it. The whole damn staircase was like a large intestine. The woman shot us in dramatic positions from above, leaning over the bannister and popping flashbulbs for a fare-thee-well, but now she squeezed past us and went down the next flight to get some angles from below. This flight was where the murder began.

We had the keyboard riding inside, toward the bannister, and the back, the heavy corner, against the wall, and I had fully as little help from Art as I expected — though of course it wasn't his fault that he couldn't wedge in beside me on the turns. He did little more than help steady her on course, reaching over from behind me, though doing his share of "Whewing" and "Jesusing" as always. I don't think he carried more than ten percent of the load, and since top man can't manage more than thirty or forty due to his position, that left me with a good half of a fiddle weighing damn near half a ton, and I mean I could really feel this one in my grapes. We took her down four and set. After this the pretzel work began. The fiddle was still on end — the turn was too sharp to carry her any other way.

"Want to take her two more, or is a step at a time enough?" McGurk asked, knowing what I had. "This is the bend in the river."

I was a second in answering. I leaned my head on my arm, holding onto the feet of the piano till a twinge in my groin subsided. I was afraid I had strained my milk this time. I had done it once before years ago and gone around for 6 mos.

40

with the family jewels in a sling. From below came a chipper voice: "Now, I want to get the sense of weight from underneath, the tension of back and thigh in a perspective looking up — the whole tremendous sense of a Burden being come to grips with."

"You've come to the right place, lady," says the page turner, adjusting the pad on his shoulder. He spat on his hands. "What say, shall we try for two or just take her down one? What does the old Waltzenheimer think?"

I knew I was wasting in anger energy desperately needed for my work, but this habit of Art's irked me. It hit me where I lived. My name is obviously an abbreviation of Waltzinski or probably Walzinski, by ancestors who weren't ashamed of it but who did Americanize it by hacking away some of the underbrush. Why not? I thought I would teach the page turner a lesson. Also there was your sexual motive here, the feeling that he was a potential rival for his wife. So after we got past the turn and he had his shoulder wedged in beside mine again, more or less, I decided I would give him a little more of his legitimate share of the piano. This I did by tipping it ever so slightly over in his direction.

The result was a howl of protest from the page turner, who at the same time staggered against the bannister, grabbing a spindle of it. It come off in his hand with a snap like a firecracker. In a twinkling we were in trouble. The fiddle (still on end remember) wobbled off course, and with a terrific heave and a very loud "For Christ *sake!*" McGurk tried to steady it back on. Without much luck. There was another crackling sound which was either some more bannister giving way or somebody's neckbones grinding. Losing Art's carrying support of course lost the piano that much more equilibrium, that much more steerability, which rapidly sent the whole situation to hell in a handbasket. With McGurk's labors (and Herculean is good) concentrated for the moment solely on pilot work, I now had damn near that whole fiddle on my back. I could feel muscles coming away from my bones from the heels up. I was convinced I could hear them, though that may of been the blood throbbing in my head. We couldn't set the piano on the step because of the way it was swaying crazily in midair. For me to set would lose it the little support it had because, from that far down, I simply couldn't heft it. It would have listed out of control completely and toppled over the bannister and gone crashing to the floors below, probably taking half the stairwell with it. That was the reasoning sheer instinct did for me. I didn't think it out, it just went through my mind like a streak of lightning. So the same way you have to paddle a canoe faster than the current to keep control, we had to go down those steps like a bunch of drunken sailors. The very momentum of the piano made us speed up to keep control. Through some superhuman effort McGurk finally got the piano righted away from the bannister and toward the wall, along which it bumped, but now suddenly the top was tilting dangerously *forward*. There was a split second when it could of somersaulted down the stairs behind us. But then, summoning all the strength I had out of muscle, guts and bones, in one agonizing single heave I somehow managed to hump it back to McGurk, who of course was pulling back on the top himself. Even Art Salerno came through in this pinch. Like three men fighting a monster we stumbled down the stairs in a kind of insane trance and dropped it on the landing with a thunderclap that shook the whole building.

42

"That was excellent, but, shoot, I'm afraid my bulb didn't go off," came the cheerful voice.

None of us said anything. Art and I sank down on the top step of the next flight and sat with our tongues hanging out, gasping like fish out of water. Our arms hung limp between our knees, our eyes bulged, we breathed in death rattles. Mc-Gurk was draped in a collapsed state over the piano, which was still on end. His head was cradled on his arms, and he was whimpering softly. For a minute there was only that and the sound of Art and me's death rattles.

"I assume you'll have a similar maneuver on this next flight? I mean you'll do the whole thing over again? The light is better here, and we'll get a longer, more theatrical sweep."

I raised my head in my own good time. When I spoke my voice was without tone.

"Lady," I said, "in a minute we'll all pick up this here piano — the three of us. When we do, you'll put the dolly under it. Then we'll roll her around the landing and come downstairs, and when we do, you'll be waiting there for us with the dolly again, to slip it under her. And so on. That's the way it's going to be all the way out to the truck."

"Oh well, perhaps a shot of you loading it on the truck will be more to my purposes. Yes, suddenly come to think of it. The furniture actually leaving, the moving van the symbol of the mobile society. That's much the best. And it goes without saying you'll get the twenty dollars I've saved, to divide among you."

Taking our time, and with frequent rests, we finally got the monster out of that hallway and on the truck. After getting it on the tailgate she asked us to hold the pose while she shot us from various angles. Which was no sweat, except for the

43

tedium of the posing. In fact with the piano resting at last on the tailgate there was no sense of strain in our positions, so she got us to fake it. "Could you put your foot way back and your shoulder here," she asked me at one point, "so I can get a continuous sweep of line from your heel upward?"

"That's not a natural way to be shoving a piano on a truck lady," I said.

"That's all right. It's the artistic authenticity I'm after. Whether it's literally valid doesn't matter."

She bustled around and got set, squatting down in a variety of angles while we sustained poses that weren't literally valid.

"Lady," I said at last, "for a bunch of guys symbolizing a mobile society ain't we standing a long time in the same place?"

At last she got what she wanted, and then insisted on riding along to the city dump. There she got some interesting shots of three mystic figures carrying a piano acrost a blasted landscape in the fading light of day. The long shadows we cast gave it a haunting surrealist quality she called out as she darted around clicking the shutter. I could see she was more excited by this sudden development than the Labor poses. We were three allegorical symbols of the general human enigma, carting their mysterious burden toward the slag heaps of oblivion. Garbage was dumped here as well as junk, so we sank to our knees in vegetable matter as we plodded toward the brink of doom, the veins in our necks standing out like whipcord and bucking for ruptures to a man. Once we stumbled and the page turner pitched forward on all fours, covering himself with glory. "Let's leave her here," McGurk pleaded, sinking in fruit peels and inner tubes. "No," I said stubbornly, "we'll take her to the edge. I want to see this sonofabitch go over." Salerno begun to vomit, contributing his bit to the eternal conundrum.

Seeing that Mendenhall roll end over end down that mountain of filth was one of the most satisfying moments of my life — my professional life anyway. With a last jangle of music it keeled over on its back, castors up, and laid there. That finish seemed an echo of the question left suspended in the summer air among the droning flies by the three men with their mysterious burden — "Why? To what end? What for?"

"I want you to see the pictures when they're ready," the woman told me when we walked back to the truck. "I'll call you the minute they're developed, and then you can come up to the studio and have a drink."

four

THE SHOTS of the dump come out beautifully. One in particular had a haunting quality of world's end, the woman said in describing what she would shoot for in the oil she was now definitely going to base on it. The views on the stairs and truck were only routine studies for composition. "It has a magic approximating the effect of painting itself, don't you think?" she said of the city limits shot. Hazy air and smoke from scattered fires softened the setting sun to a red coal. And who were them mystic figures carrying their enigmatic burden through the rubble of the universe in the evening of Time? Were they pallbearers transporting into oblivion the instrument of song? Were they phantoms wandering through the World Ash of Goderdamerung? Were they, these men drifting with their backs to us as if in a dream, the executors of some inscrutable design to whose meaning they themselves lacked the key, or the exemplars of some voluntarily assumed despair, bearing to the edge of Hell the last artifacts of human longing? These were some of the things the woman who was going to paint the picture wanted to know. I may not have them all straight or in the right order, but that was the general drift.

"I'm thinking of calling it 'And the daughters of music shall be brought low,' " the woman said.

She left the studio couch where we were looking at the prints together to fix us drinks. I could hear her clattering around in the kitchen. I couldn't take my eyes off the picture. There we were, McGurk, Art Salerno and me, exemplars of some voluntarily assumed despair or whatever, phantoms in a surrealist landscape. And here I was sitting up here looking at myself in a setup just as fantastic and surrealist. A thought within me struck a sour note: they like men from the lower orders, these upper-crust women.

"You must of had lots of interesting experiences with pianos," she said cheerfully coming back with two whiskey highballs. She handed me one as she joined me again. She sat down the same way she had before. She first knelt on the couch and then sat on her legs. This produced a hollow in the upholstery like another pit for me to fall into. The springs twanged eagerly to make room for me.

"Oh I don't know," I said. "It's just work. We don't generally wind up lugging them acrost symbolic landscapes. The only interesting thing I can think of offhand, we got stuck in a turn once with an upright we should of swung and had to

46

saw the toes off the legs at either end to jockey it around. The people gave us permission of course. It was no trouble to glue them back on, and probably cheaper than swinging. We all laughed like hell when we did it, including the owners. She was a fat jolly woman."

"I'd like to play a piano," she said, and sipped thoughtfully. As I watched her I remembered she hadn't paid her bill yet, nor had another word been mentioned about splitting the twenty bucks among the crew. Reflections like these slow down sexual stimulus. "It's a secret regret I always have, not learning to play an instrument. It must release an awful lot pent-up within you. Sort of ventilates the spirit."

"I have only one secret yen involving pianos. I'd like to drop one off the roof of a building and see what happens. All them wire guts spilling in all directions."

"You're probably very complex," she says, sizing me up again. "Full of dark impulses and mad desires. But I understand the destructive urge. We all have it in us — creative people most of all. I have a writer friend who has this irresistible urge to drop his typewriter out his fifth-story window. I suppose he'd like to see its innards scattered around on the pavement, on much the same principle as yours."

When we had exhausted the subject of stuff we'd like to drop out of windows there was a pause. I took a large, loud gulp, sensing the woman taking me in again.

"What about this posing?" she said.

When I left it was with the understanding that I would think it over in terms of when I could work such a thing in et cetera, by which time I got the hint that she meant modelling in the altogether, an anatomy sketch, which in turn had implications to be read into a kiss and some hurried necking

47

on a couch that could plainly be pulled out into a bed. She had a husband who was not on the scene, was all I found out about that. We talked some more about my secret leeric desires and I left.

The question that remains in my mind to this day is, what if I had jumped in? Would that of had more or less repercushions than the thing that developed out of our preliminary skirmish? I don't see how it could of produced an explosion as devastating as what resulted from a chain reaction it set in motion indirectly. She led to something worse, like the atom bomb needed to trigger the hydrogen bomb. The man who gobbles sex indiscriminately is not to be justified. He is either a fool or a knave, no two ways about it.

I went to air my problem with the only person I could let down my hair to — Lena. By that time I had given Art one of the extra set of prints the woman had made. He showed them to Lena, and in doing so must of told her about my going up to the woman's flat for a drink, because by the time I got to see Lena again she seemed to have the lay of the land and was spoiling for a discussion. "She probably *is* the lay of the land," leave it to Lena not to fail to get in with typical malice.

We were talking the whole thing over like two civilized people early one afternoon at her place. I had walked home from the warehouse for lunch and was walking back when I bumped into Lena as she was turning into her house with her arms full of groceries. Art I had sent on a long haul to Chicago, to give his hernia a rest after the recent exertions. He had strained his milk on the Mendenhall, all right enough, either getting it down the stairs or into the dump. Well he had earned a nice long ride to Chi with five, six easy rooms

48

of furniture and no piano. Lena invited me in for a cup of coffee, either because her scruples about this had changed or her curiosity had proved too much for them, and so there we were now in her living room, hashing over my dilemma. Should I have an affair with this woman? Lena gave her opinion very forthrightly.

"Show your true masculinity. I said true, not obvious or superficial, or purely animal, masculinity. Show you're a man not down here," she said, laying a hand on her loins, "but up here," laying it on her bosom. She indicated the male heart as best she could through the contents of a jumbo size brassiere. "There lies the true virility."

I sat nodding, finishing my coffee as she developed her point.

"These affairs are always shabby. They get sordid in the end, and found out. They're bound to. Then they blow up marriages worth two, three times the affair. Oh the jewels that we exchange for bawbles! Then there are the taxing scenes that lay people waist, emotions boiling over, friends in on it and neighbors listening, and finally somebody getting drunk and riding off into the sunset. No, it's not worth it, Stan. The game isn't worth the candle."

I couldn't help feeling she was right. The decision to pass this thing up suddenly gave me a warm feeling inside. It rapidly grew into a kind of elation quite unlike anything I had ever experienced before. I was tasting my own merit, along lines laid down by Lena. At the same time I had a sense of compatibility with her that made me positively glow. Who else could I talk to like this? Nobody. Not my wife. I became emotionally drunk with this feeling — that sensation of kinship with another party that is one of the greatest things in

49

life. Impulsively I reached across the coffee table and took her hand. "You're so right, Lena," I said.

She returned the pressure of my grasp, leaning forward out of her chair a little the same way I was. Together we rose and kissed across the table. Holding my mouth to hers, I maneuvered around the table to get closer to her, stretching my neck, our lips sort of corkscrewing together. She mumbled something I didn't get as I reached blindly to put my arms around her. In doing so I tripped against a table leg and stumbled into her arms, which made her lose her balance and fall backwards onto a sofa, pulling me down on top of her.

"Oh, Lena."

"This has been brewing for a long time."

"We tried to fight it but it's no use. When two people feel that way about each other, what can they do?"

There were several of those kisses that drain the glue from your joints. I unbuttoned her blouse and reached my hand inside, then into her brassiere, plundering its treasures after managing somehow to unhook it. When I lowered my head to her breast she sat up, not to interrupt what was going on, or rather coming off, but to argue that what we were doing could be perfectly sanctioned on intellectual grounds — that I could rest assured it had every justification.

"Have you ever read Bertrand Russell?"

"No I haven't," I answered as best I could with my mouth full.

"Huxley?"

I shook my head, still feeding.

"Over there is a book you must read. It's called *Something for Mrs. Grundy*. Do you know who Mrs. Grundy was? What the title is taken from, the idea behind the book?"

Again more mumbles in the negative.

"Do you mean to sit there and tell me you never heard of Mrs. Grundy? That was never part of your childhood? Why, she's folklore. 'What will Mrs. Grundy think?' 'Leave something for Mrs. Grundy.' Kids were told that at supper, to leave a little on their plate to appease her. Well it turns out Mrs. Grundy was a character in an old English play who stood for bluenose disapproval. Conventional censorship of other people's conduct."

I felt a stir that wasn't amorous, and I guessed Lena was trying to reach over to the table for a cigarette. I kept her firmly pinned down.

"Funny you never heard that when you were a kid. I did all the time. Anyhoo, that's the point of the book. That with all our vaunted freedom we're still scared of Mrs. Grundy. Still afraid of *what people will think*. Or would think if they knew, which comes to the same thing and is just as strong a check on what are perfectly normal desires for perfectly legitimate pleasures. It's deeply, deeply embedded in the American conscience due to our Puritan heritage, which has got a strangle hold on us. I want you to read that book. It'll clear a lot of cobwebs out of your thinking. I know it's helped me."

"But my conscience is clear!" I said coming up for air. "I got no qualms. What are you wasting valuable time preaching to the converted for? I don't need any convincing."

"Nonsense. Didn't you just have to come and talk to me about your doubts and anxieties over another woman, and you not even in bed with her yet?"

"I did not! You wormed the whole thing out of me."

"Nice worming, that it could come out so easy it proved you wanted to get it off your chest. There was no resistance whatever, only a great eagerness to talk, only a great relief to get it off your chest. No, you'll be racked with guilt, and I don't want that. You'd never forgive yourself — and then you'd never forgive me, and then *pfft*, the end of a fine friendship. You'd end up hating me. Adam has blamed Eve from time immemorial."

"Then it goes a hell of a lot farther back than the *Mayflower!* Why pin everything on this country?"

She shook her head with a patient laugh. "Stan, Stan, you need work from the ground up. Honest." She swung her legs out onto the floor and tucked the contents of the rifled blouse back into place. I watched her light a cigarette and pace the floor. Not agitatedly, but thoughtfully, looking at the carpet.

"I don't want this to leave a bad taste in anybody's mouth, Stan," she said. "Entire couples have come to hate each other because they've rushed into something without thinking. And why do you think you can just come barging in here, have a quick matinee and barge off again — like somebody dropping in somewhere for a short beer? Just a matter of refreshment, mere appeasement of the senses. A woman isn't flattered by that, Stan. We have our pride. We're not animals."

This I understood. This I appreciated. A woman's pride naturally resists being possessed in a casual way, at least not taking much time. While they enjoy being swept off their feet, they do like preliminaries. They like the overtures to be made with some sort of style, and an affair to be conducted with gestures and flourishes. Plus with Lena this sort of thing is all very well in practice, but what about the theory?

We agreed to have a rendezvous soon, at a time and place to be agreed on later and in keeping with the facts of the situation. I could slip into her house as I had today, after grabbing a bite of lunch at home, or we could, when weather permitted, meet by the river, though that would have limitations unless we rowed out to a densely wooded island upstream from Slow Rapids. Art I could keep out of town indefinitely by sending him on long distance hauls as long as his hernia held out as an excuse. Certainly in his present condition I would not send him on anything "to Valparaiso." "Going to Valparaiso" is movers' ironic slang for a job to be unloaded around the corner from where it's been loaded, thereby offering no respite in the shape of a ride on the truck. At least it's Midwestern slang. Out east they probably have a different expression.

"I got a job booked to Muskegon next week," I said. "I think Thursday. Could we make it tentatively then?"

Seeing the amount of plotting and fenagling and sheer botheration I was prepared to go through in order to possess her softened Lena, and she whispered in my ear, "All right," giving me another kiss. I went into the bathroom to wash the lipstick off my face, neck and even hands, which looked as though I worked in a slaughterhouse, and then after pocketing my homework — the book — I went back to the warehouse.

I hadn't read many pages in *Something for Mrs. Grundy* before I came across several phrases and even ideas Lena had already voiced as her own. If I wasn't emotionally involved with an adulterer, at least yet, I certainly was with a thief. She never bothered to give anybody credit for anything, or even state a source, but simply tossed off as her own anything she helped herself to. That was why fine thoughts and fancy turns of speech kept cropping up in her conversation, to the embarrassment of all. The material in this book was so familiar to me as filtered through Lena that I saw no real need to read it. I just gave it a skim and put it aside. Why should you have to cram for the sack? It seems to me life is hard enough without that.

Tom was sitting in the parlor with me, and I turned my attention to him. He had his heels hoisted up on the edge of his chair, and between his knees he was holding a comic, his elbows resting on the arms of the chair. He had a sucker deep in one cheek.

"Have you ever heard of Mrs. Grundy?" I asked him.

He shook his head slowly, after the fact that the question was addressed to him had penetrated it, and without removing his eyes from the comic or the lollipop from his cheek.

"Well she was an imaginary woman people use to be scared of, or at least scare each other into being good with. Kids at least. Well no, grownups too. A superstition. Like the old witch. Or . . ."

His mother appeared in the kitchen doorway drying a pan. A figure materializing. She kept an ear cocked not only for my infidel ideas, but for any turn in the conversation that would give me a chance to slip them in. There was now open warfare between us over the kid's upbringing. If she took him to the mission, I would take him out for a soda and some indoctrination. If she gave him one of her religious tracks, I'd counter with some propaganda of mine in the form of one of the many free-thinking Little Blue Books I got by mail. She started it. I was only asking for equal time.

"Or a god who looks down at us and writes down everything we do in a book," I pushed on.

"There is one, Tom," she said as he turned a page, "and

54

he knows your every thought. And to him you'll have to give account some day."

"Bunk. When you're dead you're dead, and you damn well better live while you can, because you only live once."

Elsie came all the way into the parlor. She wore a flowered wrapper and her hair was drawn up in a roll on the exact top of her head. She smiled down at the little fox-faced version of herself with the perpetual grin that was his trademark. He was grinning now, but whether about a development in the comics or something else was hard to say.

"Wouldn't it be ridiculous to create something only to have it die?" she said. "Wouldn't that be foolish, now? Even a child knows that — and a little child shall lead them. These things are hidden from the wise and prudent and revealed unto — "

"Boobs and sucklings."

"Mock all you want."

"I am. Life perpetuates itself in offspring. That's how it doesn't die," I said, "and that's the only way it doesn't!"

"Don't believe him, Tom. No, Tommie. You have an immortal soul that you have to give account of. When you die or when Christ comes on the clouds of glory."

"Maybe tonight."

"Maybe."

I was thinking of that religious nut who predicted the end of the world that spring. He had been patrolling his beat every day downtown. "Where is that pamphlet of his?" I said, shuffling through the pile on the parlor table where everything usually lay in a heap. I finally found it, and now read it really for the first time. "June 11 he claims. That's today. Well today's over."

55

"The *week* of June 11," Elsie said. "I told you I didn't approve of trying to predict, but he didn't say anything more than that. I don't think either that you can figure these mysteries out — after all it says that Christ will come like a thief in the night, when we least expect it — but there's no harm in trying. It keeps our minds spiritually occupied."

She went back to the kitchen while I read the pamphlet through, wondering if the nut was still downtown parading around with his placard now that it was zero hour. Tom hadn't raised his head from the comic during the entire discussion. How much had he taken in? How closely did he listen to these debates he seemed to totally ignore? It was hard to say. You couldn't get under his skin.

"Put that down!" I barked. "Do you want to be a Polak all your life? Put that down and just listen to this drivel."

He put the funnies down with a sigh and paid some attention while I read the nut's prognostication about the last days. Eschatology it's called. When I would look up Tom was either licking his sucker or contemplating it for the next lick. The time schedule for the Last Judgment, based on an analysis of the pipe dream in Revelation, was something I didn't feel the need to reply to, it was its own reply. But when I finished the kid gave a nervous giggle and said, "What if it *is* true, Pop? You say everything is a mystery we don't have an answer to, so what if this turns out to be the answer? What will you do then?"

"He'll say to the hills 'Cover us,' and to the mountains 'Fall on us,' " came from the kitchen doorway again. "He won't be such a Bill Blowhard then."

I remembered reading an argument by a philosopher

56

named Sidney Hook on this very subject. I tried to explain it to the kid.

Hook's reasoning runs that if an unbeliever died and woke up to find there was a God after all, he would still have a right to tell Him, "You didn't give me enough evidence." A scofflaw in such a jam could fairly insist that the facts in his possession during his lifetime justified his unbelief, and that if he had it to do all over again he would reach the same conclusion because reason dictated it. If Hook's logic is valid for something as vague and general as the idea of God, how much more for anything as specific and fantastic as the Second Coming, which is as far down the scale in probability as you can get. To punish a man for failing to draw supernatural conclusions from natural facts would be an injustice for which there is no punishment.

"*That's* what I would say then," I told Tom. "What Professor Hook says."

The kid nodded, regarding his sucker with a grin before poking it back in his mouth. One minute he'd seem to be giving his mother's notions house room, the next mine. Bed wetting had had a slight revival when his mother began stirring the place up with salvation and sin and heaven and hell, but that had subsided, and he seemed to be doing all right in school again, except that he was constantly being sent to the principal's office for what he called "injecting a little humor into the discussion." I didn't dare look into that too closely, knowing full well what his humor ran to around here. "Ma did you know Pa's arthritis comes from drinking? He's stiff in a new joint every night." Was this kid a Mess? He needed more of his father's companionship — a decent paternal figure to set an example. I myself had been going to town a lit-

57

tle oftener each week, and coming home a little more loaded every night. Why not take the kid with me?

"Let's go downtown and see if the nut is still there. Then I'll buy you a soda."

The night was hot, and we sauntered coatless under the maples. Houses were open, people sat on their porches. I glanced into the Salernos as we went by, seeing both Lena and Art behind the lighted curtains. Main Street was half a mile down. The nut was not there. Since this was the only beat he ever worked, he was nowhere.

"Let's go in here," I said, leading the way into a Greek's where they served both liquor and ice cream. While Tom sipped a chocolate soda I had a whiskey. If I'd been alone I'd put down two or three.

He got drowsy on the way home and I gave him a horse-back ride. He was fast asleep when I tumbled him carefully onto his bed, and he didn't wake up when I undressed him. I wandered out to the back yard with a bottle and glass, and fell asleep on the glider somewhat drunker than I had expected.

I was awakened some time after midnight by a tremendous crash. My wife was standing over me shaking my shoulder. The noise was repeated, or rather prolonged, one great blasting roar echoing another. There was a fiery glow in the western sky.

"It's the end of the world," she said. "You better get up."

I climbed to my feet and looked wildly around in utter panic and confusion.

"How do you know?"

"It can't be anything else. It all fits. Christ has come back. This is it, Stan. The Second Coming."

So the nut was right after all. I had slipped off my shirt and pants in the heat, and now I climbed back into them with the speed of a fireman answering a 4–11. Elsie was in her nightgown and she ran down the hall to get Tom up and dressed as well as dress herself.

The sounds continued, one crash after another that shook the earth. The light in the sky was a weird succession of colors, vivid red and ghastly green and then sulphurous yellow, all smothered in billows of smoke and shot through with flashes and sparks like brimstone raining from heaven for a fact. Lights were going on in all the houses around us. People appeared in back yards or ran up and down stairs shouting and screaming and wringing their hands. "Oh my God have mercy!" a woman in a nightgown on a porch across the alley said. The pandemonium was unbelievable. How many would be redeemed? How many damned? How would the whole thing be managed? Would we all literally be separated into sheep and goats, some herded to the right, some to the left? What about Sidney Hook? Would his logic, so crystal clear in the light of day, stand up under this terrific beating, this truly ghastly blood and thunder? What would his reason avail him now? Or mine avail me, on a more modest scale of course. Were the graves opening in the cemetery and yielding up their dead?

I hurried into the house in time to see Elsie leading Tom from his bedroom. He was white as a sheet, but she had him dressed and ready. Even his hair was brushed.

"I repent," I said. "I take back everything I said. I am sorry

59

for my sins and accept the Lord Jesus Christ as my personal savior, now and forevermore. Amen."

"I hope it isn't too late for that," Elsie said. She had hastily dressed too, but I noticed she had slipped into something comfortable. None of the vanities of this world now. "For myself I have no doubts. I know that my redeemer liveth, and because he lives I too shall live. Tom has said his prayers, and I think he understands. He's not of the age of discretion, anyway. I had him baptized, by the way. I didn't tell you because I knew you'd object. But how about you?"

"I never was."

"Don't you think you should take care of that now?"

"Check." I ran to the kitchen tap and put my head under it, saying the words as I knew them and turning the water up full force. Elsie said she didn't know whether it would hold up, a person baptizing himself, but agreed there was certainly no harm in trying. And while it might be too late for prayer too, there was certainly nothing to be lost by dropping on our knees together, and maybe something to be gained. I led us in prayer, as head of the family, babbling out penitent entreaties and pleas for mercy for all of us above the noise of the nightmare still going full blast outside. Where at one point I heard a neighbor call out, "It's dat great gittin' up mawnin'!"

"Christ coming alone?" Tom asked when we were on our feet again.

"We don't know yet. It's too early to tell. The best thing to do is sit tight and see what happens. All we know is, we acknowledge him lord and master."

"And how!"

"I'm not making any excuses," I said through chattering

teeth, "but he did tell his disciples he would come back in their time. I merely raise the point. That and a lot of other discrepancies — *from a human point of view* — naturally made us figure the Bible was untrue, but it turns out that they are all part of the divine mystery, which I now accept lock, stock and barrel."

"You could be a credit to the church."

"I wonder how the Salernos will make out."

"Never mind them. We have to put our own house in order. I think while we're waiting we'll just sit here and sing a hymn. It's impossible to know how long it will take. Did you see anything while you were out there?"

I shook my head. I really didn't dare look. I was shaking in my shoes, which I now noticed I had on but hadn't tied. I stooped to lace them, and when I stood up again I glanced through the kitchen window out of the tail of my eye. There was no sign of anything yet but the flashes and the explosions went on full blast. How would he appear? Would he come floating down, surrounded by angels, the way you always saw it in paintings? Or would he simply materialize miraculously in all the houses in all the world at once?

I took the initiative in singing "Nearer, My God, to Thee," giving the pitch and leading off as we raised our voices in the grand old hymn together as a family. In the middle of it the telephone rang.

"You'd better get it," Elsie said.

I answered. It was Art Salerno.

"I just wanted to make sure you weren't missing the show, *paisan*," he said. "Afraid you might sleep through it."

"What show?"

"The fireworks factory. The whole thing is going. Can you

61

see it from there? Otherwise come on over. We got a perfect view."

"Why don't you and Lena come over here."

"Well I think it's better here. We even thought of going up on the roof."

"Look, why not pile into my car and drive over."

"I don't know how close you can get. They've got all the engines in town there and it looks out of control. Well all right, let's."

I took Tom and the three of us went over. Elsie refused and Lena didn't want to go either. The streets were full of cars tooling like mad toward the river where the factory was. It was a sight of course you'd never see in your lifetime again, and a night you wouldn't forget, but we couldn't get very close up. The cops had roped the area off for a square block around to protect sightseers from injuries by explosives going amuck, because not all of them went up of course, but sideways and all around in crazy circles, causing some damage to surrounding buildings but fortunately not injuring anyone seriously. We all stayed well inside the car with the windows up. One or two firemen were hospitalized, and several people were hurt in the jam. By the time we arrived most of the explosives had gone off, but we did see a few rockets streak across the sky and a few last star shells burst over the rooftops and drift in dreamy showers toward the ground.

By three o'clock the factory was a faintly smoking shell itself, like a firecracker shot off, and we drove home. I put Tom to bed for the second time that night, and dropped in exhausted beside Elsie. Her eyes were shut, but I doubted she was asleep. They were shut a little too tight, and her position seemed a little too rigid for relaxation. I put an arm around her and soon dropped off myself, sleeping the sleep of the just till nearly eleven o'clock the next morning.

five

I MARCHED PAST Lena when she opened the door to admit me for our rendezvous and was waiting for her in the middle of the parlor when she came in after closing the door.

I jerked my coat open to exhibit what was holding my pants up.

"Look," I said. "My birthday present."

"What? What are you talking about? What's the matter with you?"

"What's the matter with me? Come closer. Bend down. Peer at it. Take a good look at the latest outrage perpetrated on human intelligence. This." I snapped the buckle with my thumb. "This is what I get for my birthday."

"A belt?"

"Not just any belt, but something special. This is — listen carefully, make sure your ears aren't deceiving you — *a Bible belt!* Yes, it's true. A leather belt with Scriptural texts tooled into it all the way around. No, your eyes aren't deceiving you. What you see is really there."

Lena had to put on her glasses. She sat down on the sofa to read, pulled me toward her by the waist. "Come over here, do you want me to get down on my knees?"

Holding the skirt of my coat up, I revolved slowly before her as she scrutinized the texts tooled into the leather for my

63

edification: John 3:16; Matthew 16:26; Psalms 51:2; I Corinthians 13:13, and many more.

Lena took her glasses off and set them down as I let my coat drop.

"How did you ever get mixed up with such a woman? Why did you marry her?"

"That's not the point — we'll come to that later. The first thing that must rouse your curiosity too is, do they know what the term Bible belt means? These people she's mixed up with, these Fundamentalists, do they know what it refers to? Or are they so dumb that even — what's his name who coined the term?"

"Mencken."

"Mencken. That even Mencken didn't fully realize how dumb they were when he pinned the label on them. Or — or," I said, walking the floor, "do they know what it means and they're being clever. Turning it back on the intellectuals, they've got that much sense of humor. Or is it neither but they're just piously hitting back at what they know is a term of ridicule. It's hard to know which way to be disgusted. But here I am, the recipient, wearing the article of apparel with texts carved into it instead of figures like on a cowboy belt."

"What does Elsie think? What point of view did she give it to you in?"

"She doesn't know anything exept that they were selling them at the mission for gifts, souvenirs, and thought it would be nice to give me one. She doesn't know anything about Mencken and all that, the original Bible belt. Besides she's not in a very talkative mood since the other night when Christ didn't show up."

"What did you ever see in such a woman?"

64

"What did I see in her? She thought the sun rose and set on me, that's what I saw in her. Also she gave off a little gurgle of bliss every time you kissed her, like the sound you hear when you shake a ripe honeydew."

"How do you feel about her now?"

"Sexually or personally?"

"Sexually."

"How the hell do I know?"

"Well then personally."

"I don't know that either."

"Then why do you ask me to be specific, since the answer is the same for both?"

"Darling, our first quarrel," I said sarcastically. Then I relented and reminded her how sweet Elsie was when we were all young, and that (to answer her original question) I didn't marry her when she was a woman but when she was a girl. An important point. "You remember her then, *zaftig* and warm — "

"You keep using that word as though you think it's Polish. It's Jewish you know."

"I know that very well. She was no brain, but soft and warm and friendly, and always neatly dressed. Now she clops around in a wrapper with her hair twisted up in a bun, Christ's bride. How does she expect to hold a man? Could I have a drink? I know it's only the middle of the day, but I feel the need."

Lena seemed slow and more than usually deliberate as she went to the kitchen, from which she returned with a whiskey and water for me. Nothing for herself. I didn't like her mood. She looked like something was eating her. I noticed it the minute I came in. I was now sitting on the sofa, and she set the drink in front of me and took a nearby chair — the one

65

I'd been sitting in last time — and watched me while I drank.

I took a generous swig. "I'm married to a woman who never heard of Mencken."

"Did you when you first married her?"

"No, that's right. I didn't. Or lots of things that you've taught me, Lena. Oh Lena — " I reached to take her hand across the table again, but this time she pulled away. "What's the matter?"

"Matter?" She reached for her cigarette holder and in a twinkling was walking the room again snorting smoke. "You come in here to what's suppose to be a rendezvous going fifteen to the dozen with complaints about your lot. Did you give any evidence that this was a love trist, carefully prepared for and long looked forward to? Did you even greet me? Did you even notice what I'm wearing?" She had worked around behind me and now clapped a hand over my eyes. "What have I got on, you who so notice what a woman wears that you can give me blow by blow details about your married life. What have I put on for you?"

"I don't know, Lena. I'm sorry. I was just too upset."

She restored my sight, allowing me to take in the green and red silk lounging pajamas, the golden slippers and the crimson band around her hair. She was really gift-wrapped. I whistled. "Lena, you're gorgeous."

"It's a little late for gorgeous. The whistles are quite tardy, you had your opportunity several minutes ago. No, you don't want me — you just don't want somebody else. You just come in here to complain about what your wife gives you for your birthday and what she wears, not to see me. How does your wife expect to hold you, you say. How do you expect to hold me if you don't notice what I'm wearing, who went to all the

66

trouble to pretty up for her gentleman caller. How do you think that makes a woman feel? What am I, a woman or an emotional dumping ground?"

"You're a woman, Lena," I said with a catch in my throat, "and what a woman."

"Do you realize what it is for a woman to give herself to a man? What's at stake?"

"I'm not asking you to give yourself to me, only lend yourself."

"Oh my God! You're getting to be a born fool."

"Over you, Lena, over you."

I tried to take her again but she backed off once more, and once more circled the room, breathing fire and letting me have it. Suddenly I drained my glass and set it down. "I'm going out and get drunk."

I started for the door, but her next outburst stopped me cold.

"Go ahead! You're all alike. Prove conclusively what I'm trying to say and what you're leading me right up to, go ahead, save me the trouble. Spoiled children! Punks with infantile motivations, not masterful lovers having poetic affairs. You don't want to add a little poetry to your life, you just want to subtract a little of the prose. You just want a shoulder to cry on, 'My wife doesn't understand me.' Why don't you be a man once. Admit you behaved poorly and apologize. Then I might relent and admit I was probably a little hard on you, but you deserved it. In that way clear the air — for the triumphant gesture. Instead of running off like some high school kid that didn't get his way, why don't you begin over? We might have what you came for, we might yet touch the stars, if you'd behave for once like a lover. Go on, why

67

don't you sweep me off my feet and carry me to bed in triumph?"

"All right, I will!"

But that was easier said than done, as I saw when it was too late.

I strode briskly toward her, but began to slow down thoughtfully as I got close to her. I have given a rough idea of her size, from which her weight can be imagined. I slung one arm around her shoulder and the other under her knees, in the traditional manner, but the instant I picked her up my own knees buckled under me and I gave an involuntary grunt that didn't set very well either. At the same time I felt a sharp twinge in my groin that made me think of Art, now joyriding through lower Michigan in the cabin of the truck. I had forgotten that Lena is to the average woman as a Mendenhall is to an apartment spinnet. It was the strain of carrying a heavy weight out in front of you that I explained was my objection to topping a piano.

My legs sagging, I staggered toward the bedroom. It was a good thirty feet away, and it seemed like thirty miles. It was very embarrassing, but we were both stuck with it. "You're a magnificent hunk of woman, Lena," I puffed, but it was little use. Halfway there I had to ease her down and readjust my grip. I let her feet down to the floor but kept her weight on my knee, so that she was sort of sitting on my lap for a moment. Then I heaved her up again with another grunt and plodded forward some more.

The rest of the journey I managed better, but when we reached the bedroom door a fresh embarrassment greeted us, the worst of all. I couldn't go through it. I had to maneuver us through sideways, and that extra effort disorganized my grip completely, so that this time I had to let her slide all the way to the floor. Since there was no room in the doorway to pick her up again, I stepped around behind and dragged her across the threshold by the armpits. "I'll never forgive you for this," she said. So to make a joke of the whole thing, a lark, I slung her over my shoulder in the fireman's carry, or, as you might say, like a hunter bringing his kill back to the cave. I dropped her over onto the bed and flopped down on my back beside her, puffing like a steam engine.

"I guess I'm out of condition," I said. "Been in the office too long."

She got up, climbing over the foot-end of the bed to avoid stepping over me. "Thank you," she said, and marched out of the room.

"Now what?"

"If taking me to bed is compared to moving furniture, then I doubt whether I'm interested," I heard from the parlor.

"That's not what I said," I answered from the bed.

"It's what you inferred. You say you've been in the office too long, meaning not working on the truck. On the truck you handle furniture. If you were still handling it you'd be in better trim to handle me. The parallel is clear and I thank you."

I got up, after another four or five minutes lying there arguing across the two rooms. The look of her sitting there in the parlor told me clearly enough the afternoon was a dead duck. My parting shot was that *she* was probably the victim of Puritanical guilt, and that all these methods of throwing a monkey wrench into the romantic works at the last minute were excuses for avoiding the climax her conscience refused to permit. "You're the one who's afraid of Mrs. Grundy, so

I'll return the book as soon as possible," I said, and slammed out the front door. The last thing I saw was a foot in a golden slipper, tapping the floor. She looked as though she'd like to get into the car and ride into the sunset, only it was only 2:30.

There was no doubt I had ruptured myself carrying her to bed, as a trip to the doctor proved. "It's not too bad," he said, after poking me around a bit. "Just go easy for a while. I see by your chart we had a little hernia there several years ago. More or less standard — a loop of intestine dangling through the abdominal wall. What we call acquired hernia. Comes from straining or lifting a heavy object. Why don't we fix you up with a little support?"

I wore a truss for a while, which was uncomfortable at first, but I gradually got used to it. I didn't let on to Lena what had happened of course, as that would of been a breech of gallantry. Thus the one chivalry I did extend her she would never know about because it was impossible to tell her. I called the other woman's studio several times but no answer, meaning she had probably gone to the artists colony on the Dunes where she said she might spend part of the summer.

I now drank moderately all day instead of heavily in the evenings and nothing before. One night I came home about ten o'clock to find Elsie just returning from the mission with the kid. This was a direct violation of her agreement not to take him to any of the midweek revivals in return for my permission to go to Sunday School, those being the emotional whoopups I wanted to keep him free of. Elsie said, "I notice we don't object to a little reviving when we think the world is coming to an end."

"What you saw was not a sinner reviving," I said, "but an atheist backsliding."

Psychologists tell us we come down on people twice as hard when we know we are in the wrong. So I let her have it. I backed up what was a rather neat point, I think, with far more muscle than the case called for, reminding her of my basic principle: That it takes a lot more faith to live this life without faith than with it; that I may of lost my courage momentarily in what was admittedly a night of grade–A confusion, but that I instantly repented of my remorse (another pip) and that it gave her no legitimate excuse for reneging on our agreement about midweeks after having already done so by having the kid baptized behind my back. "I therefore hereby revoke my permission for him to go to Sunday School."

"Did you expect me to leave him home alone?"

"I'd of stayed home if I'd known you wanted to go. You knew that perfectly well, but you purposely let me go out without mentioning it so you'd have an excuse to take him with you. We're back among Christian ethics I presume. Right in the thick of it again. What a summer! The kid'd been better off back at Tippewawa," I said, a camp that was so awful even the counselors got homesick.

"You can't veto the Sunday School now, that just won't do, mister man. They only tell them Bible stories there, and you say yourself you have no objection to children learning them as stories."

"Well he don't need no sob sister teaching him. I can do that myself."

An unfortunate experience arose out of this. After the others went to bed I sat in the parlor brooding about the latest skirmish. The more I thought about it the more I was ready to stack up my knowledge of the Bible with anybody else's. The only thing is I discriminate, I don't swallow the hogwash and tribal superstitions along with the high moral teachings. So I carried a can of beer into the bedroom where Elsie was reading in bed and repeated that my position was not based on ignorance of spiritual matters, like I was often accused, that I knew as much about religion as the next man and maybe more. That I didn't know whether she could recite all the books of the Bible by heart but I could, and would. Only, to keep my intellectual integrity, I was going to belch them.

She looked up at me in alarm. "Stan, you wouldn't."

"One point. I won't in so doing be ridiculing the contents of the books as literature, only the use their put to by the gullible and the undiscriminating, who swallow the baby with the bath. Its time the human race became mature. Ready?"

"You wouldn't do this if you weren't drinking. Stan, you'll live to regret it."

"That will prove my point exactly. Because lets call on gods the way they did in the Old Testament which we'll begin with, and allegedly got answers. Fire from heaven and what not. If this being exists who you claim punishes people for their sins, let him strike me dead before I reach the end. Let him give me a sign. You see, I have *my* faith too. Now I'll begin."

I took a slug of beer to fuel up, so to speak, and made a good start. Say I got to Deuteronomy on the first lap. Then I took another pull of beer and let go with six or seven more books. But here a development occurred I hadn't figured on.

I began to get a little dizzy from being winded frankly. Lack of oxygen will do that to you, as anyone knows who has attempted this type of thing, or even just breathed in short pants for a while. The result — gasping for air like a stranded fish while the room and contents are starting to go bye-bye — hardly becomes a stormy petrol they call them. Iconoclasts willing to go to bat for their convictions. I was prepared to go whole hog and no pussyfooting. So I struggled gamely on. But halfway through the minor prophets I started feeling definitely faint and had to lay down. By this time Elsie was out of the bed and running around to my side.

"Stan, are you all right? Speak to me!" she said chaffing my wrists.

"I'm all right," I said, heaving myself up onto my elbows. But I wasn't. There were spots dancing before my eyes. My head swam and the room went around in circles. The empty beer can dropped from my hand to the floor. I blacked out altogether and fell back, cracking my head against the brass rails of the bed.

I came to I don't know how many minutes later, with Elsie slapping my face and calling to me in a panic. My shirt and tie were loose, as well as pretty well stained, as I had evidently been drooling a good deal out of the corners of my mouth.

"Promise me you'll never, never do that again."

"I never knocked the *contents of the books as such,* only the frau — frau — "

"Quiet *please.* If you don't stop this you'll be called to judgment. Maybe you are right now. Called to account for your sins and mockeries."

"Only the fraudulent uses their put to by *some but not all* religious leaders." No harm in qualifying. "Bamboozling suffering humanity into false hopes, feeding empty bellies with

73

promises of heavenly feasts. Two, as poetry a lot of the Old Testament is second to none. I've always said it."

"Don't bother with no fine distinctions now. Its no time. Just say you're sorry for the whole thing and it will never happen again, till we see what's what. I think you got your sign. You were struck down. So repent. What harm can it do."

"I suppose your right."

"Oh, thank God! Oh, what a house for a boy to be brought up in."

"I disagree. He'll be the stronger for it. Let him learn there are different points of view in the world, right in this house. Me the intellectual," I said as she wiped my chin with my tie, "you the believer. That gives him both sides of the age-old conflict."

"You've had your say, now let me have mine. I want to say a little prayer for you. Close your eyes."

I did, no objection to that. While she prayed for me, there was another embarrassing development arising directly out of the first, and of a piece with it. On account of the large quantities of air I had swallowed, I got the hiccups. Every few seconds out would come that sound like the *putt-putt* of a motor boat. Worst of all, the hiccups didn't blow over. They wouldn't stop and they wouldn't stop. Normally an attack will run you five, six minutes — ten at the most. An hour is bad enough. But occasionally it continues for days, and that can be very serious.

All night I laid in bed hitting on one cylinder. A minute might pass and I would think at last I'm over the hump, and then *putt*. I'd start to doze off and *putt* — wide awake again. By morning I was a wreck. I phoned the office to say I wouldn't be in, doing so myself rather than let Els, in hopes that the physical act itself would straighten out what was haywire inside me (irritation of the diaphragm to be accurate about it). I started to tell Stella, the office girl, that I was a little under the weather, but my condition made itself obvious over the wire. "I've got a bad case of the hic-*putt*-cups," I finally admitted.

"You've got the hiccups?"

"Oh, yes. And I'm sure it'll clear up soon. You carry on, and I'll keep in *putt* touch. When the crew gets back from the Willis job send McGurk and Desmond out on the next one and have Art Salerno crate the lot going out to Shaker *putt* Heights.

Two days later I was still in bed, making like an outboard motor, and growing steadily weaker. I tried not to think of all I had heard and read about this affliction, the dire consequences it might have. To no avail. I was haunted especially during the haggard night hours as I recalled how people had died of it, or anyhow with it, including one pope. It would be ironic if I went the same way as a great religious leader — not that the gulf between us was as wide as it had once been. No sirree. Daylight hours restored a measure of sanity. Kind friends volunteered remedies — all the usual things such as sips of water taken a certain way, sudden frights and so on. One neighbor blew off a shotgun under my window, with no results exept a near heart failure. On and on I *putt*ed, like a failing engine. One gossip, a woman Elsie had the sense to keep in the parlor, brought an almanac over with interesting medical oddities including the longest-running hiccups cases on record. I quick plugged my ears so as not to hear the top figures, but I thought I caught something about forty-some days, rung up by a woman in Ohio. Maybe I heard wrong, and maybe I misunderstood the motive in bringing these statistical tidbits to our attention. The friend may only of meant to show how long you could live with them, but uppermost in my mind was the understanding that you could die of them. I later learned you don't die of them, but of the things that cause them, or in a general deterioration of which they are a part. As a last resort they can cut something called the phrenetic nerve or something. Els was the soul of kindness and patience, sitting with me and sometimes taking trays into the bedroom so we could have meals together, over which we said grace believe me.

She had called the doctor but he just gave advice over the phone. Now she said, "I'm going to make him come." She went to the telephone and did so. But by the time she was through with the call, the hiccups were gone.

I didn't dare mention it right away, for fear of false hopes, but it was true. I counted off ten minutes, fifteen, then twenty, before telling her. I lay back on the bed in exhausted relief. "Thank God," I said.

"I hope you will, Stan. God's hand was in it. He laid it on you — and he took it off. The Lord giveth and the Lord taketh away. Blessed be the named of the Lord."

"Amen."

As the day wore on, though, I began secretly to feel it was the fright thrown into me by the almanac entry that did it. The thought that you might break the world's hiccup record is enough to scare hell out of anybody. But I said nothing about it. I kept my own counsels.

That night I slept like a log, twelve hours of solid oblivion. But in the middle of it I had a brief dream, like a small picture in the center of a blank canvas, that I could remember in vivid detail the next morning. It was about what I occasionally imagined in real life — that Lena Salerno was on the piano crew. There I was working side by side with her, with one important difference however. She was on heavy corner while I was carrying keyboard. McGurk was topping, and kind of grinning down at us, or at me. Then the scene changed as it will in dreams, and instead of moving an upright we were moving a grand. A grand of course is hauled with the legs off, on its side, with the same weight to carry for all, roughly speaking. Which would seem to mean that the dream had to do with equality between the sexes — but wait. Hold it. Topping the fiddle is now none other than not McGurk at all, but Elsie. My wife. She's on top.

An example of the way she has of staying there (by remaining downtrodden) took place at dinner the next day.

I had been griping about how familiar a sight Polish sausage and bean soup was getting to be on the kitchen table, and now was dismayed to see it on deck again. I had seen a silver candlestick on sale in the window of an antique store and gone in to buy it. One of those impulses. I let Elsie unwrap it for a surprise. Then I put a candle in it that I had also stopped for, set it on the table, and lit it.

"It's still light," Elsie said.

"It's not to supply illumination, it's to add a touch of romance. Women complain their life lacks romance after three, four years of marriage, so what could be more romantic than dinner by candlelight?"

"Especially with you eating in your undershirt."

"It's hot in here."

"So the heat of the candle will help cool it off."

"Not as much as a good pot of hearty sausage and bean

soup left over from last night, and the night before that."

The sausage was dreadful. I finished mine with a solid sense of achievement. Elsie wonders how anybody can eat anything as piping hot as me without scalding the roof of their mouth to death. She doesn't see how they can be human. Still I was feeling good and I said to Tom, "Ma claims the missionary told a funny story at the tabernacle the other night. Can you repeat it? Let's inject a little humor into the discussion at home, the way you say you do at school."

"Sure," said Tom. He set his spoon down and, looking across the table between the two of us, told the following.

"There was this colored missionary — the one who spoke — who had a congregation of converts in the African jungle. Or has rather. The story's a true one. So once some ministers from America who were traveling in the Congo came to visit his church, of thatch and straw, and all during the service the members of the congregation kept turning around to look at them. They had never seen white people before. So finally the missionary — he was preaching — stopped in his sermon and said to the congregation, 'Never mind them. Their skins may be white, but their souls are just as black as yours.' "

I roared. "That's a good one," I said, slapping the kid on the back. "And well told." He beamed with pleasure, and as usual in such moments of delight and amusement his nose seemed to get more pointed, increasing his resemblance to a fox. I suddenly felt he would come out all right in the end. His sense of humor would keep him from taking religion too seriously, or being damaged by an unfortunate home example. A new evangelist was on the horizon, Billy Graham, and I even thought of giving Elsie permission to take the boy to Chicago to hear him. What harm could it do? He couldn't be any worse than the local Bible banger, a self-righteous character who you knew was always thinking, Why can't people be more like Jesus like me?

But now I sensed a subtle shift in mood elsewhere at the table: Elsie feeling excluded from the comradeship between father and son. It had sprung up around a story from her end of the battlefield, yet I think she detected in the way we shared our appreciation of it an element that left her out in the cold somehow. Maybe she guessed my secret line of reasoning about the kid: that my tolerance would win him over in the end. I don't know. At any rate she was quiet the rest of dinner, and when it was over made a move that really took the cake. It was one of them marital chess plays that freeze the opponent on the board. She rose, shoving her chair back, passed her hand across her brow with the put-upon look, picked up the candlestick with the still burning candle in it and carried it to the sink to do the dishes by.

Top that if you can. As for the kid, I was glad to see by the toothpaste and shaving cream tubes that he was his old self again. He would secretly twist the caps on with a pair of pliers, so tight that you had to use pliers to screw them off again. The only thing, I wished he would smile once in a while, instead of just grin all the time.

six

AS FOR LENA, there were times when I wished I was married to that battleax. I'd show her a thing or two. Or was I boasting? Who did I know that had ever gotten the best of her — or even the last word? That temper, those comebacks.

79

Lena was like those litter bins with the swinging tops that you have to pull your fingers out of quickly before they get bitten off. Lena snapped back at you in the same way before you even finished what you were saying. Then there were the towering rages she was nice as pie in between.

I didn't see her alone all that summer and fall. Aside from everything else, I hardly fancied the idea of going to a rendezvous in a truss. Nor were there those brief moments we use to snatch together when the four of us went out, the whispered exchanges and the melting glances. So the affair simmered down, though I suppose each of us in his mind kept it on a back burner.

One day Art stopped in the office at quitting time to see me. I knew he had something special on his mind from the way he hung around till the office girl left. When she finally did and we were alone, he said, "Stan, I've been thinking about my life and future. I don't think it's in this business. You, yes, you own your own, but there's not enough security in it for a guy who doesn't, especially if he's married. When you get to be forty you suddenly realize it's now or never if you want to make that switch into something permanent. Besides the question of security, the furniture gets heavier as you get older. And I have got this rupture."

"I know how you feel."

"Even just crating, you have to handle the stuff. So if you told me no more truck, it still wouldn't meet these objections."

"I understand that perfectly, Art. Just what do you think you'd like to go into? You talk like you've got something spotted."

"I've been looking into the vending machine game, and it

looks pretty good, at least with the company I've been investigating, and who've been investigating me. They have a nice little deal they'll set you up in, if you qualify. What they do is, they supply the candy and cigarette machines on a kind of loan basis. You pay them off out of your monthly take. They even find the locations for you. It's an outfit in Chi. I've been in to see them a couple of times, and since things look like they might be firming up, I thought I owed it to you to tell you."

"Are the locations they find you in Chi?" I asked, locking the office vault. "Would you have to move out of town?"

"They might be anywhere. They're a nation-wide outfit, expanding in the big cities in every state. They could find you something around here or a thousand miles away. Yes, we might be transferred."

The shock this gave me made me realize how my recent indifference about the Lena affair was based on the assumption that she'd always be around, always there for me to go back to. That dream was shattered — so rudely that I had her on the phone before Art was two minutes out of the office.

"What's all this about vending machines?" I said. "Why didn't you tell me?"

"I thought it was better this way. Art didn't want me to say anything till something seemed to be jelling. Even despite that, I had half a mind to tell you anyway the other night when we went to the movie, but you didn't seem to know I was alive, so I skipped it. It really is better this way in the long run."

"Better! Long run! Do you realize how I feel about you? Oh, what fools two people are not to seize every moment they possibly can while there's time."

"Yes. Yes. Of course," she said, suddenly catching the same urgency that was seizing me. "The wine of life keeps oozing drop by drop. The leaves of life keep falling one by one."

"My sentiments exactly. Lena, how you can put things."

"Stan."

"When can I see you?"

"Anytime. I mean any time you can arrange it — you know, safely."

"I've got four rooms going to Fort Wayne tomorrow. McGurk and Art can handle it nicely. It won't be overnight, but it'll be all day."

I slipped into her house about one o'clock, taking the risk of not even going home for lunch and having that as an excuse for being in the neighborhood if seen. I carried two broiled lobsters which I got from a fish store near the office where they cooked them, and a bottle of cologne as a present. I was determined this time to do it with all the flourish and style at my command. All the graces. It was a real occasion, a real love feast. Not being animals, before going to bed we first polished off a whole lobster each, together with a quart of potato salad and half a huckleberry pie. Lena had made the potato salad and even baked the pie. She was quite a dish herself today, too. She had on a whole nother pair of lounging pajamas, scarlet silk edged with gold, with a gold sash tied tight like a cummerbund to hold her bulging middle in. I thought the whole rig was going to bust when she sat down on the floor to eat like we did, off the coffee table, just explode somewhere or other with a report you could hear across the street. I wouldn't of minded, and didn't mind the spectacle that made me afraid it might. I like a full meal in bed as well as at table. You can have your *Vogue* and *Harper's Bazaar* two-dimensional spooks Lena calls them. Which she's right — not just rationalizing her own heft. Give a man something he can get his mitts on, not some scarecrow you can see the Plaza fountain through that she's posing by.

But Lena has her spiritual side, and so when the meal was over and I had given her the cologne and was casing the place to decide how I could steer her toward the workshop on her own steam this time, no more hernias please, that'll be quite enough for now, thanks just the same, she says, "I have something for you too."

With that she hands me an envelope, in which was folded a sheet of paper with a poem written out in violet ink, in her own handwriting.

"It's beautiful," I said, even before reading it. "Lena. You wrote a poem to me?"

"It's a sonnet. To remember me by. Because — well I might as well tell you. The vending machine people called this morning to say Art's definitely in, and they want him to move out west. They're booming in the Pacific states."

"Oh, my God. What'll we do, Lena."

"No. No tears, Stan. No regrets. Let's not spoil this moment. Read the poem."

I smoothed the paper out and read it. It went:

> *How do I love thee? Let me count the ways.*
> *I love thee to the depth and breadth and height*
> *My soul can reach, when feeling out of sight*
> *For the ends of Being and ideal Grace.*
> *I love thee to the level of every day's*
> *Most quiet need, by sun and candle-light.*
> *I love thee freely, as men strive for Right;*

I love thee purely, as they turn from Praise.
I love thee with the passion put to use
In my old griefs, and with my childhood's faith.
I love thee with a love I seemed to lose
With my lost saints, — I love thee with the breath,
Smiles, tears, of all my life! and, if God choose,
I shall but love thee better after death.

"It's beautiful, Lena," I said when I finished. "But I'm surprised at you."

"Why? What do you mean?" I thought she looked away a little guilty.

"This last part, above loving better after death. I didn't know you believed in an after life."

She twisted a cigarette into a holder and we were once again on the march, snorting smoke.

"You can *really* be the *most* — " she said, not finishing the sentence, but I suppose the next word would be exasperating or infuriating, judging from her look. She grit her teeth and rolled her eyes to the ceiling as she paced. In one hand she angrily twirled a tawsel on the end of her sash. "You always have to foul things up with this — this compulsion to bring up some totally irrelevant thing. The last time we had a rendezvous you came barging in here complaining about your damn Bible belt, not even noticing me, let alone remembering what you're suppose to come for. Now I give you a poem — *hand* it to you *personally*, in my own *handwriting* — and instead of responding to it romantically for what it's intended to be, you pick on some little detail and make an issue of that, thereby screwing up another precious hour."

"Lena, I'm sorry," I said, getting up off the floor where I had all this while stayed squatting tailor-wise. My napkin was still hooked into my waist, as I didn't realize till later. "It just struck my attention because I always thought of you and me as seeing eye to eye on things. That we were kindred spirits, and that's how all this got started. The poem is very well worded. It's beautiful. I could never write anything like that in a thousand years. I don't know how you do it. Forgive me and let's — "

"No. It's too late. You've spoiled everything again. I'm out of the mood."

This got my cork, wrong as I may of been in not complimenting her first and then bringing up the other matter later. She always made a federal case out of everything — as I now bluntly told her. Passions were being roused of one kind anyway. "Lena," I said, "if you're going to converge on me again with this kind of talk, then I don't know why I came here."

"Well don't look at me, because *I* wouldn't know. Why did you? Why do you bother, if you can't behave like a lover?"

"Things are just like usual. I come here in good faith, and all I keep is getting criticism."

"Did it ever occur to you that you deserve it? You invite it. Cordially! Why? Because you can't think in terms of Us — only of Me. You can only see the elements of a given situation, relationship, that affect you personally, and these you select as your picture of it. The rest is unimportant. It bespeaks a self-centered and very unadaptable mind. One incapable of the fine give-and-take of human relations."

"I suppose you've got loads of personality."

"That's typical of you too — changing the subject. Switching things around to suit your convenience. I'm beginning to see there might be Elsie's side of the story. That the grievance

85

is far, far from all yours. She might a tale unfold too, if she was the type to come complaining. But she keeps things to herself. She suffers in silence."

"It's a lesson you might learn from her! What have you been doing just now but complaining. And it's not the first time. What you want is a wailing wall yourself, not a lover. You've never been treated right by any man, to hear you tell it."

"You're all alike!"

"In a minute I may never come back."

"It's what I suspected right from the first. You're not a man!"

She shot this at me with such violence, wheeling away, that I stood stunned. Motionless between fury and desire. I watched her squash the cigarette out and throw the holder down on the coffee table we had a moment ago been happily tucking in lobsters at. It bounced to the floor. She kicked at it, but missed. Something in the scene checked the anger inside me, this 2-way traffic of rage and desire, giving desire the right away. What a tumultuous bedful this woman would make, if you could only shut her up and get her into it. Get her off of theory and into practice. Hunger rolled like a breaker, sweeping me to her side.

"Oh Lena, what are we doing?" I said. "Our last chance and this is what we do with it. We could have so much. Let's not squander this hour in another squabble that we might as well be married. Let's take our happiness while we can."

I lunged out to take her with every indication that I intended to act on this advice, but she sidestepped me so neatly that I charged right past her, like a bull past a toreador. I turned around.

"Look baby," I said, "I've had just about enough of this. This time I'm going to gore you." I got her around the waist and held her in a vice-like grip. I suddenly felt capable of rape, which I think she sensed. Because there was a stinging blow on my jaw, dealt with the sharp edge of her elbow. I don't know whether she intended it or whether it was a result of her general thrashing around to get free of my grasp, but the surprise made me let go, and then, seizing the advantage, she shoved me back against the wall with a thud that knocked a picture askew.

I stood there glaring at her, like an animal pawing the ground preparatory to charging again.

"Stan, Stan," she said, "control yourself for God's sake. There are prison terms for this."

I came back in slowly, like a wrestler. "And prison sentences there ought to be for a lot of other things too. You've teased this man long enough, baby. Now you're going to lay it on the line. So if you don't take those slacks off, and now, I'll be glad to save you the trouble."

With that I reached out to tear them off, but my hand was arrested in midair by a development that saved *me* the trouble. It was the embarrassment you had all along feared. Under the strain of her defensive contortions they gave way at last with a loud rip, opening a gash that exposed a good twelve inches of the divine flank. It was the climax of our affair. Lena had burst her seams at last. She gave a little gasp of surprise, looked down to confirm what had happened, and then put her hands to her face and with a loud wail of humiliated fury threw herself on the couch.

I came over to try to console her, to express a tenderness I had not hitherto felt, but it was no use. "Go away! Oh go

*8*7

away! What's the use! Everything is so awful! Everything is so absolutely and utterly hopeless!"

No exaggeration, at least of the present situation. She was really hysterical. She laid on her back with her hands over her face and kicked and thrashed around on the couch, carrying on like a Crazy Woman with a stream of incoherent jabberings punctuated by shrieks I was sure could be heard in the street.

"Lena I . . . Let me just . . . You're a big beautiful bundle of . . . You really are you know, and I would like nothing better than . . . I'll always," I said, making several starts, but they were all futile.

I murmured some parting sentiment that I knew wasn't heard above the uproar either, and it was looking down at her there that I noticed the napkin still tucked in my Bible belt, and yanked it off. I said goodbye and started toward the door. Then I remembered the poem and went back for it. I folded it into the envelope, put it slowly into the breast pocket of my coat and went out. I hated like hell to see me go, I can tell you, because she was the only mistress I ever had.

seven

SO THE STINKING summer wore away, and fall came, bringing with it not the clear sharp days that brace the spirit, but long weeks of the kind of drizzle old country Poles call "korsniak," or cabbage soup. It began to rain like that as I hurried back to the office, a foretaste of what was to come when autumn really settled in. Good thing I had to get back to the office that afternoon or I'd gone on a binge right then. What I hurried back to now was an office girl who was beginning to get on my nerves, probably in part because others were wearing them thin.

Stella Kovacs was the soul of efficiency, but she had a habit of conducting a conversation almost exclusively by repeating what you had just said in question form. "Stella, I'm going to lunch." "You're going to lunch?" "Yes. If McGurk's crew get in before I do, tell them to load that lot of furniture that's going out of storage. It's on the elevator." "It's on the elevator?" "Yes, it goes out next." "It goes out next?"

The guys called her Echo Lake, but it didn't amuse me no more. Stella was a thin, giggly girl who was saving up to get married. I could imagine what domestic life was going to be like for her swain. It was going to be like those vaudeville routines where the straight man repeats what the comedian said, on and on, till the payoff comes. I knew that when I got back to the office I was going to take my mood out on her, for years of living have given me a low opinion of this species.

She was sitting at her desk, which was front-to-front with mine so that we faced each other, stamping tags for a new lot which the other crew was bringing in later in the afternoon. Every lot going into storage gets a number, and every article of furniture is tagged with it. Stella had a couple dozen of these tags laid out in rows on her desk and was stamping them with the adjustable rubber stamp used to number them. I sat across from her with my hat still on my head, watching her bring the stamp down on the ink pad, then the tag, alternately, thud, thud, thud. She gathered the batch together like a deck of cards and laid out a new one, and then again, thud, thud, thud.

"Stella," I said at last, "this lot has only two rooms."

"This lot has only two rooms?"

"Yes. A kitchenette. Really only a room and a half. You saw it on the bill you gave the crew. You made the bill out yourself. Now you've already got enough tags there for five, six rooms, but away you still tag, knowing we will again have to throw the surplus away. You overtag."

"I overtag?" She giggled, as though I had complimented her on some erotic tendency or other. It made no sense, yet now it suited my mood to pursue the needling along sexual lines.

"Do you realize how many kitchenette jobs we're getting in lately?" I says, tipping back in my swivel chair and putting my feet on a corner of the desk. "Does it suggest anything to you?"

"Does it suggest anything to me?" Christ! I thought, she even repeats questions into new questions.

"Yes. Think. Kitchenettes are what people first rent, so households of that size splitting up means that divorce is on the increase among younger and younger couples. Kids in the first stages of marriages, not the last. They don't wait ten, fifteen years any longer. Life is too short. Seize the moment! Get divorced while you're young. Well besides divorce and separation, there's death, sickness, poverty and husbands running away never to be seen again among some of the other reasons why stuff goes into storage. The bulk of our business is human misery. Have you ever stopped to think about that? That we're vultures?"

"We're vultures?" She giggled again, positively shimmering at the enlarged scope I had given her life. I was opening vistas for her. I sat there gorging myself on irritation and annoyance. I *wanted* her to annoy me. I looked for it, I cultivated it, I fed on it. I decided to toy with her a little more.

"How long is your marriage going to last?"

"It's going to be permanent," she replied with spirit. "I'm not going to get divorced."

"At last a direct answer!" I said, banging the desk with my fist.

"What do you mean?"

"Nothing."

She had now stopped stamping tags and was doing something else. I glanced over at the office safe.

We needed a walk-in vault, not only for our own records but to store things of special value in for customers, such as silver. It stood open much of the day, and it had more than once crossed my mind what a convenient place it would be for holdup men to shove you if you were ever robbed. I had often thought of having a phone extension installed in it so you could call for help. I didn't want to rouse any fears needlessly in Stella, who might get scared and leave me without a bookkeeper. But now I said to her, "Stella, have you ever stopped to think how much of human life is based on trust? We have to trust people we don't know a single thing about. We trust restaurant chefs not to poison our food, service station attendants to give us full measure. You trust a boy friend enough to marry him without really knowing anything about him, and you trust a boss who, for all you know, might be criminally insane. It happens every day, people nobody would dream suddenly going berserk with their family or pedestrians out walking. How do you know I won't attack you and drag you into that vault and lock you up inside it. My prisoner."

"Your prisoner?" she said, drawing her shoulder up in a titter.

"Yes, my prisoner." I rose slowly and stood over her, giving my belt a menasing hitch. "The fact is, that's just what I'm going to do. Not kill you. Oh no, I have better plans than that. I've secretly dug out another room that communicates with the back wall of the vault. I've been working on it nights, and in it are all the necessities of life to keep a nice luscious young girl alive *for a purpose*." I chuckled like a maniac. "It's furnished with a couch, air conditioning, a refrigerator for food and champagne, all the comforts of life. Even a telephone. But you can't call out with it. I can only call in. To keep in touch with you." I laughed like a fiend again, "Mbwaahahaha," then added: "Needless to say, it's an unlisted number."

"It's an unlisted number?"

"Oh Christ," I said, thinking it aloud to myself more than saying it. I put my hat on the rack and went up the back stairs. "I think I'll check on Lightning. See how many fingers he's smashed by now this time."

Lightning Walters was an old timer who had worked on moving vans for forty years. He was semi-retired now, but he helped me out during the rushes and between times when I needed an extra helper, or to crate a job — as was the case today with Art Salerno in Fort Wayne. (All the good that did me!) At seventy he was pretty slow with a hammer and saw, but he could still get five rooms wrapped and boxed in only half again the time it should take, which isn't too bad by today's standards.

He was on the second floor, halfway through the job. The hammer quickened its tempo at my approach, iron doors giving their usual warning. I sat on a finished crate and chewed the rag with him for a few minutes.

"How are things, Lightning?" He got his nickname ironically of course, but not because of the speed with which he weelds a hammer, but because he never strikes twice in the same place. He bent three or four six-penny nails while I watched, and had to pull them out and start over again, though that was probably nervousness at having an audience.

"Oh, I'm feeling fine," he said, showing an assortment of teeth as black as watermelon seeds, as well as some glimpses of watermelon pink in the wide open spaces between. You will notice that he answered a question about how things were by telling how he felt — a typical response. People constantly bragging about their health are just as hard to take as hypochondriacs. "Never felt better in my life." He pulled a bandanna from his hind pocket and wiped non-existent sweat from his brow, then tobacco juice from his chin which was plenty existent. I knew the peon of praise to his superb physical condition which my question touched off would be climaxed by the inevitable statement: "I never had a sick day in my life." Well it was no secret why he never. He smoked cigars and a pipe as *well* as chewed tobacco, and as one of the boys on the van remarked, his filthy old mouth was probably the most sanitary place on earth. No germs could possibly live in there.

I took about as much of Lightning as I could, but when I left he had contributed his bit to the deterioriation of my mood — which was what I wanted. People bent on a self-destructive tear often find their spirits soaring at the same time they're plunging, in the heights and depths at once somehow. Frank Novak, whose place I stopped in on the way home from work, wasn't pleased to have me get as expansive as I did on three or four quick drinks. He kept the afternoon *Blade* spread out on the bar, and added nothing to the conversation except a few occasional remarks about what was in the news. He seemed interested in a prowler around town. I told him to forget the prowler and join me in "Sto Lat," the Polish drinking song that says, "May you live a hundred years." With a good-natured laugh he said no, it was too early, and refused to serve me any more — or rather diplomatically persuaded me not to ask him for any more. I know the signs. I laughed comparatively, to show there were no hard feelings, and told him he could expect me back after dinner.

I walked in a little after eight o'clock, to find a bunch of the boys talking about the prowler as if there had been no interruption of the discussion. Frank was in the thick of it. There was the usual variety of viewpoints. Some said he was a Peeping Tom, which started a general free-for-all on what motivates people like that. Frank said he thought it was the secrecy of it. "That's a thrill in itself to them — having to do it on the sly. Like children doing something, or just *being* somewhere, that's forbidden. There was even a murderer some years ago who said that just breaking into a house satisfied some kind of sexual urge. The danger of it and all."

"Then why did he kill? Why didn't just breaking into the house satisfy him?" another guy said.

I listened to the discussion swirling around me for about two or three drinks, and then put in my two cents. I suggested that all these abnormalities, from harmless peeping to rape and murder, were exaggerations of normal instincts. That we're all prowlers, thieves, rapists and murderers at heart, or have a dash of it in us. This is the beast sleeping in each of us, dozing lightly in some. Long before I finished my remarks I noticed Frank waiting impatiently behind the bar to answer me.

"Now wait a minute," he said. "Just a minute. You're saying two different things here. First that the criminal in each of us has gotten out of hand, second that each of us is a criminal under control. Which of these two do you mean?"

"It seems to me they're the same thing said two different ways, or maybe it's sometimes one, sometimes the other. But if you want me to vote for one, I'll say the first. Most criminals do in deed what we do in thought all the time. That was Christ's basic principle, the big truth he got hold of. Everybody commits adultery in his heart. The peeper is corrupting a perfectly natural and normal thing: curiosity. The instinct to look at a woman. If you walk down the street and accidentally see one undressing behind a window you'll stop and watch. Set out to find one, and you're a peeper. But the impulse is the same."

It was a stimulating discussion, and I had a good evening with my cronies without getting stewed. Yet when I left the tavern I walked home in a depressed mood. I had written the whole Lena business off, she was washed out of my life on a tide of events over which I had no control, and now my thoughts kept returning to Elsie in a general feeling of guilt. Guilt isn't the right word, but there isn't any for the vague, uneasy sensation I was experiencing, so it will have to do. There must be something to the Mrs. Grundy business after all, and to the Christian principle I just found myself citing (speaking of Christ purely as a moral teacher of course). Maybe there's sound psychological reasons for leaving something on your plate, for a sop to the gods even though they

95

don't exist. Now I felt unhappy that things had come to such a pass between Elsie and me. There was no love life between us save for the purely physical satisfactions, mechanically sought, mechanically given. Yet now that the distraction of Lena was out of the picture, I could begin to see that what had soured me on Elsie sexually was the religious war, which was really irrelevant to it, or ought to be. Elsie was more attractive than Lena when it came right down to it. She was better looking, or would be if she learned to dress and make up, and her figure was better if only by virtue of there not being so much of it. If you saw the two of them lying on a beach I think Elsie would draw your eye more or hold it longer — it was only when you stopped to talk to them that you could see Lena had more style and pizazz. And there I had been going to all that trouble to see Lena, who I didn't really like. Obviously I was drawn to her by the style and pizazz — and because she was something new. Ah, there you have it, the all-important and never to be underestimated factor of novelty. Familiarity is an alienator of affections, no use in denying that. The author of *Something for Mrs. Grundy* made the point that variety is as much an instinct as sex itself, hence all the hightailing for new pastures and fresh objects of desire.

All these things were churning through my mind in the chaotic jumble we call thought when I got a novel sensation from a totally unexpected quarter.

I always came home from Frank's place through the alley. I closed the gate behind me and had just passed the garage and was walking across the yard toward the back porch steps when a noise in my bedroom made me stop. It was just the scrape of a chair, but there was something so secret and mysterious about it that I stole over and stood quietly under the window. The shade was almost, but not quite, drawn. By taking a step back and standing on tiptoe I could just look under it into the lighted room.

Elsie had just undressed, and was standing at the foot of the bed, ready to get into her nightgown. As I watched, she slipped it over her head and wriggled into it with her arms in the air. It was a charming feminine motion, and supposedly done every night at this time and often in my presence, but did I ever notice it? Had I ever? Watching her when she didn't know she was being watched — least of all, of course, from out here — that was what gave the scene an extra flavor. In fact there was an odd thrill about it, a dash of secret excitement quite unlike anything I had ever experienced before. It remained with me after I had locked up the house and gone to bed myself, causing me to take Elsie in my arms in a way that, I guess, I hadn't done in some time. I slept a little better than I had in some time too, and without getting up for any extra nightcaps.

The next night, about half past ten, I was stretched out in bed with my clothes on looking at an art magazine when I glanced up to find Elsie sitting at the dresser in her shift, brushing her hair. Funny, I thought, here a man will pour over cheesecake when the real-life article is in the same room with him. All he has to do is lift his eyes from the page and there's the substance, but no, he prefers to feast his eyes on the shadow. I remembered my little adventure of last night and had a whim to repeat it. I got up, putting the magazine aside. I hovered around for a minute, giving the drawn window shade a slight hitch up so it would clear the sill, and said

97

something about going outside for a breath of air before locking up. Smoking a cigarette, I drifted down the porch steps into the yard and resumed my post under the window.

She was in profile to me this time, but the effect was if anything that much more provocative. Her pink slip fell away above her crossed legs, offering a tantalizing glimpse of plump white thigh. She was slow in undressing, and I noticed for the first time, appreciated, a certain thoughtful leisure in the way she did things when she was by herself. She may of been half-hazard in the way she put her hair up, but not in the slow, methodical way she brushed it. She seemed to enjoy that. She had a cigarette burning in an ashtray, as always when at the dresser brushing her hair or manicuring her nails, and she would interrupt what she was doing to pick it up and take a drag, each time watching herself do so in the mirror. Eternal charming feminine sight!

I crouched there in the shadows watching for fully fifteen minutes before being rewarded with the crowning sight. She stepped out of her underthings, as women do, put her nightgown over her head, and then there was the same delightful wriggle as the silk slipped down her flanks and settled in folds about her with a secret whisper I fancied I could hear out here. I couldn't wait to get back to her. It was only afterward that I got up again and locked the house.

This went on for several nights. Sometimes I would go out when I knew the charming performance was about to begin, sometimes I would lurk around the back yard without knowing, adding a tingle of uncertainty to it. I would smoke a cigarette and wander along the fence, looking idly at the view across the alley. A number of shades were up, and I saw from two or three windows how careless people can be, but that was not what I was out here for, and I would turn away. Old Mrs. Stepanek could be seen ironing in the kitchen in her slip, not a sight to detain anybody for long. Once she put her iron down and went to the window to lean out of it, spreading her hands on the sill for a look around. When she withdrew she pulled the shade down. No need for any such precautions, Mrs. Stepanek, I thought sympathetically.

I pursued my new-found fancy for the better part of three weeks I would say, not regularly by any means, that is to say not nightly, but when the mood took me, and while I cannot recommend this rather sophisticated practice indiscriminately and without regard for the individual temperaments concerned, it did add a certain zest to my own domestic life. It is a taste for special palates, an extra fillip for jaded sensibilities.

One night about half-past ten I was crouched in the shadows at my customary observation post when there was a rustle of footsteps behind me and a hand gripped my shoulder. I saw the glimmer of a badge and a cop's face, accompanied on the other side by another. "All right, that's about enough of that, don't you think?"

"What do you mean?" I asked as I was hustled away between them through the alley gate, and then toward a squad car parked some distance down with the motor off and the headlights out. "What is the meaning of this?"

"Oh, cut it. Let's not play games."

"You don't understand," I said. "I live there. That's my house."

"Then what were you doing looking into it like that?"

"None of your beeswax."

I was helped into the back seat and joined by one of the cops while the other got in behind the wheel and drove off.

99

"You'll have to do better than that, Mac," the driver threw over his shoulder as we turned onto the street. "We're cracking down on altogether too many prowlers lately. I don't know what it is. The weather, sunspots, world tensions, or just a run of something you get now and then for no reason you can explain. What's your name?"

"Stanley Waltz."

"Got any identification?"

My wallet was in my coat, which I didn't have on, so the answer to that was negative. "But if you drive me back I'll get it and show you."

"Where do you live?"

"*There!*" I turned and pointed back in the direction we had come, and with considerable spirit, for I was getting my dander up. "I live there, that was my back yard. That's what I've been trying to tell you."

"Then why were you acting so suspicious?"

"I was only doing what I have a perfect right to do. It's my property and I'll prowl on it all I want, and I'll act as suspicious on it as I goddam please! As you'll learn to your regret," I said with heat, for we were slowing to a stop in front of the Third Precinct Station. "Who reported this?"

"I don't know. We just got the call on the short wave."

"Mrs. Stepanek? Because she don't have to worry anybody will bother her."

Much has been written about the subject of reality and allusion, and how the two merge into one in an individual's life. I wouldn't know what to call this as I was escorted up the station stairs. They were real enough, and so was the broad doorway through which we walked — yet the whole thing was a fantasy. The main desk was on a raised platform behind a massive wooden rail that would give anybody walking up to it, even someone lodging a complaint, the feeling of a wretch before a high tribunal. A Sergeant Michaelson was on duty, according to a name plate on the desk, which had a short wave mike on it and a mess of papers he was working at. Two smaller desks behind him were unoccupied at the moment, though in the course of the next few minutes a sleepy looking cop entered from a back door and sat down at one of them. The cops who were running me in steered me up to the main desk.

"Charge?" said the sergeant.

"Peeper."

The sergeant gave me a glance before pulling a form sheet toward him, murmuring something like "At last." By now I had hit on my plan.

"That was what I had gone out to look for, Your Honor," I said. "I thought I'd heard a noise outside, and it was in all likelihood him, since there was this call reporting him. So I stepped outside to check. But I saw nothing. He had apparently escaped."

"You didn't look as though you were seeing nothing in that window," the cop who'd been driving said. I now recognized him as a blond Polak I had seen around town. "You looked as though you were seeing plenty — and getting your fill. We watched you ourselves for a couple of minutes to make sure. You weren't looking for any prowler. You were watching a show."

"It was my own house, which I understand is a man's castle. That includes the grounds I take it."

"What were you watching?" the desk sergeant put in.

"I was watching my missus prepare to retire for the night."

"Couldn't you do that from inside?"

"It's not the same thing."

"I see." He stroked his chin in a way that indicated he didn't exactly, but was trying to. "Do you make a regular practice of this?"

"I don't see that my private life is any concern of this department."

"You may be disturbing the peace in some way."

"*You're* disturbing the peace. I'll make this a test case in any court you care to name. And I may also sue you for false arrest if you don't stop this nonsense and let me go."

Losing my temper was all to the good, since it indicated that I was telling the truth, at least to the desk sergeant's satisfaction. It was to him I addressed my plan. When he asked for my identification I told him it was at home, then gave him my name, address and telephone number and suggested a simple call there would clear this all up. "Doesn't 922 Sparrow Street sound like the number of the house where you picked me up?" I asked, turning to the driver of the car. He allowed that it did. The other cop had disappeared, but a man in plain clothes had joined the group, taking notes of his own. His interest seemed to me sympathetic and intelligent as he listened to the questions and answers. I now proposed to the desk sergeant that he check the phone number I reeled off to him against the name and address I gave him by consulting the directory on his desk. He did, and they tallied of course. "Now why don't you call my house and ask the lady who answers to give you a description of me."

That was how it was all straightened out. The Mrs. Stanley Waltz who answered said it was true her husband had stepped out of the house for a minute and had not been seen since.

She described me, a square-jawed man of forty with dark eyes and kinky black hair parted on the left, and calloused hands, but what he was wearing when last seen she couldn't for the life of her say. Showing that we never look at one another. A few questions about our private lives (such as her maiden name, etc.) and a comparison of her answers with mine satisfied the desk sergeant, who then told her she could come and get me any time. But he didn't dismiss me immediately.

After he had hung up, he lit a cigar stub that had gone out. He watched me through the flame as he puffed to get it going. The man in plain clothes was still jotting his notes when I turned away and started toward a bench on which to sit down and wait. "Just a minute," the desk sergeant said. "I'd like to ask you a few more questions. Personally."

"What do you want to know?"

"How long have you been married?"

"Twelve years."

"Have you been engaging in this practice for long?"

"I've said that that seems to me none of your business."

"Well now just wait a second. I could make it my business. I'm only asking these things personally, not as an officer of the law, but I'm not sure that your behavior isn't a violation of some statute or other at that. Not at all sure. I can still book you if you're not cooperative, and put bail at five hundred dollars, which you probably can't scare up in cash at this hour of the night. So why don't you just try to satisfy the law's justifiable curiosity?"

"Am I to understand that you use your job as a cloak for peering into other people's emotional windows?"

"He's got you there, Sarge," said the man in plain clothes,

103

moving in a little closer with his notebook and pencil. I figured he was making the full official report, and since he had such a friendly face and manner I decided to go along with him. He was a young man of about thirty-five, with a lean ferret face but twinkling blue eyes that you instinctively trusted. The diplomatic thing would clearly be to go along with him as a means of smoothing the whole matter out on an amicable basis. "You accuse the sergeant then of morbid curiosity?" he asked with an extra sparkle in his eye.

"I wouldn't accuse him of anything. I just raise the point."

"I'm only trying to grasp his exact motivaton," the sergeant said to him, and then to me, "What exactly do you feel when you steal outside and watch your wife under these conditions instead of inside the house where you're perfectly free to feast your eyes on her to your heart's content?"

"She's my lawfully wedded spouse, and I have a right to look at her any way I wish."

"Do you pretend she's a stranger or something? That you've never seen her before? Or that you don't live there but it's somebody else's house and somebody else's wife? Or what?"

"I've never thought it through in any such detail. All I can say is, well, it puts a woman in a new light. Gives her a new dimension."

"Spices up a relationship. Hops up the domestic grind," the sergeant said, nodding to himself. "Yes, I can see that."

"Gives an old and familiar dish a dash of the garlic of the forbidden," the other man said. He was evidently the intellectual of the bunch. "Would you say there's that in it? I mean that part of the thrill *is* the pleasure of the forbidden? Pretending that you're an evildoer?"

"I've told you I don't analyze it that deep. I just don't go into it. If you want to, go ahead, but leave me out of it. You're parlaying a little thing into something it was never intended. My original defense still stands. I was picked up for skulking around private property, but it's my property and I'll skulk around on it all I goddam please. It's my right under the Constitution."

"But what if everybody did that?" the sergeant asked. "What if this became a universal habit, and all the back yards in town were full of husbands peering at their wives through the bedroom window to give them an extra new dimension? Where would civilization as we know it be then?"

"I have no idea, and it wouldn't be my problem in any case. If you'll excuse me I'll go outside and wait for my wife. I don't want her in a place like this."

"Have you ever been psychoanalyzed?" the guy in plain clothes asked, following me.

"Not yet," I said, going out the door, "but you may drive me to it."

"Do you care to amplify your statement about 'a new dimension'? Define that a little more closely?"

"No."

I was waiting for Elsie at the curb when she drew up, a few minutes later. I hopped in and told her to step on it.

She accepted without any questions my explanation that I had gone out to check on a noise in the yard, not saying anything to her about it because I didn't want to frighten her unnecessarily. "Well I'm glad the police department is efficient in some ways," she said, "even though they nab the wrong person."

"I may sue them for false arrest," I said, not really meaning it, but just to get it off my chest.

"No don't, Stan. Forget it. Just stay in the house nights after this. It'll keep you out of trouble."

As it turned out, I stayed in not only nights but days as well for some time to come. Because while my explanation held water on the domestic front, there was a story on page five of the Slow Rapids *Blade* the next day. The young fellow in plain clothes with the trustworthy eyes taking all those notes was a reporter, as you may of guessed. That I never tumbled is indicative of my state of mind at the time.

eight

THE STORY WASN'T featured or played up in any way, and thank God not on page one, but it was long and detailed, and followed by opinions of my behavior from local leading authorities. The reporter had got right on the blower and asked lawyers and judges and psychologists to give their views on exactly what constitutes disturbing the peace, and just how far a man's privileges on his own property go — to what extent, in other words, a man's home *is* his castle. The head of the psychology department at the local college, Polycarp, gave his slant on my behavior.

"I would say there is nothing morbid in this practice," his statement ran, "not seriously so at any rate, except to the degree that it may be a kind of fetishism. Although here too we must proceed cautiously. Fetishism, classically defined, is the compulsive use of some inanimate object in attaining sexual gratification, such as a shoe, a lock of hair, an undergarment, etc. Here the object is not any of these, but the naked body, which can, of course, also be associated with sexuality. Perhaps new ground is being broken here, or should be broken in our continuing attempt to understand the whole complicated mechanism of *special detail* in sexual gratification. Simultaneously, there is another and contrary element to be taken in consideration. In obtaining sight of the sexual object under simulated surreptitious circumstances such as these, there is doubtless also at work the degradation principle; that of making a member of an alliance a *temporarily anonymous object*, and so reducing her in status, a form of violation in itself. Even more cardinally, perhaps, is the wish to divest her of familiarity as such. The husband symbolically converts her into a stranger. This may be the beginning of a trend. A woman in Pennsylvania was recently granted a divorce on the ground that her husband insisted on giving her a new name each week. These attempts to freshen up a familiar object, even confer a new identity, by imposing a novelty it does not intrinsically possess, is a reversal of the usual function of fantasy. Instead of living in an imaginary world, one makes the real world imaginary. But it remains to be seen whether any new ground is really being broken here, whether the incidents cited are straws in the wind. Certainly a close watch should be kept to ascertain whether a trend is in the making."

There were several angry letters from readers, some demanding a return to the McKinley and Coolidge eras when life was less complex, some asking when it would be safe for women to go out on the streets at night. As I say, I kept out of them even during the day except when absolutely necessary, walking and even driving around when I had to in smoked glasses and a soft hat pulled down over one eye. The guys at the office razzed me, talking about what some people will do for hacks, but Stella looked at me askance, casting apprehensive glances at the vault. Finally I said to her one day, "I'm going away on vacation."

"You're going away on vacation?"

"Yes. For a few weeks. You're in charge of the office and Art Salerno of the crews. He can do the estimating too. And while I'm gone you might be thinking how things aren't all black and white. There are intermediary grays."

"There are intermediary grays?"

"Oh my God!"

I went to Florida. But I no more than stepped off the plane than I realized you can't run away. I telephoned home every evening I was there, which turned out to be exactly three. Then I packed up and went back. That was just as frustrating. Nothing was said about the recent events — which was the trouble. I wanted to talk about them but Elsie wouldn't. I wished she would tell me what she was really thinking instead of maintaining this patient and enduring — and no doubt Christian — silence. As a sheep before his shearers is dumb. Every time I started to explain the newances of the thing she'd say it wasn't necessary. She understood. It was perfectly all right. My hunch was she secretly thought any scrape I got into got me that much nearer the fold. In the end I would stumble into the everlasting arms. It was the kid I was most worried about. All he still ever did was grin, so nobody could have the slightest inkling what he was thinking. I'm sure we kept the newspapers from him till that part of the notoriety blew over, and he never brought the subject up himself or gave any hint he had ever heard about it. But it would be too much to ask that he would never in later life learn about his father and the blot on the family escutcheon. That his name had a stigma attached to it.

Because I soon realized I was a marked man. Most of all from the expressions of the people who tried to be natural about it and laugh it off. They included Art and Lena Salerno. Maybe they did look on the whole thing as a crazy lark to be laughed off. In any case they left early that winter — for Arizona of all places. That was where the firm sent him. They were out of our life. The last we heard was a card saying Art was happy as a clam servicing a flock of vending machines in and around Tucson.

Conversations at Frank's tavern weren't what they use to be, or so I imagined, which came to the same thing as far as my life was concerned. People there, like everywhere else, either avoided me or went out of their way to be nice. Which of these was the more annoying I was never sure. I couldn't be sure of anything again.

The drizzle in which summer had passed into fall continued while autumn became winter. But just before Christmas the weather changed, and one Saturday afternoon when the house was full of Elsie's relatives and mine, all trying to get into the Holiday spirit, it suddenly began to snow. "It reminds me of Poland," an old aunt of Elsie's said. They talked of the old country customs, how they had observed the approach of Christmas there in the church and in the home. They did this without trying to tread on anybody's toes. They knew I was an atheist, and were careful not to say anything to offend me.

Elsie clapped her hands and said, "Why don't you all go down now and get your trees together, you menfolk. Take the kids and walk together through the snow to Pete Lubek. He's got a lot full down by Sycamore Street."

"Why, yes," I said, "I'll help observe the pagan custom of taking a bit of green into the house, which is one of the heathen odds and ends that the Christian religion was put together out of, some of which also include the birth of a god witnessed by shepherds, a ceremonial last meal — a notion that was knocking around the ancient world before the Galileans took it over — and Poseidon walking on the water, all of them and a lot more adapted from heathen cults flourishing at the time. Sure, let's go. Get your coats and hats everybody!"

But throwing myself into the spirit of Christmas didn't help much, and bursts of enthusiasms always wore off soon. My mood would fall back into one of brooding anxiety and concern, always on Tom's behalf, always in terms of his future. I didn't want him to grow up and find he had a name with qualifications passed on to him. Sometimes I thought of moving out of town and setting up a business somewhere far from Slow Rapids. But that was completely impractical, and it would be running away. I wanted to stay here in my home town, somehow, and lick this thing. That was why even though others forgot the incident, or seemed to on the surface, I became more and more obsessed with the idea of clearing my name.

One evening I picked up the *Blade* and saw, boxed on the front page, an announcement of a poetry contest. It carried a five hundred dollar prize for the best poem submitted in a competition sponsored by the owner of the paper, Walter Wetzel, in memory of his late wife, who had been a clubwoman and ardent poetry lover herself. Since he wanted to be sure the prize went to something "of a traditional and not experimental nature, in keeping with the tastes of the deceased," he would judge the contest himself.

To win such a thing would certainly clear the family name. But for me to write a poem was just as certainly out of the question. Then, slowly, the idea began to creep into my head of using the poem Lena had written me and left behind. Why not? Who would be the wiser? She was out of my life and Slow Rapids was out of hers, forever. She would never hear of it away off there in Arizona, while the honor to the family would clear its name with a little left over — not to mention the five hundred dollars toward the college education I was now more than ever determined Tom would have. He was already in junior high, none too soon to think about it. As for me, the poem was now one of the more useless items among my souvenirs. I typed it over on the office typewriter, signed it, and submitted it with an entry blank cut out of the *Blade*.

It won first prize, and I think it won hands down, judging from some of the runners up and honorable mentions they printed along with it. It was splashed on the front page along with a glowing letter from the publisher saying what pleasure it gave him to find he could award the honor to a sonnet "so conspicuously embodying the ancient merits of beauty and meaning which the late Leona Wetzel cherished, and to the end of her life championed against the ugly and the incomprehensible." Alongside it was a picture of me accepting the five hundred dollar check from Mr. Wetzel.

I don't know whose phone began to ring first. Probably his, and not long after the issue hit the streets. Because when I got back to the office after looking at a job there were several messages waiting for me, one from him asking me to call back immediately. The phone rang as I was reading it, and it was Wetzel.

Thus I learned from an apoplectic publisher what a plagiarist Lena Salerno really was. The best. Wetzel kept spluttering something about Browning, about whom he had just been briefed by readers eager to perform the task for him. Browning I'd heard of, of course, but I hadn't realized he had a wife who wrote too. I said it was a rotten coincidence, and regretted the whole thing more than I could say. I would certainly give the money back, not being a crook. "It's not the money anyway, it's the principle of the thing," I said.

There was a statement in the paper the next day, Friday, rescinding the prize and talking about *Sonnets from the Portuguese*, which enough of his readers were familiar with to make Wetzel proud of the paper and its clientele. There were quite a few letters again. One of them complimented him on his good taste, and said his picking a classic far outweighed his ignorance of its already having been one for a hundred years. One was in *my* favor. It was from a guy who said he'd rather see somebody steal an old poem than write a new one. But by that time I already had my head in a bottle. And I didn't take it out till Tuesday morning.

This was not only the longest single bender I was ever on. There was something else about it.

Up to now I had never suffered from hangovers. I always had a quick rebound, no morning after regrets, and a head sometimes clear as a bell no matter how much I took aboard. But this time I really did it up brown. The result was that I still hadn't gotten out of bed by Thursday morning, or Friday, or by the end of that week — or the next.

Elsie pitched in at the office, doing a surprisingly swell job.

She turns out to be a wonderfully efficient woman with a surprisingly good business head. Also a tower of strength in a pinch. She has never bawled me out for what I did, knowing full well why I did it, except to criticize the deed as dishonest and therefore a sin — which was only to be expected in her case.

So far I have not only not gone back to the office — I haven't even been out of the house. The hangover has proved chronic. Again kind friends have come forward with remedies — again the usual ones familiar to everyone — and again to no avail. The nausea, dizziness and headache persist. The room reels every morning when I awaken, and it's an hour before I can so much as move my head, let alone get out of bed. That I accomplish joint by joint, limb by limb, very slowly, till finally I am on my feet and can stagger down to the bathroom. Because I have moved alone into the little upstairs bedroom we've made in the attic, away from callers. Some of these are medical men interested in my case. They have never seen an incurable hangover before. When they are let up it does no good; they are powerless to affect any change whatever in the symptoms. I lie with my face to the wall, no longer interested. All I think is, Now I've left a worse stain on the family name than the one I tried to wipe out. Now no girl worth marrying will ever want to marry him. No girl worth wanting will want him.

Before Elsie goes to the office, she usually leaves a sandwich or something in the icebox for my lunch, which usually as not I have no appetite for. Sometimes when Tom can get away from high school on his lunch hour he'll run home and fix me a little chicken soup. I can keep that down.

So the seasons flow into one another, the years come and

go, like the tide. Sometimes Tom will try to tempt me with a TV program, or regale me with a tall tale from school, or come to say that Pete Potmesil phoned again to offer to take me for a spin. Spin! With the whole room going around like a carousal. But that is not the point. The point is that I have at last learned what it is all about. It can be put in a word, the sum total of human truth and wisdom. Love. That is everything. We have simply got to learn to put up with this mortal stuff, to make do with one another. Only love enables us to go on. Simple human love that asks no quarter, seeks not itself, is not puffed up. Loyal and abiding love, love that never stints, never begrudges. Love that helps us bear with one another and that makes us do for one another — make sacrifices, even, when the time comes or the occasion calls. That at least I have learned as I sit here thinking of my wife pitching in at the office, and hearing Tom come up the stairs with a little soup for his father. Simple devotion we have got to learn to give or we are through. Sunk. Kaput.

Oh that the hiccups had carried me off! Then would I sleep in the merciful dust. And the doctors as they go away shaking their heads, what shall we say of them now? What good all their learning, their degrees, their Fie Beta Kappa keys? All as nothing, nothing, before a soul in hell.

TOM

nine

WHEN I WAS twenty and a senior at Polycarp I rather fancied one of the many fetching motorists to be seen driving about the campus and the town, often in convertibles. Such was the blue Buick that nearly ran me down as I walked across the gravel drive near the Administration Building, brushing my coattails as I sprang to safety on the wet winter sod. The incident ended a long period as a pedestrian, wandering about in a fume of provincial resentments and unaudited sorrows. The driver was a good sport about it, leaning from the car like a nymph in a cigarette commercial and offering me a lift. She was a senior too but new here, having switched to Polycarp because the philosophy head was an idealist and the climate here more congenial to her interest in comparative religion. That was her major. She was an ash blonde of medium height, with a small waist and haunches that turned observers ill with longing. Hysterical welts appeared on the palms of the Dean's hands in his sleep, I believe. Need I no longer moan license numbers into my pillow?

I am a prey to fantasies. I imagine that there are people on this planet named Max Planck. I imagine that all matter is reducible to units of energy whirling in submicroscopic orbit, of which balls of roaring gas form the delirious counterpart in outer space. I must curb these delusions or see a doctor. I sometimes fancy that I am supported on a jointed improvisation of Tinker Toy called "bones," and then must pause and pass a hand across my brow till the conviction subsides. Where will it all end? Now I imagine that I am riding with an Evanston girl of good family in a contrivance propelled by the measured explosion of vaporized gasoline. Overhead cloacally powered jets streak across the continent in five hours while around us clothed mammals alternately lose and recover their balance in a regulated error known as "walking." Ought I to seek professional help? Only a moment ago I was myself a pedestrian, who had thought the girl the property of a sculptor recently in residence at the college, a young Italian held to be already enormously gifted in the art of twisting metal into disagreeable shapes. A great future is envisioned for him. Dark-eyed, with glossy waves of black hair, he has that animal magnetism that can be so repellent, especially to another man. Who am I? A student without a car, let alone a chosen career. I was about to call my father a humble piano mover until I remembered the arrogance with which he practiced that occupation, which he could make sound as arcane as that of a concert pianist.

"You mean. To sit there. And tell me," the motorist is saying a few days later, her tongue sensuously coated with ice cream, for we have stopped in at Tony's after a movie, "you mean to tell me that your mother picked up this candlestick from the table — "

"Where my father was eating in his undershirt."

"I understand. And carried it to the sink to do the dishes?"

"By its romantic light."

I had launched a series of questionings aimed at extracting as intimate details about her private life as possible — with this result. I was spilling my guts. I had ashamedly tried to hide my past, till I realized that nothing in her own Chicago Gold Coast childhood could begin to match it. She was absolutely fascinated. I was dining out on every gamey morsel of a heritage hitherto cloaked from snobs not secure enough in their own standing to dispense with the outward symbols of appearance. I appealed to her in a way that a prune-eyed wop with an acetylene torch never could. I dated other motorists, keeping one or two on the string, but this could be It. For me she was a kind of security, or anchor, or toggle. I got carried away with my subject.

"My mother once said she was going to complain to the President about something — I forget what — and if that didn't do any good she was going to write to Uncle Sam." But the motorist, while not underestimating such a nugget, remains mesmerized by the preceding, the haunting tableau of the candlelight dinner.

"Was she trying to be funny?"

"That's the thing. How will we ever know?"

"Didn't you *ask* her? I mean weren't you curious?"

"I was only eleven at the time. Twelve at the most. Oh. I forgot. My father once gave my mother a complete medical checkup for Christmas."

"Your mother's still alive. Why don't you ask her?"

"You can't go home again."

"But you still live there!"

"What's that got to do with it? *Emotionally* you can't return to something. I have that truth rubbed into me every day precisely because I'm on the scene."

"Because if she was being funny, then there is a woman with a gift of irony second to none. If not . . ." The lovely motorist sighed. "Then life is too sad."

It is the latter note that now dominates my memory of exactly how my mother carried the candlestick to the sink, the put-upon note. Yes, I remember now the characteristic single sniff with which she set it down, the isolated snuffle so much more wearing to my father than outright tears would of been. Would have been. Living with unripened hysteria drove my father crazy. "Why don't she break down and *bawl* for God's sake, like any other woman. Have a good cry and get it over. No, she has to be a martyr, make me feel guilty. They're all alike," he would say, contradicting himself. "Make their husbands blow a gasket, like it stands in a lot of magazines, then wonder why they die young," he went on, graphically warning that his own veins lacked the resilience for domestic life, and that she would one day wake up to find herself taking in washing.

My father took a special interest in his bodily organs, and considered detailed accounts of their behavior and function to be equally fascinating to others. Apparently his food entered his stomach after being swallowed, where it was worked over by digestive juices and chemically altered for transmission to the intestines (of which he had several yards) and ultimate absorption into the bloodstream, for use as energy. It was a cycle in which he took pride, perhaps justly. He would invite us to watch him hold up half an orange and squeeze it dry in one fist, an act made possible, he explained, by the metamorphosis into energy of fruit and other foodstuffs assimilated in days gone by. His reproductive and urinary systems were entangled in an arrangement that taxed credulity.

"Then why don't you get down on your knees and thank the God who made you?" my mother would put in. "If you're so wonderful. I should think you'd worship your Maker instead of sitting in taverns abusing the body he give you."

Later that month I was crossing the bridle path in the town park when a horse galloped into view without a word of warning and nearly ran me down. I wheeled about after leaping to safety and recognized the woman astride him. It was the motorist. There was no doubt about the tweed figure bent dramatically over the flying mane. Gaining the sidewalk after a plunge through some intervening shrubbery, I sprinted on through dense traffic to the security of the other side, where I fetched up before the window of an automobile agency. I wistfully took in the glimmering models, the hope of one day owning one a kind of fixed point of reference, or toggle. Something drew my attention from them. It was my own reflection in the glass. A dopey elongation of my face told me I was in love. Even the prospect of one day owning something out of which you could get no more than ten miles a gallon faded beside it.

My hallucinations continued unabated, if not more feverishly than ever. One of the most overwrought of them I experienced the next evening at a violin concert. I had this weird idea that sounds felicitous to the human ear could be produced by a man trained to draw tautened strands of horsetail hair across the dried entrails of cats, arranged in groups of four on fluted wood. This is crazy, I said to myself. This has got to stop. But not even closing my eyes and giving myself to the strains of Mendelssohn could dispel the insane chimera. I gave my head a slight shake to rid myself of it, drawing a worried glance from my friend in the seat beside me. The motorist again, as I knew without looking.

Now an unnerving thing happened. Instead of being calmed by the hand laid on my arm my fantasies took on an even wilder tone. I imagined that her father had mounted her mother to produce her. That this was the manner in which the world was replenished. I had seen her parents, and these thoughts had got to stop. They were rum notions and no good would come of them. They were patently the product of a morbid mind. Nor were they the limits to the riot of fancy to which I was now subject. That invisible organisms infested the palm of my hand, that people joined mouths in unlighted places preparatory to exchanging lavish tributes to one another's appearance, indeed protestations that they could not live without each other, these were among the other figments of my imagination. I am a sick man. I must make a genuine effort to return to reality.

Afterward at Tony's I remark, "How delightful for two people to break bread together, once in a while."

"They can do it every night."

"It's not the same thing. We have it on the best authority." Now I crane across the booth table and kiss the motorist, one of those long, eviscerating kisses from which I draw back and say, retrieving my necktie from the coleslaw, "It's no good."

"Why not?"

"I've told you how pious my mother was, and how I was dragged to those ghastly revivals that have so turned me against religion that I could never possibly be happy with anyone who believed in a supreme being, my dear Marion, as you do. Or make such a person happy. You're Episcopalian I know, and while it is admittedly a pallid sect, nothing to it, and you're not hidebound, I am. I should always be mocking and ridiculing something sacred to you, so that inside of six months . . ." With a gesture I evoke marriages demolished in that time by discordant intellectual outlooks. "Not that I don't get a bang out of Jesus . . ."

"That's very interesting. Because the story is that you broke up with Sarah Feldman for the opposite reason. You could never marry an unbeliever, somebody from a freethinking family like hers, because you're rebelling against a father who was a bigoted atheist."

"That is correct. I'm rebelling against both parents."

"In other words you have two upbringings."

"These two backgrounds, that I'm in revolt against."

There is more to it than the niggling matter of personal adjustment. There is the underlying reality of Everything As Such. The difference between a major truth and a minor one is after all simple enough. A major truth can be contradicted, while a minor one cannot. With trivial statements of fact such as "It's raining out," or "She's taking a bath," there can be no quarrel. But the large verities, like God is love, Life is good and Honor above all, stand each in the shadow of its opposite: there isn't any, all is vanity, and honor is a word. Thus there are two sides to any question of any importance, and the only thing for an honest man to do is take both of them.

"What about a middle course?"

"Laodiceanism? That I particularly abhor. To the angel of the church of Laodicea write, 'Because thou art lukewarm, and neither hot nor cold, I will spew thee out of my mouth.'

No, don't come to me with your tepid accommodators, committing themselves to nothing, willing to come to grips with nothing. Perhaps you'd better take me home."

The motorist sits back with the last of her glass of milk in her hand, to watch me. She drinks, her gray eyes never leaving my face, no change in her expression of thoughtful regard as she gulps the milk. She sets her empty glass down. "In other words, you're a mess."

Tony's is jumping tonight, and smilingly I watch a group dancing near the jukebox, the dregs of my coffee at lip. I drift to a particular aspect of the subject and talk about my father, filling the time while she eats the ice cream on which she again insists.

"Why don't you ask me in to meet your family?" she says. I stiffen against the back of the booth, like a condemned man through whom a current of electricity is being passed, my eyes shut. After a moment I resume the narrative on which I have embarked, and am not far along in it when I sense that I have again passed the point where I am documenting our incompatibility, and am once more kindling her fascination.

"Wait. Hold on there a second. Let me get this straight." She shoves dishes aside and leans forward with her arms on the table. "Do I understand you. To be telling me. That your father has been laid up with this hangover for *nine years?*" For dramatic emphasis she draws not only on this habit of spaced deliberation, which gives phrases and even single words the value of entire sentences, but also on an exaggerated enunciation, of a kind that makes "nine" come out something like a telephone operator's: "niyun." At crucial conversational junctures like this she talks as though we are communicating through a thick pane of glass and she has to make herself understood without being heard. "The same. Identical. Hangover?"

"We've tried everything. Prairie oysters, massive injections of vitamin B, hair of the dog of course," I answer offhandedly, modestly disclaiming that we Waltzes are all that special, "but to no avail. His condition remains unchanged. It is the same to this day."

She indulges in the average girl's habit of sitting on her heels with her legs tucked under her, but in the process of shifting about she seems like some highly intelligent momentarily distracted young puppy, crawling about in search of a comfortable position. "And he has never left the house in all that time?"

"That is correct. People are kind, and for a long while offered to take him for rides or sit with him and play cards, but eventually they forget. They have their own problems, and he says he can't do any of those things, though you do see him read. And now I really think you ought to take me home."

"The symptoms stay exactly the same?" she says softly, as though a word too much, a single overemphasis will blow the wonder clean away.

"The symptoms classic to hangover persist. Dizziness, nausea, headache — you know that katzenjammer just above the eyes."

"Yes of course, but I mean now wait." She is now the intellectually kindled college senior. "You surely must have explored the possibility that it's emotional. That he's punishing somebody, or himself. Is he atoning for something?"

"He's too hung over. Waiter. Check."

125

"Now Tom, let's stop this foolishness right away. When do I get to meet your parents? I introduced you to mine. I know they happened to be visiting the campus, it's not quite the same thing. Still in all. Now when?"

I lean my head against the wall, which is made of tin and painted the color of Pepto-Bismol. "How's Saturday morning? I'll give you a ring or something."

ten

THE MOTORIST SPRANG up the cottage stairs two at a time, her head down and laughing to herself as though in anticipation of something. Where did I ever get the idea she was patrician? Perhaps from snapshots of her father's horses. I had been watching for her at the front door, which I now rather testily opened by way of welcome. Grabowitzes, Wishnotskis and Yablonickies have come through this door in quantities, but never a Wellington. "Can't you see we're Poles apart?"

"You wait here. I'll bring him down. But first a few rules. Don't ask him about himself — especially none of this atonement stuff — and don't look at him directly, or do anything to make him self-conscious."

We descend the stairs at about the pace of a bridal party. My father staggers down them with his feet apart, as an aid to equilibrium, clinging to the bannister with one hand while steadying the icebag on his head with the other. I shall watch to see whether he doffs it at the sight of the caller, for doubts about his sanity are beginning to creep in. If I keep imagining that the light by which we now see Aldebaran left it at the time of Nebuchadnezzar, then I shall be ready for the cuckoo hatchery myself. No doubt about that. I am not pulling myself together at all. Yesterday I saw a man in the street trying to put out an umbrella that had caught fire. That part was all right. Nothing unusual about that. But for a moment I thought that these details were being photographically registered on some kind of aspic embedded in two sockets in my head and transformed into comprehension by a scoop of albumin directly behind them, and that was scary. I had had to wait till the sensation passed.

My father progresses by careful stages, making the necessary turns without turning his head, for vertigo is still his chief morning-after symptom. He sways against the wall of the living room along which he gropes, pausing occasionally to grasp an object of furniture. I hold his elbow lightly, my hand in readiness to do so more firmly if need arises. He doesn't see the motorist, who stands at a table with her gaze bent over a magazine, idly letting the pages fall, her hair hanging along one side of her face. I adopt the shuffling rhythm of infirmity myself as we creep at snail's pace toward my father's chair, a wide armchair near the window which he backs painstakingly around to before plopping himself into it with a hideous grimace.

"Pa, I'd like to present Miss Wellington. She's sophisticated without being stuck-up."

He smiles wanly in response to a greeting from the slender young woman in the blue serge suit, settling the icebag on his head with the familiar rustle of cold cubes but not, thank God, tipping it. I draw up a chair for the motorist to sit in facing him squarely, their knees almost touching, like two pas-

127

sengers in a railway coach. He must not be required to turn his head, and so it is in this attitude that she must adhere as best she can to my warning not to look at him too directly.

She talks mainly of the campus and how it must have changed since he last saw it, as though he was a student there. The hope is expressed with a gingerly smile that he will be up and about again soon. Here a momentary sparkle returns to the dark eyes which, together with the still abundant brown hair, contain an echo of the "spiffy gink" he once was. I can remember him sucking in his gut and throwing out his chest for the benefit of local scholars. He has the broad face and high Slavic cheekbones that are a staple of the family album, and the contrast with the motorist's obviously Anglo-Saxon features has a kind of theatrical simplicity about it. One half expects a director to stride in and propel the scene forward on lines of stylized absurdity by saying, "When you ask him whether his brains aren't freezing, try unscrewing the cap and dropping an ice cube from it into your highball. *But don't hoke it.* I want a compassionate chuckle here, not a laugh. Let's try it that way tonight and see what we get."

My mother is at the warehouse but will join us for lunch. I go rustle that up, listening alertly from the kitchen but hearing nothing impolitic from the motorist. She gets him to talk about the books he is reading. Apparently once he has his posture established and his eyes focused he can read. Once I imagine I hear the word "Lourdes." Can it be that she is proposing he make a journey there in hopes of curing his trouble in its healing waters! I hurry in with a tray of sandwiches and a pot of coffee just in time to see him clap his hand over his mouth in the gesture common to portrayals of seasickness, as though we are already pitching toward Europe, at the same time pinching his nose between thumb and forefinger, like one who has arrived at a decision to cut off the respiration that alone perpetuates this farce.

We are preparing to eat our lunches from individual knee-high folding tables when an oblong woman appears in the hallway and shoots her arms into the air to draw a pin from her hat — my mother. "Hello, all." I feel a spasm of filial irritation. I am always irked by the way she takes for granted all the lunches I fix, and have fixed over the years, often trotting home from school to do so. She accepts as a matter of course also the fourth table snapped open for her to join our picnic in the parlor. Well, why not? She is the breadwinner — a term given an almost ludicrous literal pertinence by the mountain of ham and cheese sandwiches round which we now ring ourselves. The family car is hers for business use, even evenings, when she makes estimating calls on people moving. It is an old Chevrolet on which I scarcely have designs anyway, since you would never ask a girl into it. One could better advance his romantic aims from behind the handlebars of a bicycle than at the wheel of anything so square as that.

There is no doubt that my mother, who has saved us from "bankrupture," has herself been redeemed as a person. The crisis has drawn out her character, given her a new definition. She rose to the occasion beneath which my father sank — whatever it was. They seem to me like two figures on a seesaw whose relative positions have been abruptly reversed. Ten years ago she would of taken Miss Wellington in deferentially, would of answered all the questions shyly. Now she puts them herself. A quick, acute appraisal suffices to assure that the caller is not slumming; a crafty question or two extract her church affiliation. There is a certain hilarity in the way my mother, tugging her skirt down, tolerates the other's high Episcopal connections, and just look at us eating off of this nest of tables from Pete Potmesil's dreadful furniture store. Miss Wellington's glances I return with shrugs that I dimly sense to be Jewish, unconsciously picked up from Jews I know or have seen in television plays. We Poles have no lore, no stamp, no color. We aren't even a minority group. There aren't enough of us.

My mother typically taxes her caller's own Christian charity by talking about her faith at the rate she does. She hopes in open company that her husband too has found Christ through this visitation, or will. I am grateful for this demonstration of how any toleration of even diluted high church is out for me. Out! The hope that the afflicted has seen the light prompts Miss Wellington to turn to my father and ask him point-blank, out of something more than idle curiosity I think, "What about it, Mr. Waltz? *Have* you found Christ?" He grabs at his nose again as though to cut off his breathing, reaching up with the other hand to steady the ice-bag. "We don't always talk freely about what we feel deepest," my mother says. "He don't mock and blaspheme like he use to, and he hasn't touched a drop in nearly ten years. Would you care to say grace, Miss Wellington?"

I marvel at the grace with which she says it. As we bow our heads over the sandwiches (which we are well advised to give thanks for in advance; I bow my head more in shame than reverence) I have one of those sudden visions that set young men aflame. It has nothing to do with anything going on here. It is an unexpected sense of vocation at last, as complete and arbitrary in its inspiration, I suppose, as my mother's conversion. It is almost mystical, and certainly religious.

I have been feeling my eye being irresistibly drawn to our Globe-Wernicke sectional bookcase. Something is telling me to look there. Lying on top of it is a fat green volume, a text-book we have been using for senior English. And at that precise moment there pops into my mind Hopkins's remark about Browning — my term-paper subject. Browning reminded Hopkins of a man bouncing up from the table with his mouth full of bread and cheese and saying that he means to stand no blasted nonsense.

I laugh softly to myself as I know that literature is my field, and that I must teach. I shall dedicate my life to instilling into the young an appreciation of the glories of poetry. I do believe there is something Pentecostal in these visions that turn us on, that fill us with a sudden sense of our personal part in the divine plan.

And now, ladies and gentlemen, a word from our alternate sponsor, the Devil.

eleven

ALL MARION WELLINGTON'S ideas about my father proved as vain as such speculations had always been. She did advance one interesting theory, that he is the victim of Ménière's syndrome, the affection of the inner ear that disturbs the organs entrusted with equilibrium. But since this complaint is, like migraine, in turn regarded as emotional in origin, we are back where we started.

Only in that regard. It is a few years later, and I am an instructor in English at Polycarp, where the motorist teaches comparative religion, all more or less according to plan. She spent a year getting her master's at the University of Chicago while I was working on mine at Michigan, from where I sent her ardent letters advising that silk not wed canvas, etc. She must think me right, judging from the way she sits up front in assembly chapel today between my departmental head, Dr. Norman Littlefield, and the current artist in residence, a poet. The intellectual stimulus afforded by first acquaintance with my family would seem to have worn off. Now it is the twenty-third year of my life and the twelfth of my father's hangover. I am still a humble pedestrian but I shall get a car yet if I adhere to my budget, according to which I put aside three dollars and fifty cents a week. I have just been to my doctor, and apparently I must avoid foods. That will be another great saving. Meanwhile the campus is full of lovely motorists, with whom being a member of the faculty is sometimes an advantage, sometimes not.

The poet in residence looks as though he could do with a good meal himself. He pursues the contemporary personal ideal of abrasiveness, though enemies have been circulating malicious rumors that he is a hell of a swell guy underneath. Dr. Littlefield my boss is the reverse, bland as a banana. There are reports that his gallbladder is in upside down. Still, that's not as bad as some of the things you see on television. Why does Goldwater not go to Russia to live? It seems to me he would be happiest in the Soviet Union, where they prize doctrinaire mentalities of that sort.

Dean Shaftoe rises with a sheaf of notes and we know the announcements are about to begin. I lapse into woolgathering. I pretend that the room is full of something called "air," an element of which, oxygen, it is necessary for me to inhale through two holes in my nose in order to keep going. I even invent a name for this pipedream: breathing. I really must pull myself together. The Dean is dug in for one of his explanations in depth, this one about the use of special research material in the library, and I lean back in the seat and close my eyes in death.

In the course of his three months' hitch, the poet in residence has done very little but reside, as a colored dining-room waiter entrusted with his comfort observed. Trotting through the snow with yet another tray for him to have in his dormitory room, Harvey remarked, "Dat man sho' know how to reside." This was the same employe said to have answered sightseers inquiring about the rotunda dominating one end of the campus quadrangle, what it houses, or what, "Ah don't rightly know. Ah reckon dey uses it mostly for a rotunda." The resider affects garden gloves and a green bowtie, of which there is now unimpeachable evidence that it is pre-knotted and fastened around the neck with an elastic band equipped with a hook and ring. So now as the Dean drones on about the library I reach in from the aisle and pull the bowtie out as far as I can and start running, the resider scrambling to his feet and hotfooting along in my wake as fast as he can in a desperate attempt to close the gap between us, so that when I finally do let go (this is the humorous implication) it won't hit him in the Adam's apple with quite so hard a smack. In this manner I force him on a tour through town, and in fancy I can hear him yet, panting as we cross the C.B. and Q. tracks into my old neighborhood, like a vaudeville team whom the impulse of one has taken beyond the limits of the act and clean out of the theatre — to see those simple folk of whom his verse offers such a thoroughly synthetic love. He is to have all that rubbed into him now.

133

"There's the fireworks factory where I worked summers. There's Lichtman's dry goods store where we bought ties like this — we called them Jazzbos — but with pennies saved up in order to look decent on Sundays, not for snobbish monkeyshines, you son of a bitch!" Labored heaves alternate with the steady spank of feet behind me; a whimpered plea to sit down and rest a minute, not heeded. Rounding the turn at the City Hall now, moving nicely in our second wind, not an inch gained or lost since Waltz snatched the bowtie and started running, the advantage seized by surprise neither extended nor diminished. "There's the Gospel tabernacle," I puff, "just a rented store. To this I was dragged as a boy in the ceaseless struggle between my parents. You can hear the service through the open door now. There's the old hymn, 'Gladly the cross-eyed bear.' And if I'm a mess, have you ever known anyone before who went through the Second Coming? Well, you do now."

Dusk. The streetlamps glowing like a row of dirty moons to the river's edge. There we sink upon the bank and I let go the tie, hearing precisely the flat *splat* with which the elastic would of caught him in the Adam's apple had I done so at the very outset, in the chapel aisle where in my Polycarp dreams it still seems to me that our phantom run began. But then he'd not have had this instructive tour of the town. As we drop, exhausted, on the riverbank I bring out: "I'm one of your admirers." The death rattle which accompanies the mute gaze he turns on me prompts me to add, "You see, it was I who urged your appointment. I have great influence in the English Department."

He sometimes wore a ring on his thumb, the resider. Shrill as are all these claims to individuality, they none of them compare with the affectation to which we now come. I am conscious of having to state it simply, letting it speak for itself. He spelled his name with an exclamation mark behind it — Hodges! Some said he did it for the additional panache that would in consequence adhere to it, others in order to shed the "Jr." hitherto required to differentiate him from his father, a Chicago industrialist against whom he was, of course, in revolt.

I opened my eyes and snapped erect in my chapel seat, with the unmistakable conviction that I was going to create a disturbance. More: that I was going to make a shambles of my life. The moment was charged with the most extraordinary sense of *déjà vu*, the certainty that we know exactly what is going to happen in the next few seconds, as though we have lived through it before. The motivational pressure behind what I was going to do was resentment. It was no doubt the sight of the lovely motorist sitting up front between Hodges! and Dr. Littlefield that made me flip. She was too good for me, a poor hunky who could only window-shop for standing, who could never be part of such charmed little groups. That was the implication in the laughing head turned now this way, now that. My back seat became symbolic. How could a woman who liked me also like an ass like Hodges!? Admiration for his work was not enough to explain it. I admired his work too, and that was why I was always glad to see it clobbered in print. I had, oh, thirty seconds of freedom left.

"The importance of original research varies with each subject, of course," Dean Shaftoe was saying, "and so all of that should be gone into with the department head or teacher in question before taking your request for special material — especially material we must borrow from other libraries — to

135

the librarian. Every department has its own norm." Here I apparently leaned forward and through cupped hands shouted at the top of my voice, "And we've got Norm Littlefield!"

You begin with the fact that everything is awful. That any two people are mismatched, that nothing will work. You go on from there. In the hush that followed, me alone grinning richly about, I began framing the letter of resignation which I would now not in the least mind writing, for, yes, I hated teaching. The whole approach is wrong. College professors are judged not by the impression they make on their students, but on one another, and on colleagues not on their own campus, but elsewhere. As though this were not sufficient idiocy in high places, their fame depends not on rumors of classrooms kindled with the thirst for knowledge, but on those lucubrations in academic quarterlies of which not the least part are them solidly caked masses of ordure in 6-point known as footnotes, like some waste extruded by the main text above, you know. No, the whole thing is screwy, and I can only hope that my suicidal blurt has struck a martyr's blow for sanity, since Norm Littlefield is precisely one of those bogging us down in the principle of research for its own sake. I knew that Norm had got his Ph.D. in something to do with weak verbs. I had vowed to make it my life's aim to die not knowing what weak verbs were, but some fool blabbed. They are verbs inflected with suffixes, without inherited change of the root vowel, as *walk, walked,* in distinction from verbs inflected with changes in the root vowel, as *sing, sang.* Now he had gone so far as to suggest in no uncertain terms the field for me on which he would look with favor as my sponsor: "The Clowns in Shakespeare." Oh, my God! Well, nobody is giving me those bores for lifelong companions. And I trust everyone within the sound of my voice realizes that the pun we have just heard ejaculated is part of the self-immolating satire? For that is the point: it is not only Shakespeare, it is Shakespeare at his worst. One of the clowns might have been guilty of it, but not me *I hope*. Then why this ghastly silence that envelops us like a fateful cloud as we shuffle out of the chapel like mourners into the February cold?

Eyes avoid me. Faces whisk themselves away on pretended missions elsewhere. Scraps of comment reach my burning ears. " — on earth got into —," " — for his sake he's drunk." This last is probably a reference to another disciplinary case here, a student recently up for hurling a brick through the window of a downtown store, for which he was threatened with expulsion unless he could prove to the faculty's satisfaction that he had been drinking at the time as well. One more element in the crisis should be noted. Norm Littlefield is just then himself under fire for the choice of writers he is bringing on for spells of residence among other things, therefore a more sensitive time could not be imagined for an underling bucking for promotion, or even interested in holding onto his job, not to appear to be rallying to the support of the department head — good old Norm Littlefield with his pepper-and-salt suits and his curved pipes and his seriocomic gallbladder.

I walk on alone in my exile. For ridicule banishes us from the human community as surely as pain binds us into it. The smiles I know now to be openly proliferating behind me, the headshakes, send me into the wilderness as surely as the stones that drove ostracized ancients from the security of the tribe. I agree with Samuel Johnson that there are not six consecutive lines of good poetry in Shakespeare. Yet what move us are the peaks, for which we endure the stretches of claptrap and the tiresome clowns and the idiotic plots. But my plight is well put in *King John:*

> *Thou wear a lion's hide! doff it for shame,*
> *And wear a calf's-skin on those recreant limbs.*

Limbs is good. As I hurry across the late winter ice my feet shoot out from under me and down I go in a comic-strip sprawl that breaks my leg with a snap I can hear. I lie writhing in agony, thank God. An undergraduate medical corps is hastily formed which carries me to a doctor's office down the street. In what a twinkling our luck can change! Lolling in anguish, my useless limb dangling from the knee, I taste restoration to the human community through pain — serene in my purchase of absolution. I make a face at the Psychology Building as we go by, as much as to say, "And I suppose I willed the patch of *ice* to be there too?"

"No Toby Belch today, eh, Fenton?" I say, recognizing one of my bearers as a student in the Comedies class for which I would now otherwise have been girding myself. "Or very soon. Can you see it sticking through? The bone I mean." He threatens like the others to vomit as they stumble through the snow. "Why, they have those walking casts you know, sir," he answers. "They'll have you back in circulation in two shakes."

Fears of that are soon allayed. The x-rays in the doctor's office show a nasty triple break he can't possibly set there, so off we go to dry dock for some surgery.

As I roll toward the hospital in the ambulance, pleasantly numbed by the shot of Demerol administered by a nurse with two breasts, I try to put this whole situation into some sort of appropriate Shakespearean claptrap:

Frail crockery that in a trice can splinter thus
'Pon the glib surface underfoot, poor frame
On which is hung this mortal pulp that e'en thou
Outlasts i' th'earth, couldst thou while we're above't
Bear me no better hence? Damned wickerwork my flesh uphol-
*   ster'st,*
Amid whose members no longer in good standing
Thou thyself so ignominiously sprawl'st,
How swiftly I am redistributed, to compound the general mess.

I could even imagine the idiotic footnotes required to make this rubbish intelligible to students. 1. CROCKERY. *Here, as in* WICKERWORK, *Shakespeare is employing an imaginative metaphor for bones, the skeletal framework as such.* 2. GLIB. *Slippery, slick, referring to the ice on which the victim falls.* 3. NO LONGER IN GOOD STANDING. *This shows again Shakespeare's comic genius for puns that shade into metaphor and vice versa.* MEMBERS *is used in the sense of limbs, no longer in "good standing," i.e., now that they are sprawled on the ground.*

"God," I groaned, but good-naturedly, smiling serenely with my hands folded above the blanket. Who will take my classes? Norm himself will undoubtedly be stuck with the Comedies, with Blodgett and McGeese doubling on the Life of Shakespeare and Introduction to Elizabethan Poetry.

I turn and gaze dreamily out. Why do ambulances have picture windows? I have often been a pedestrian gaping morbidly in, now I can look out. I put on a show for the benefit of an old lady at an intersection where we are momentarily slowed. I grit my teeth in a horrible grimace, as though I am writhing in anguish. She shakes her head in friendly pity, blowing me a kiss. Yes, there *is* a human family. Then the wail of the siren again and off we bowl along the river road to the hospital, the Demerol now flooding my limbs with a Lethean peace. A compulsive habit carried over from my teaching chores makes me instinctively grade everything I see, and in my mellowed mood I give Him a straight A for the day, also mentally jotting the word of constructive criticism. "A rather striking mezzotint effect in which the gray values of a February morning are effectively contrasted with Your blue sky and the subtly distributed blocks of lemon yellow sunlight on the buildings. Keep up the good work. The handling of the gloomy-bright combination of middle values is a little contrived, a little reminiscent of Burchfield. Watch that."

I am given pre-op tests and medications, rolled down to surgery, and back up to my room, where I awaken with my leg in a hip-length cast. Seeing that I have come satisfactorily out of the anesthetic, the hovering nurse departs, to let me sleep again.

Evening, and I am awakened from a doze by visitors, hoping I have shut my mouth in time. Smiling from the foot of the bed is the motorist in one of those suits that always make me want to ask the name of her tailor, while beside her Hodges! wears that impish grin which he owes to the two incisors standing slightly forward of the rest of his teeth. Why are other people so much more special? I try to be lonely in the midst of crowds, to laugh at points in the movie where other people don't, but it is no use. I snatch the bowtie and off we are again like the wind. "Don't worry about it. Everybody is reminiscent of somebody," I pant over my shoulder as we tear down the hospital stairs into the street and strike out at a steady lope along the river drive. "You've been imitating MacLeish so long you sound like Eliot. That's Nestle Down, an oubliette for nervous cases we're determined to keep my father out of. That's the Lamartine estate where I cut grass in summers — "

"Tom, you poor. Poor. Thing. I only learned about it late this afternoon, and so when Arthur picked me up for dinner I said we can't go before looking in on poor Tom."

"I couldn't have eaten a thing," says Hodges!, as though priding himself on this unexpected evidence of humanity in his makeup. "Pretty awful for you, Waltz." The bowtie turns out on closer scrutiny to be not a Jazzbo with an elastic band at all, but a handsome foulard very possibly selected and even tied for him by a woman. He shows a woman's civilizing touch. Also he has dispensed with the buffoon's canvas gloves and is in general a much nicer person. I do not like this development at all. Nor the manner in which they talk, after finding chairs. Their glances are not forthright but keep sliding off me, as though I am coated with invisible grease in layers too thick for their gazes to obtain a purchase. They likewise avoid mention of the chapel incident with an obviousness that only indicates the scale on which it is being discussed outside. Damn their eyes! I cling the more savagely to my sanctuary, the haven in which alone I can postpone being held to account.

"The doctor said he never saw such a filthy break and that it will take months to heal. He drove three spikes into my leg to hold things together down there. They do that now, you know. And when the leg's all healed I'll have to come back for another operation to have the spikes out. And so on."

The motorist rises to inspect the cast, bending near so that I catch a deranging whiff of her scent, as well as a glimpse of the little doves I have felt fluttering in the palms of my hands. There has been one kiss so ecstatic that, scarcely able to breathe, I raised my head and said, "This is no good." She knows that only supreme moments wring this hard truth from me. I get rid of Hodges! by significantly clacking the lid of my water pitcher with a thumb, to show that it is empty, watching till he is safely out in the hall looking for a utility room before turning sharply to the motorist.

"Well, I must say it's nice of you to bring a friend when you visit a chap in the hospital."

"Well, of all the. After I explain expressly that I came to see you even *though* I had a date. I mean here you go switching it around to that." She shakes her head, sadly but at the same time briskly, and continues in the polemic vein so natural to her, though I know very well that I am hearing a playback of some Ethics class notes. "How narrow to look at affection always in the purely sexual sense anyway. That's the curse *even of sexual relations,* have you ever stopped to think of that, Tom?" Is the phrase "even of sexual relations" underlined in her notes too? "Love isn't just a physical bond. It's got to be part of man's whole. Spiritual. Makeup." This plenitude is illustrated by a rounded gesture of both hands rather unfortunately like that with which lewd men carve a nude in the air to dramatize the concept of voluptuousness. "It's why we're sick. We think we can separate the two. You can see the havoc being wrought by this attitude among young people. Remember as recently as when you and I were in school there was all this talk about how serious kids were because they got married so early? Well, the first precincts are coming in, and they're getting divorced just as fast."

"Sometimes with children. It's outrageous. I've just learned that two of my students are divorced. I have a friend in the graduate department at Columbia who says five of his classmates are divorced. Five!"

Hodges! returns, his errand of mercy accomplished with amazing speed. "Getting lectured, Waltz?" he says as he sets the pitcher down. This means that he has come to know my sweet driver's habits rather intimately. I cannot let this pass. "Marion's on the side of the angels," I tell him quite crisply.

My reward is the light in his eye that I have come to recognize as a sign that he has seen a way of snatching the conversational ball and running you back eighty yards with it. He gives the impish smile that helped more than any other single feature to bring off his "clown" period, now, apparently, a thing of the past, another shell outgrown and left beside life's unresting sea. Before that there was said to be a brief spell on the road as a beatnik, one of the Telemachus types engaged in the symbolic search for a Father figure, the inadequate original of which is luckily back home wiring the dough so the Quest can go on.

"Now there's an expression there's something very interesting about — 'the side of the angels.' Not one in a thousand knows where it comes from. Do you, Waltz?"

Since Waltz is hanging like a bat over the side of the bed, looking under it for something to hit somebody over the head with, he does not reply save for a grunt of generalized distaste. Being the salt of the earth entails certain obligations, so the other's ignorance is not reproved by any outward measure.

143

"Disraeli said it in a speech in England," continues our nonesuch. "The controversy about Darwinism was raging at the time, whether man is an ape or an angel. 'I, my Lord, am on the side of the angels,' Disraeli said. Meaning he believed in the traditional Biblical view of creation, nothing more. Not what people usually do by the term at all. It's one of those things that have been completely corrupted by popular usage. Did you know that, Waltz?"

"Ah, water." I gratefully pour myself a glass, which they watch me gulp thirstily. I make a mental note to check Hodges!'s facts, to see whether in truth Disraeli coined the phrase or was simply ringing a change on it. "Well, what more can you expect from a century like the nineteenth than confusion like that?"

"I'd like to have lived in the eighteenth. That's the century for me. How about you, Marion? When would you like to live, if you could have your choice?"

"The eighteenth century," I interject while she sits mulling this, as though Hodges! has asked the restaurant at which it would amuse her most to dine, "had a splendid physique but a rotten constitution. The seventeenth century had a splendid constitution but a rotten physique. The nineteenth century had a rotten constitution *and* a rotten physique. The — "

Hodges! looked at the clock and yawned. "We really must run along, Marion, if we're going to the Half Moon. Andrew doesn't like to serve after nine, you know, and it'll take us a good half hour to get there from here." My phone rang just then and they made their escape in a flurry of whispers, leaving me alone with the voice of Dr. Norman Littlefield. I groaned in my teeth. Would the scope of my folly mitigate the enormity of my crime in his eyes, by entitling me to pity in addition to that accruing from the broken leg? That was the continuing and at last now critically focused sixty-four-thousand-dollar question.

"Waltz, how are you?"

"Oh, Dr. Littlefield, nice of you to call. Yes, I'm in pretty bad shape to hear them tell it."

I lay like a corpse in whom remained some vestigial knack for receiving impressions through a mechanical contrivance while Littlefield made formal expressions of condolence, in a voice betraying, I must say, nothing of the emotion he must have felt at being publicly pilloried by an underling and assumed protégé. With closed eyes I learned that Blodgett and McGeese were indeed taking my classes in my absence. At last I heard what I expected.

"Of course I have something more to say to you, Waltz, a good deal more, but that can wait until — "

"Oh, how can I ever, how could I ever, I mean a man all his life thinks he's a rational being, and then *kablooey*, this thing comes out of him from God knows — "

"Later, when you're feeling better. You sound a little dopey still. We'll go into the whole thing then. All I want to say now is that in a way I'm glad it happened, much as it gives aid and comfort to enemies in certain quarters. Brings everything out in the open if you know what I mean. The thunderclap that clears the air. When you find out how somebody really feels about you — "

"Oh, Dr. Littlefield."

"But I'll say no more tonight. You need your rest. You sound rather rocky. I'll look in on you in a day or two, and then we can talk the whole thing over. Good night."

*   *   *

Waltz spends the laudanum hours mentally drafting letters of application to other institutions of learning, or rather one master letter which he spends the next day putting down on paper. He tries to give some idea of his pedagogical worth, as well as his accumulated background for teaching the specialty for which he has a special zeal — Shakespeare. He assures prospects that he has in hand a long-range research project, the Clowns in Shakespeare, work on which goes forward with its customary relish, and on which articles should soon begin to appear in the better academic quarterlies, complete with offal in 6-point at the bottoms of the pages. It is wisest to keep lines out in your present profession in case no openings develop in another — like lawn maintenance or snow removal.

Growing drowsy in the late afternoon, Waltz lets the pencil drop from his fingers as he muses on the pioneering contribution he has made to that scholastic ideal, small classes. The best schools like a pupil-teacher ratio of seven or eight to one. Waltz has improved on that in his Dramatic Poetry Workshop, an elective, in which an enrollment of two the first semester has dwindled to none now. That is carrying the ideal of small classes a bit too far, admitted, and he has tacked to the bulletin board an announcement that the course has been withdrawn owing to a conflict in the instructor's schedule.

The Dramatic Workshop was normally offered by a woman teacher now on leave. I ruefully ponder the term "normal." The poor thing is at Nestle Down now, to which she was forcibly removed after accusing one of the students of blowing gas under her bedroom door at night in order that he might ravish her in her sleep. Momentarily roused from my doze by the arrival of afternoon juice, I work out, as I sip it, a little episode as the Bard would have done it. First I fashion a straight character of the kind who are always trying to outdo the clowns, thus making matters twice as bad, to say, "Call'st that a normal college?" So that the clown named, oh, Stumble, may answer, "Hath it not the customary deficit? It would be state-supported were't not for the state it's in."

"What state art thou in, fool?"

"Desperation, for I must seek another position. An't please thee, I'll assume a lying one to rest a bit, and think on't."

"Dost do anything but lie, fool?"

"Marry, 'tis sometimes necessary, and I'll stand on that. I can be upright when needed. But as to positions, I must find a new one or be state-supported myself, i' faith."

"What wilst do, ass?"

"I will lift up mine eyes unto the Hills. Dost know the Hills, varlet? A most wealthy and influential family in this town who could re-enstate e'en an ass were he to bray ardently enough."

"Thy faculties are wandering, fool."

"Worse, oaf, my students are."

I shake my head, amazed again that grown men can take such bilge seriously, even devote entire professional lifetimes to learned dissertations on it. I lift up mine eyes unto the ceiling and emit an inarticulate howl of rage and despair, which brings a nurse's aid in at a gallop to see if anything is wrong.

The hospital's general level of functioning I have decided to give a C−, with floor care itself a D+. The place is no worse than most institutions of mercy, from what I hear. The trouble is apparently understaffing, and being in such demand has made registered nurses somewhat choosy and fastidious as well as bossy. They are always working on charts and feel their next most important function to be that of safeguarding the doctors from demands on their time by the patients. Physical contact with the sick is now pretty much a thing of the past among them; that is largely relegated to the practical nurses and aids, or, in extreme conditions, the mortician. The unregistered personnel are all that save the hospital from a flunking grade, the A— I give them pulling the overall mark up from the F it would otherwise have rated. At least in my estimation. There are other nurses besides Miss Wurlitzer and Mrs. Dart, and perhaps patients by the sight of whose flesh they are not so openly repelled as they seem to be by mine. The woman I like best is one in charge of a department on a lower floor called Therapy, to which I am periodically trundled for instruction in the use of crutches.

By evening I had rough-drafted a letter that satisfied me, which I then neatly rewrote, remembering to round out the characters in my handwriting so as to reflect warmth and generosity of spirit, being especially careful to avoid those breaks in the downward loops, as in the g's and y's, which indicate sexual disorder. Who wants that? I had by now nearly eliminated my naturally neat and persnickety t-bars, said to betray a confined and unimaginative nature, in favor of quick spearlike dashes — sometimes entirely missing the main body of the letter — so suggestive of creative spontaneity and romantic flair. I put the result by, with the warning to myself to get copies off to the colleges I wanted to apply to the minute I get home. That done, I turned onto my side, as well as my encumbered limb allowed, and looked out the window at the fading day.

We at Slow Rapids lie cupped in a shallow valley formed

by a confluence of low hills merging in the near west, from which river mists arise to meet the cold air above, so that we are continually treated to a succession of sunsets now largely out of date. Generally Pre-Raphaelite in feeling, they sometimes descend to the level of Corot, and bad Corot at that. At their worst they are sheer calendar art. I often tell Him as much. "The straightforward romanticism at which You persist is by now basically uncongenial to the modern temper, which aims rather at implication and understress, as I have told You before," I mentally jot by way of helpful comment on what I see now, "while the sun centered so exactly between Your banks of lilac cloud (suffused with rose yet!) is quite contrived. This kind of sentimentalization of nature is simply unpalatable to contemporary taste." I then add the helpful criticism. "If You wish to pursue the pantheistic vein I would suggest study of some of the painters who have done so to their profit, and to ours. The trees in the foreground are nicely executed, though of course reminiscent of Renoir. C—."

The dawns are not to be believed. More women to whom the human, or at any rate masculine, form is repugnant enter and with averted eyes set down pans of water, with a clatter serving the simultaneous function of awakening you from a much-needed sleep. The soap floating in the pan completes its resemblance to the dumpling soup served for dinner the night before. This is all part of a general, well-orchestrated hubbub commencing suddenly everywhere. The rumble of carts supplements the reports of curtains shot back from between beds in double rooms and wards, like artillery fire supplementing infantry. To this is added a steady muffled beat from directly below, where the kitchen is said to be located.

It is of course all part of the notorious dawn barrage of hospitals.

No one bathed me with the water mysteriously brought in by the one evangel who set it down and fled. I finally gave myself a cursory sponging, also giving the bed a very satisfactory soaking. The cart delivering breakfast trays passed my door, till a well-placed shout brought it back. My bed was not made, the request for Demerol, to which I was entitled every four hours, went unheeded. It was all this that prompted the farewell with which I took leave of the hospital the following Saturday morning, four days after I entered. "So long, everybody," I called to the other patients as I was wheeled down the corridor. "Take care of yourself."

As I bounced over the threshold of the elevator I collapsed, my head dropping onto my chest. I was going home! Home!

twelve

I WENT BACK in an ambulance too. This seemed best owing to the flights of stairs to be dealt with at the rooming house where I now stayed. I had left home on beginning my career as a teacher, when I had been asked to move into a dormitory as housemaster. The building had recently caught fire, scattering a hundred of us into temporary private lodgings. Instead of returning home I had found a room at Mrs. Duncan's, conveniently located on the corner of a street bordering the campus. As long as I was in a cast that prevented bending my knee, it appeared that I must go up and down stairs in a sitting position, which was all right inside the house but another thing outside, with all the onlookers gathered around the porch steps to witness my delivery.

The ambulance was owned and driven by a local garageman named Mr. Hines, who was given to misguided religious zeal. He called his repair shop the Christ and Holy Trinity Garage, after the church next to which it stood — one of those examples of backfiring sincerity, since this expression of his piety had in the end not a pious air at all, but a frivolous and even blasphemous one, especially with the neon sign garishly proclaiming his place of business.

The policeman arranged for by telephone to help Mr. Hines carry me in was waiting for us in front of Mrs. Duncan's rooming house, along with the motley collection of pedestrians, which swelled rapidly as the ambulance stopped behind the parked squad car in which the cop had arrived. One spectator was an organ grinder with a monkey on a string — or I should say two spectators, for the monkey himself watched with that intent blinking stare peculiar to his kind as I was drawn out of the ambulance and carried to the house, while the music from the hurdy-gurdy remained respectfully suspended. There was a sprinkling of college students, at whom I smiled wanly as I was borne past them to the cottage. It was a white clapboard with a bay window in which a shingle hanging between lace curtains read: ROOMS FOR SELECTED GUESTS.

The formidable figure of Mrs. Duncan awaited us in the vestibule. "It's good to have you back, Professor Waltz," she said, smiling severely down at me. I had given up trying to make her understand that I was only an instructor, realizing that the dignity of the house, as well as her own ego, were nourished by use of the more prestigious title.

As we mounted the stairs to my bedroom a sudden apprehension seized me.

Mr. Duncan was a reformed alcoholic whom Mrs. Duncan regarded as in mortal danger of backsliding. For that reason she was an inflexible advocate of temperance — if that is ever a good term for the fanatical extremes usually characteristic of people so minded. My mother was a member of some temperance society or other, and I can remember my father flinging pots and pans about as he tried to explain to her that in order to be temperant one had to indulge in alcohol, not proscribe its use absolutely. It was certainly absolutely barred from Mrs. Duncan's premises, the pledge not to have it about in any form being one of the conditions of admittance as a lodger. I had quite understood the policy aimed at safeguarding a husband from temptation, and it had never bothered me since I did all my drinking at bars. I had simply never given the matter any thought. Now that I was trapped here, with the emotional strain of a very possibly deepening personal crisis added to the physical one of near-immobility, the problem became instantly a major one. I felt that I could have done with a stiff one even at that early hour. After devoting her mornings to the light housekeeping entailed by the rental of two rooms (only one of which was occupied at the moment, either for want of interested applicants, like my Dramatic Workshop, or because those who applied had failed to meet Mrs. Duncan's exacting standards) she would have lunch and then set out for a local department store where she taught knitting from one to five. It was clearly in those afternoon hours that I must have liquor smuggled into the house. Mr. Duncan worked in the office of the fireworks factory past which in fancy I trotted the exasperating Hodges!

The first thing I did when restored to the privacy of my room was to rub contraceptive jelly into my toes. These alone protruded from the cast, and I had begun to feel there the numbness against which I had been warned to be on guard. Some lubricant such as cocoa butter had been advised as an ideal massage, and since the preparation was composed largely of this ingredient, according to a declaration on the box, I used it for that immediate purpose, working it well into the crevices between the toes. I had bought it some months before, for use in a relationship that had never materialized, and saw no point in wasting it since it filled the bill from a practical point of view now. It came in the form of pellets in a brightly colored packet, which I kept hidden under a notebook in a desk drawer.

As I massaged my foot, I reviewed the arrangements hastily agreed on with Mrs. Duncan a few minutes before. Meals were not provided here unless a guest was sick, but under the circumstances she agreed to feed me for the few weeks in question. In return for this concession, I would try to be reasonable in the number and frequency of my callers, and in the hours they stayed, as well as apply the same standards as to the "sort" of visitors I had in my room as she did to roomers admitted to the house. I anticipated no difficulty in this area, since all I wanted to do was stay in bed with the covers pulled over my head and not see anybody again, ever. I promised again solemnly to observe the injunction against alcoholic beverages.

Removal from the human race has the compensating merit

of at least enlarging one's inner resources. My happiest hours, I think, were those of early afternoon when I had the house to myself and could prowl it unmolested. It was then that I solved some of my drinking problems. Such problems in logistics refine themselves further, to a man on crutches, into makeshifts of sheer animal survival. The following brief scene will be instructive, if not edifying.

At two o'clock sharp the next afternoon, I was waiting in the vestibule to receive the first quart of bourbon ordered by telephone from a neighborhood package store for that time promptly. I was watching for the delivery man through the curtained pane of the door when he pedaled up on a tricycle cart of the sort ridden by ice cream vendors. I thrust the correct money plus a tip out to him in return for the bottle, which he handed to me in a brown paper bag. After closing the door, I folded the bag into a pocket of my bathrobe, set the bottle on the floor, and worried it toward the foot of the stairs with the tip of my crutch, like a puck with a hockey stick. Leaving it there for the moment, I hobbled to the kitchen where the paper bag disappeared among a collection Mrs. Duncan accumulated in a broom closet. After filling my pockets with ice cubes at the refrigerator, I returned to the vestibule stairway. Now began the laborious ascent, backwards in a sitting position. With each few steps I would have to pause and shove the crutches up another stage ahead of me — or more literally behind me — doing the same with the bourbon of course. Erect once more at the head of the staircase, I nudged the bottle down the passage and into my room with the tip of a crutch again. I was soon lolling gratefully in my window chair, sipping a highball from my bathroom tumbler.

154

In this way I gradually worked out some sort of convalescent routine for myself. At first I debated asking Mrs. Duncan to supply me a regular pitcher of bedside ice water, but decided against introducing into my habits any innovations short of those making actual clinical sense, so as not to generate speculations in one all too suspicious by nature — one who administered her domain with the general air of a policewoman. There was risk enough in having to hide a bottle in a drawer where already a packet of contraceptive jelly lay concealed, along with a notebook of poems on which I was at work. They were mostly drafts, in varying embryonic or finished stages, of sentimental ballads in a vein of old-fashioned innocence Mrs. Duncan would not have appreciated. A sort of hobby. They bore self-explanatory titles: "That Little Bed of Myrtle," "Christmas at the Whorehouse," and "Why Is Daddy Walking Funny?"

An extra tumbler I was presently assured, by Mrs. Duncan's insistence that I daily drink the water in which my breakfast egg had been boiled, for the calcium so vital to knitting bones, with which she herself toiled faithfully up the stairs each morning when it had cooled. Whether her assumption that the boiling water actually extracted this substance from the shell was scientifically valid or an old wives' superstition I do not know, but in any case, since I had no intention of hastening my recovery in any fashion whatever, I poured the water either into the bathroom basin or out the bedroom window each day, a fate also reserved for the milk with which she tried to ply me for the same curative ends. I thought first of asking her to put ice in the milk, but decided in the end against risking any such odd request simply as a stratagem for smuggling cubes into the room. It was easy enough to carry them in my robe, or even in my coat and trouser pockets. Luckily both Mr. and Mrs. Duncan were heavy drinkers of soda pop and iced tea and coffee, so there was always a supply in the refrigerator from which my own modest needs could be met without risk of detection.

Into my pockets I also stuffed such snacks as could be abstracted from the refrigerator without arousing supicion — slices of cheese and cold meats to be eaten with crackers, or some of the pumpernickel to which Mr. Duncan was loudly addicted. This indulgence was of a piece with my traffic in alcohol, and like it a problem in logistics. This not only because picnicking in bed became part of the sybaritic ways into which I fell, in my general retreat from the world to which I would soon enough be recalled to account, but for another reason having to do with house rules. Foodstuffs were also forbidden in guests' rooms because of a spreading infestation of ants. They were everywhere in the kitchen and dining room, and would, Mrs. Duncan insisted, no doubt rightly, proceed to any part of the house where the faintest evidence of food was to be found. The only exception to this was milk, to which insects are not prone. I was for this reason always scrupulous in my regard for the way I ate anything in my room, cupping one hand under another to catch any crumbs, and licking my palms clean. This was certainly not too much to ask. I must have mashed hundreds of ants underfoot on the lower floor, where the Duncans went out of their way to step on them too, and the rooms of which were regularly sprayed with a broad-spectrum pesticide called Blast (there was also some fear of roaches and silverfish at the Duncan's in those days).

Thus nearly everything I did in my waking hours was forbidden, which added the guilt of broken regulations to my continuing shame as a *de facto* malingerer goldbricking on the proceeds of a willed mishap. Sometimes, athirst in the insomniac nights to which an inactive life increasingly doomed me, I would creep downstairs for some ice. I dislike drinking whiskey neat. I took every precaution possible against awakening the Duncans on these nocturnal excursions, after of course ascertaining that they were in fact asleep, which was easy to tell from the respiratory duet with which they obliged. Having paused at their closed bedroom door to this end, I would then proceed quietly on down in my flannel bathrobe, whose capacious pockets held all the ice cubes I needed plus any available cold cuts, pickles and other *délicatesse* I might care to take back in quantity to my lair. The hinges of my own door I kept lubricated with contraceptive jelly.

When I had telephoned to order my second quart of bourbon and saw the empty bottle staring at me, I realized I had another problem on my hands, that of disposal. This time when the delivery man handed the new bottle through the door I handed the empty one back to him.

"There's no deposit on these."

"There's no deposit on these?"

"Not on whiskey empties, no."

"Well, take it anyway, and here's a little extra something for you, my good man." Our exchanges had something of the surreptitious flavor of Prohibition days, I guess, though, for his part, he probably suspected he was delivering merchandise to some sort of disorderly house, or perhaps private sanatarium.

I filled my pockets with ice and, settled down in bed with a fine highball at elbow, did some work on "Christmas at the Whorehouse." It was a long narrative in ballad quatrains that told the story of a cruel father who drove his daughter out of the house for some minor wrong and then, years later, deserted by his wife for his tyrannical behavior, sought solace in a brothel one lonely Christmas, to find his daughter there. Writing sob ballads was (apart from the value of all hobbies as offering a relief from the rigors of reality) an extension of my interest in collecting them. I had by now amassed quite a library of records, a few of which I played on my portable phonograph that afternoon when I found composition bogging down. It was, on the whole, a pleasantly lazy and relaxing afternoon.

This whole fabric of existence, so painstakingly woven and so meticulously sustained, like a prolonged perfect crime, suddenly began to unravel and disintegrate without a hint of warning.

I was left alone at my lunch in the dining room, one afternoon during the second week of my confinement, when Mrs. Duncan excused herself, explaining that she had some shopping to do before going to work and would clean up when she returned. I was grateful for the peace, Mrs. Duncan having developed the habit of hanging about and talking after serving my food. I had come to cherish my solitude, to the point of disparaging all potential lodgers on whom I laid eyes. I had remarked that a woman who had just inspected the still vacant room looked to me like a Lesbian. Mrs. Duncan replied, rather self-righteously, that tenants were not barred from her premises on grounds of nationality.

Left alone, I began to scratch under my cast with my table

fork. Anyone who has ever had a limb so imprisoned knows this frustration, which can send the victim into a frenzy. I had found the best implement for such emergencies to be a wire coat hanger, which can be bent into a variety of surgical shapes, but I had none at hand here, with the result that in trying to reach the spot where I itched I pushed the fork down too far and couldn't get it out again. I tried to fish it out with a knife, which only made matters worse. In fact, that too was lost. The end of the handle kept slipping from between my thumb and forefinger, like a wet pip, just beneath the top of the cast, till it was too far down to recover. In a fit of pique, I seized my spoon and thrust that down into the cast also. "Get *in* there then," I said, "if that's what you want." I had no doubt I would recover them all quite readily with the coat hanger, which turned out not to be the case.

With an odd laugh, I set to work assembling my stock of provisions for the night. Suddenly parched for beer, I had ordered two cans from my vintner, due at the appointed hour also with a fresh quart of booze. I stuffed the pockets of my trousers and robe with enough ice cubes to keep one can cold in the bathroom wash basin while I drank the first, or to chill both if they arrived warm. The problem of pressing on the delivery man the empty beer cans could be faced when the time came. For snacks, I took a few slices of the ever-present pumpernickel and a can of sardines which I located so far back in the recesses of a kitchen cabinet that I was sure it had been forgotten and would not be missed. The sardines I lashed to one leg with a stout rubber band. In order to add to my store several stalks of crisp celery and a scallion or two left over from my lunch, I set them on top of my head and tied them with the cord of my bathrobe, which I knotted under my chin like a maiden tying on a bonnet. There was more to this than the instinct of self-preservation, or self-dramatization either. It was a kind of protest — the passionate outcry of honyocks everywhere. Viewed in that light, my behavior from here on became a kind of self-laceration, the urge to define plight by deliberate monstrosity. After pocketing a drumstick, I popped two or three ice cubes into my mouth for extra measure, hunched myself between my crutches, and, grasping the handles, propelled myself toward the front vestibule.

As I reached it, the door opened and Mrs. Duncan entered, her arms laden with provisions of her own, in the more conventional form of grocery sacks. I had misunderstood her. I had thought she meant she was going to shop downtown before proceeding directly to work, not that she was going to the food market and would drop off her purchase at home first.

It would be hard for us to say which of us was the more surprised. We both stopped in our tracks. I smiled, as best I could with my cheeks bulging, and mumbled something.

"Professor Waltz, what on earth," she said, standing aside to let me pass, for I had resumed my clomping if for no other reason than to get her behind me so we would not have to look at one another. I mumbled again, this time gagging, and with a spluttering cough disgorged the three ice cubes. One of them shot against the opposite wall, the other two dropping at my feet. I looked down at them with an expression of curiosity, as though I had never seen them before. "Well, of all the . . . I just thought I'd . . . And there's always so . . ."

Mrs. Duncan set her parcels on a living room table and marched back to the vestibule, where she stood, arms folded and lips compressed, and watched me back up the stairs on my hind end. When I had gone halfway, my eyes resolutely lowered, she said:

"And this is what goes on under my roof. This is how I am repaid for my kindness."

"If I could only . . ." I picked up my crutches and hurled them the remaining distance up the stairs and even some length down the hall. As I toiled along on my seat, Mrs. Duncan shook her head with the same look of sorrowing dismay, more for the ice cubes and what reprehensible use they clearly implied than for the foodstuffs stolen from one part of the house and eaten in another from which we were trying to keep vermin. I thudded along on my behind to my door, swiveled into it and disappeared into my room, cursing the day that had ever brought me here.

The mood inspired by this wretched incident had at least the merit of producing the head of steam necessary for me to sit down, with my foot on an overturned wastebasket, and write out the letter of resignation already framed in my mind. The applications for teaching posts at other colleges had long since been handed to Mr. Duncan for deposit in the mailbox outside. This being a formal communication, presumably to be handed or read to the personnel committee of the faculty, I began it "Dear Dr. Littlefield" rather than "Dear Norm":

Since I shall in all likelihood be asked for my resignation, I prefer volunteering it, and in so doing take the occasion to explain the action which has precipitated the present crisis.

It was not idle. Quite the contrary. There is a growing body of opinion sharing the spirit of protest of which my public outcry was a spontaneous, nay irrepressible, expression — long overdue here as on many another campus. It is the gathering ground swell of impatience with the dead hand of scholarship as typified in the species of research fostered and required here in the English Department as it is now run. You know what I mean. Tallying the past participles in Spenser or weak verbs in pre-Chaucerian dialect, or yet another disquisition on the clowns in Shakespeare, in preference to something really good in the new — or vital in the old — is the bane of academic life as it persists under the aegis of research for its own sake, the sacred Norm under whose tyranny, yes, we labor and are heavy laden. Have a care! Some of us younger men, weary of the whited bones of erudition and aspiring to the flesh and blood of literary tradition *in the making,* will one day turn and rend our overseers. And if that little demonstration I heard in chapel was an indication, that day is at hand. You will have noted *that nobody laughed.* No, you could have heard a pin drop, such was the stunning austerity of the occasion. That indecorous but honest ejaculation was the no longer controllable rebellion of one who speaks for gathering thousands, and who speaks for them now as he says — you and your kind have got to go!

Farewell.

Yours sincerely,
(Signed) Thomas Waltz

That done, I diverted my mind by writing another letter of quite another sort.

In a movie magazine I had seen lying about, I had come across an announcement of a contest involving a new Hollywood starlet, Angela Ravage, whom her studio was trying by this means to build up in the popular mind. A prize of a thousand dollars was offered for the best letter written in answer to a question posed by Miss Ravage: "Why can't I find happiness?" This is the kind of thing that makes one's flesh creep even while it exerts some kind of irresistible fascination over us — or at least so I have found it. Confident that I could do as well — or as badly — as the next person, I reached for a fresh sheet of paper and began rapidly to write, "Dear Angela, You can't find happiness because you're looking for it. Happiness isn't something we find, but something that finds us, provided we don't chase it and scare it away. Happiness, Angela, you see, is like a little puppy dog. If we try to catch it, it will run away from us. But if we walk along paying no attention to it, it will follow us home, wagging its," etc.

Nauseated as I was by what I had written, some genuine emotion seemed at the same time to be plucking my heart-strings and even misting my eyes. This was partly the strain I was under, both physical and mental. That much could not be denied. Nevertheless I must acknowledge some inner counter-part to the mawkish sentiments I was counterfeiting, no doubt kin to the starved emotions responsible for the taste in sob ballads (not mine alone). Too, I was myself sexually lonely; why had Marion Wellington not called, or sent me a get well card? Also mixed in this complex of feelings was a sheer resentment of the intellectual world in whose view I had made an ass of myself. The maudlin pap to which I could so readily turn my hand was a deliberate, perhaps perverse, wallowing in standards repugnant to those in whose eyes I was a laughingstock. Finally, this outlet undoubtedly afforded an appeasement of household gods, an expiatory sop to my parents for being as "ashamed" of them as I was. Indeed, one of the gems of my collection was a recording of "Just Plain Folks," so cracked and valuable I was not entirely sure of the words when, the tears streaming down my cheeks, I would throw my head back and sing along with the phonograph:

163

We are just plain folks, your mother and me,
We are just plain folks like our own folks used to be.
As our presence seems to grieve you,
We will go away and leave you,
For we're sadly out of place here,
'Cause we're just plain folks.

Consulting the magazine advertisement more closely, I noted that in addition to the thousand dollars the winner would be awarded a date with the actress if he turned out to be a man, a "visit" if a woman. This was undoubtedly an attempt on the part of the magazine, which was co-sponsor of the contest, to attract masculine readers. A meeting of that order was scarcely of interest, but I could certainly use the thousand dollars now.

There was another discouraging development. The itching in my broken leg, which was the left one, continued and intensified, and from its nature and persistence there was no doubt of the truth to be inferred: there were ants in my cast. It was definite. The sudden sight of a file of them coursing upward in a thin line from the floor to my bed confirmed it.

I rose instantly from it and went to my armchair, where I sat gravely evaluating the situation. I had had muffins and marmalade for lunch, particles of which must have adhered to the eating utensils I had thrust down into my cast, and which were still there. Truth to tell, I had noted ants in my room a day or two before, drawn by my snacks as justifiably predicted, and now they were being attracted on into my cast by the sweets there. I had no more than analyzed this predicament when the front doorbell sounded, and I remembered my vintner was due. "Coming!" I clomped and thudded down the stairs, rolling an empty ahead of me. Mrs.

Duncan had by now of course departed for work, and I made my customary transaction through the half-opened door, handing out also my manifesto to Dr. Littlefield which I had snatched from my desk on the way out, along with the contest letter.

"I wonder if you'd mail these for me like a good fellow. There's a box right in front of the house there," I said. "And here's an extra dollar for you this time. Ah, good, the beer is nice and cold."

After watching from the window to make sure the delivery man posted the letters, I went to the kitchen to spray my cast with some of Mrs. Duncan's insecticide bomb, Blast. I directed a dose of it as far down my leg as I could, drawing the rim of my cast away and my thigh muscles in, to make as wide an aperture as possible. The measure seemed efficacious, judging from the ants that were presently seen pouring, not over the top of the cast, but out the other end, through the open toe.

From here on things deteriorated in an almost geometric progression. Upstairs I found the ants swarming around my bed and, drawing from my pocket the can of Blast which I had taken with me in anticipation of this, I sprayed everywhere as liberally as I dared. I returned the can to its place under the kitchen sink, and on my next trip up took my liquor with me, a can of beer in each pocket of my bathrobe, the bourbon as always. The beers had flip-top lids requiring no opener, and I sat in my chair and drank them both, but they gave me no pleasure. I was now quite harried and at loose ends. The room smelled of the spray, and there was a revival of activity in my cast. I had some second thoughts about the direct exposure of my skin to the pesticide, and now, assum-

ing that whiskey must be as lethal to ants as anything, I un-
screwed the cap of the bottle and poured some of that down
my cast instead. Just then I caught the sound of Mrs. Duncan returning, a little early it seemed to me, and I hastily put
the bottle and the empty beer cans in a drawer of my desk.

I was innocently reading a book when she entered, presently, with my glass of milk. She stopped and pointedly
sniffed the air. She was about to make some comment when
the telephone rang and, setting the milk down, she hurried
into the passage to answer at the upstairs extension. She returned in a moment and announced to me from outside in
the hallway: "A Dr. Littlefield is on his way over to see you."

thirteen

AS I SAT waiting for Littlefield I passed the time, and be-
guiled anxiety, by again trying to put this mess into some sort
of appropriate Shakespearean claptrap:

> I shall be packed ere thou me packing send'st
> And find some place to cool my spirit's flush.
> The shade in which we lie the very sun from which
> We seek escape himself hath 'factured,
> Luring from summer boughs the self-same leaves
> That make a rustling haven from his heat.
> E'en so th'identical Power that deals us ill
> Some consolation fashioneth betimes.
> So husbandmen whose fields to drought are lost
> Will fear no more the pestilence and frost;
> And suitors spurned are banished in their need
> By rosy lips they'll never have to feed.

I shook my head again at how easy it was to turn out this stuff. Congratulating myself that I was at last out of all stifling academic concern with it.

I had drunk a good third of the bourbon by the time Littlefield arrived, and so it was doubtless this bottle courage, utter recklessness of consequence, that made me throw my crutches under the bed and crawl in after them when I heard him drawing near.

I lay there still as a mouse, listening to Littlefield come slowly up the stairs and down the corridor to my room. I could visualize him advancing with his shuffling gait and his thatch of iron-gray hair — the "literary mane." "Where's my Elizabethan man?" he sang out while still coming down the passage, in his rather affected baritone. No, he was impossible. He even *looked* like a professor. He would have to go.

I could hear him enter my room on Mrs. Duncan's shouted instruction as to its whereabouts, and imagine the baffled glance accompanying the mumbled expression of his failure to locate me anywhere in it. He puttered back out to the head of the stairs to report this lack of success to Mrs. Duncan. Next was heard her firmer tread mounting the stairs and entering the room, after perhaps a brief glance into the open bathroom. She marched straight to my bed, and I saw her policewoman's face peering under it at me as she bent down with the lifted skirt of the spread in one hand. "There he is."

By the time I had writhed out from under she was gone, leaving Norm Littlefield the sole witness of my struggles. "I was just . . . Seemed the only . . . Because she's always . . ." I explained, heaving myself up onto the bed by my elbows, like a tired swimmer onto a rock. I wriggled backward until

I lay stretched out full-length, hauling my inert leg up last, and panting heavily.

"Well so. It's nice to see you, Norm. Have a seat."

Littlefield's face, at best scarcely suited to the expression of even one emotion, was put to considerable strain now with three or four to register simultaneously. His nose was too small for his high forehead, and both were too narrow for his chin, a wide, jutting feature with a large dimple in it, like a second navel. It seemed, his face, a composite of portions of three different faces, like those combinations which participants in newspaper contests are required to unscramble and properly reassemble with their rightful components. Vice President Hubert Humphrey gives somewhat this same impression, though on a much better-looking and agreeable scale. In Littlefield's case everything was somehow, or seemed somehow, pulled together by his curved meerschaum pipe, which in his doubt he now produced, filled from a tobacco pouch, and lit. I watched him, unable to think of a single thing to say now that the dreaded confrontation was here at last. I could feel the ants stirring in my cast again, and promised myself that the minute I was alone in the house once more I would try sucking them out with the nozzle of Mrs. Duncan's vacuum cleaner.

There was some transitional talk about my break, how things were going with my classes in my absence. I held out little hope of my being once again fully mobile for some weeks, perhaps even months. Then he said something that rather took me by surprise.

"I for one can't wait to have you back, of course."

"You for one can't wait to have me back?"

He became flustered and, looking away, rubbed the stem of his pipe against his nose.

"It goes without saying that I appreciate that vote of confidence. Ill-timed it certainly was, and unfortunate in that it created a disturbance in chapel. But that makes it all the more heart-warming to me. The fact that it was so spontaneous, Tom."

I nodded, staring fixedly at the navel in his chin, my gaze just clearing the toes of my upturned crippled foot, elevated on a pillow in keeping with the doctor's instructions.

Norm continued with visible emotion.

"Yes, it makes a man feel good to know who his friends are when he's under fire, as I told you over the phone in the hospital, and to hear his friends rally to his banner. Dean Shaftoe and President Bagley now understand clearly that I do have support — "

"And if they give you the heave-ho it means, by God, that several of us — "

"No. Don't say that, Tom. Don't go that far — yet. Thankful as I am for what I know you were going to say. Let's leave that bridge till we come to it. Just let me go on with my point, that now the authorities know I have support in my department and that it has the courage to become vocal if need be. Our faction is in the minority, yes, but less so than when that editorial came out in the *Polycarper*. It's given others the guts to come out. Newcombe grasped my arm in the hall and said, 'You can count on me too, Norm.' It makes a man — "

Here Littlefield was so overcome by emotion that he brushed at his eyes, and I could feel tears welling up in mine.

"It was nothing, Norm."

"It was everything. That testimonial may have been the turning point. And it goes without saying that as soon as I reasonably can I'll recommend your promotion to associate professor. With tenure. Of course that depends on my remaining in power in the department."

"Well, here's one boy you can bank on, believe you me! And don't think I'm only thinking of the promotion as such, and hike in pay, or whatever. I even forget what it is."

"A five-hundred-dollar raise the first year and another five hundred the next. There's a regular scale for that."

What ran through my head was a hymn I had sung so often in the mission, with the line "And the burden of my heart rolled away." The tide of this ecstatic relief had no more than begun to flood me than it ebbed, as, with a sickening plunge, I remembered the letter in the mailbox.

I got rid of him as fast as I decently could, bumping down the stairs on my behind to see him out in order that, having said goodbye at the door, I could watch from the curtained pane till he was safely out of sight, and then descend the outside porch stairs to the mailbox, which was almost directly in front of the house, as I have said. I risked breaking the other leg in the speed with which I hobbled over to read the schedule on the postbox. According to it, the next pickup would be at six o'clock — five to ten minutes from now. I breathed a prayer of thanks, only hoping the mailman had not been early and already gone. There had not been a pickup since I had given the letter to the liquor delivery man to drop.

I loitered about the mailbox as nonchalantly as I could, considering that I was in a bathrobe as well as between crutches. This drew the gazes of passersby, and also, finally, that of a policeman who appeared on the corner opposite. I have mentioned that the other side of the street bordered the campus, whose square half-mile was roughly his beat. He eventually strolled over, apparently overcome by curiosity.

"Something wrong?"

"No. I'm just waiting for the mailman. He should be along any minute. Thanks just the same."

He went back across the street, but remained in view, trying to affect offhandedness himself as he paced in a narrow range with his stick dancing on its thong. I had no doubt that Mrs. Duncan was drinking in the scene similarly from the parlor window, to which I resolutely kept my back.

At last a red, white and blue truck rumbled to a stop at the curb and a mailman sprang out and came over, drawing out his key chain. As he squatted to scoop the contents of the opened box into his pouch, I said, "Look, there's a letter in there that I mailed by mistake. I'd like to have it back if I may."

He shook his head, squinting up at me. "Can't give it to you."

"Why not? If I can prove it's mine."

"It's now in the official custody of the Post Office, and my official responsibility."

"There it is!" I said, recognizing it. He drew out the letter I indicated, though withholding it from my eager grasp. "It's absolutely essential that that letter be not delivered. It's a matter of life and death. Can't I recall something that's mine?"

"Yes, but I can't give it back to you. Not just like that. You'll have to come along to headquarters with me to claim it. You've got to make out a form."

"All right, fine. Let's go."

"Don't you want to put on some other clothes?"

"These are all right. Are you about ready to pull in?"

"Couple of more stops."

I stood for the brief ride to the Post Office, there being only the single driver's seat in that kind of pickup truck. The driver was a rangy man with bushy red hair and narrow eyes, which he kept averted except when a traffic maneuver justified his turning his head in my direction in a more or less natural manner. At such brief intervals I could sense him taking me in sharply. He said nothing, save for an inquiry or two about my broken leg. We passed the Christ and Holy Trinity Garage, just beyond which he made his final pickup before turning a corner and pulling in behind the central Post Office.

I'had rather a time getting up a short flight of steps to the rear platform near which he parked, before clomping up to a desk to which I was ushered for the discharge of my business. There, under the supervision of a proper official, I made out the necessary form for the recovery of my mail, identifying myself to his satisfaction by writing out the name and address of the intended recipient in handwriting that, of course, matched the original on the envelope, and rattling off some of the opening paragraph of the letter. He then returned the letter to me, explaining that regulations required his retaining the envelope, a forfeit I was glad enough to make.

Though the Post Office was now closed, a couple of doors were unlocked for me which let me out the front entrance of the building. Fortunately the outside steps were broad and shallow enough to accommodate my descent in an upright position, though even so I attracted a number of gazes as I made my way down them toward the curb. There I presently managed to hail a cab, into which I sank with a sigh, exhausted but happy, clutching the letter in the pocket of my robe. In that was also enough for the taxi fare, a crumpled bill and some change left over from transactions with my vintner. Now I could, without a cloud in sight, sing of how the burden of my heart had rolled away. Indeed I hummed a few measures of the hymn under my breath.

There was an instructive object lesson in my deliverance — the moral of the episode it could very well be said. Salvation had come from precisely that quarter from which I had all along feared danger. Predicament and solution have often enough a common source. I had been so blindly engulfed by my own share of the bottomless folly of mankind that I had forgotten its universality. Littlefield was as big an ass as I. The next man generally is as great a fool as oneself. Egotism and vanity guarantee it.

As Shakespeare said, "Why should I fear the likes of me?" Or did he?

fourteen

ONE ADVERSARY, however, yet remained to be faced. In my elation that fact had slipped my mind, but the high heart in which I had it again forcibly brought to my attention made it less hard to bear than might otherwise have been the case. I was seated on the third step inside the house, ready to fire my crutches up the stairs in preparation for my sedentary climb, when Mrs. Duncan silently materialized in the parlor doorway, looking grimmer than ever.

"I'd like a word with you, Professor Waltz."

"Certainly."

I got to my feet again, or rather foot, and swung into the parlor with a few of the pendulum strokes at which I had become fairly deft.

"What is it, Mrs. Duncan?"

"I'm afraid I must ask you to leave. I think you know why."

The discovery that I had been drinking having already been made, along with the violation concerning foodstuffs and the attendant responsibility for ants in the upper reaches of the house, there remained only one further revelation about my habits at which umbrage could be taken — if one excepted the presence of contraceptives in my room.

"You've been reading my poems," I said, attempting to wrest from her the role of the injured party.

"I won't ask you to leave until you're physically able, of course. That should be in a few weeks, when you say you'll have your cast off."

"Another will be put on."

"I'm just giving you the notice."

"Was 'Christmas at the Whorehouse' one of them?"

"I wouldn't care to go into details about the type of person I mistakenly took into my house."

Invoking the invalid's exemption from the rules of amenity by dropping into a chair though she remained standing, I exhaled a long breath and looked at her. I sat very erect, with my hands along the arms of the chair, somewhat in the attitude of the seated Lincoln in the St. Gaudens memorial.

"Mrs. Duncan," I said, "you're not being fair. Quite apart

from the question of which is worse, writing frank poetry or snooping into other people's things, that poem is not indecent. I deny it absolutely. In fact it has a moral — or will have when I finish. I plan to show how sin never pays and evil is requited — in this case rancor in the human heart. I could prove it by the notes I have for the rest. Let me just show you — "

"No, I wouldn't be interested," she said, checking my offer to go fetch my preliminary drafts. "I've seen quite enough of everything, from drink to ants — not to mention missing silver."

I sensed the futility of trying to explain to her that the sob ballad tradition in which I was working was one of nostalgic innocence rather than salacious appeal; that, indeed, its innocence was one with the beaded lamps and wall chromos with which we were surrounded in this very parlor; with the horsehair chair in which I sat, and the antimacassar on it. It was one with the etching "The Deathbed Promise" which hung in my own mother's bedroom, part of the *mise-en-scène* of my inflamed childhood. It showed a woman ravaged by illness, gazing from her pillow at a kneeling son, while the father stands with his face to the wall in the attitude of one playing hide-and-seek, though beating it with his fists. Taken together, these constituted the kind of corn to which I was myself more than half addicted, though its victim; or perhaps because I was its victim, nostalgia being so intermingled with pain. The tearjerkers I collected in an ostensibly humorous vein actually released emotions deeply felt, though forbidden expression by sophisticated fashion and intellectual restraint.

I hobbled haughtily off, assuring Mrs. Duncan that I would

not encumber the house she ran or taint the air she breathed any longer than was absolutely necessary.

That you can't go home again is a truth inseparably linked to the fact that neither can you ever get away from it, as I had tried to tell Marion. The train of associations unloosed by my defense of "Christmas at the Whorehouse" now poured out of hiding (like ants over a sweetmeat), seeming to emerge from every crevice of memory. I remembered the time I had stood at the foot of my mother's sickbed reciting "The Destruction of Sennacherib" with all the expression with which I had "rendered" the selection at the school "Christmas exercises" which her illness prevented her attending. I remembered her wan face, framed in the pool of hair upon the pillow, so like that of the woman in "The Death-bed Promise" etching hanging on the nearby wall. I remembered my father, then in his prime, before the hangover that had so untimely felled him, sitting in a chair, smiling with the same pride as hers in the resonance of my elocution and the sweep of my gestures. "And there lay the steed with his nostrils all wide . . ." I remembered my next having to sing one or two of the carols in which we had raised our voices at the mission service from which her illness had also kept her, and to which I had dutifully gone in her stead. My mother had briefly joined in the carols, and then my father, "on a secular basis, remember. And then me and Tom will go pick out a tree, to commemorate the winter solstice like the pagans of old." I recalled hating him for the intellectual rigidity insisted on even in that sickroom — so much so that I freely gave a testimonial for Christ to make my mother feel better. I recoiled equally from that in turn, though — from her hand fondling my head after I had done so. I similarly shook my father's hand from my shoulder as we trudged through falling snow toward the vacant lot where Mr. Lubek sold his evergreens. In this way I resented all the family *schrecklichkeit* that converged on me from opposing directions in the formative years of my childhood. If formative is the right word for so chaotic and jumbled a human result as I.

Now I lay on a bed in Mrs. Duncan's rooming house, hating the hate that modern enlightenments so freely urge our airing, as an aid to the comprehension of family relationships and the cultivation of mental health. "Your conversions were aimed at your father, your blasphemies at your mother," a guidance counselor had told me when I was a student at Polycarp. He had even drawn a square with a cross inside it to illustrate the diagonal intersection of hostilities that formed my character. "Recognize that and be free." I had recognized it and was free — to attend divine service on Sunday, and on Monday to read Bertrand Russell's *A Free Man's Worship* to my English class, with equal zest and a raging fury that its dark declarations were so.

Feeling wretched now, I went out to the hall telephone and called my mother (whom I had not told about my broken leg). She was at the warehouse.

"Ma? It's me."

"Hello, Tom. How are you?"

"Fine, Ma. And you?"

"All right. Busy."

"That's good. How's Pa?"

"Same."

"I read a hangover remedy in the paper the other day. I've got it here. Shall I read it to you?"

"I'll get a pencil."

We had never given up hope. Now I read off the ingredients of something that, with the simple addition of gin, would have made one of today's more favored cocktails. So many hangover remedies have that ring. "Lemon juice, tomato juice, Worcestershire . . ." That done, my mother asked me whether I went to church regularly, and I told her yes, while bridling with resentment.

Closing the door, I lay on my bed with Chopin going softly on the portable phonograph. Poland may justly claim him, despite his French origins. His father was a refugee from Lorraine, but Chopin was a spirit instinctively vibrant to the rhythms of Polish folk songs, a heart through which flowed Slavic blood. Even the Polish skies seem to be in his delicate chromatic tints. They are not blazing azure we are told, but a blue delicate and fine. In Mazovia, his birthplace, it is touched with an exquisite mauve, the familiar hue of all his music. The miraculously hardy hybrid resulting to the permanent literature of romantic music is perhaps not so miraculous after all, for the temperaments blended to produce it are not all that dissimilar. There is a flamboyance in the Polish nature that has made people call us "the Frenchmen of the north." Viscont de Vogüe called us "the Italians of the north." The wincing strains of the preludes and nocturnes catch a certain *pathétique* that people now rather sentimentally associate with Slavic history. Sainte-Beuve said, "Even the word Poland is touching." Here, at any rate, was a level on which one could with impunity satiate the taste for unabashed emotion. Here an outlet for one who believes in the scarlet thread of pain: tearstained letters, marble fountains, maidens waiting, floating swans and people spitting blood — all that.

After an hour of this, I decided I had to see somebody, and made up my mind to call Marion Wellington. As I was thinking about it, the telephone rang, and that was who it was.

Marion said she had had me on her mind and had wanted to call on me for some days, but had been laid up with a cold herself. The next day, Friday, she was going to run up to Chicago to spend the weekend with her parents, but perhaps we could get together Monday or Tuesday. I told her I was scheduled for a visit to the doctor's on Monday at two, and that it would be nice if she could take me. To which she readily agreed.

"Where is Hodges!?" I asked.

"Gone back to Chicago. He's flying to Rome, you know. I'll look forward to seeing you Monday, Tom. If you could change the appointment to later in the afternoon, we might go on to dinner."

This development restored my spirits, and I returned to the bed to contemplate the evening thus guaranteed as in store for me. I realized at length that I was lying in the position natural to me, on my stomach, my arms embracing the pillow, so indicative of starved affection and retreat from reality into infantile evasion. I quickly rolled over onto my back in the face-up attitude which shows a more healthy masculine self-assurance together with a willingness to shoulder adult responsibilities.

I had been given an approximate date when the removal of my cast might be hoped for. I had no idea that the cast would also have to be temporarily taken off for the x-ray which was to be part of Monday's interim examination, and was therefore completely unprepared for the sight of a strapping blonde nurse, armed with a power saw, approaching the table on which I lay. Marion Wellington had moreover insisted on coming along into the treatment room to watch.

She stood with folded arms while the nurse pulled my trousers off, preparatory to the carpentry, and hung them on a hook. As the nurse plugged in the power saw and picked it up, I recalled with horror the still unrecovered contents of the cast, mentally tallying what was to fall out as it was dismantled. There was a complete dinner service for one, as well as a desk ruler, and the carcasses of God knew how many ants. As for the stains just below the groin, where the whiskey and insecticide must have discolored the orthopedic stocking lining the inside of the cast, these were of a kind that did not bear thinking about. Fortunately I lay on my side with my face to the wall for the first incision, which the nurse prefaced by saying as she picked up the saw, "Now, this little disc on here, this blade, doesn't rotate — it vibrates from side to side. So there's absolutely no danger of cutting you. The orthopedic stocking will itself stop the blade before it touches your skin. So there's no need to be alarmed."

I mumbled something into the crook of my arm, which I didn't catch. Then the nurse switched on the electricity, starting the motor. She bisected the plaster of Paris from the haunch down, lifting my shirttail up as she began the steady cutting motion. For a few minutes everything went smoothly. Then suddenly the insane whine of the saw was interrupted, or augmented, by a metallic screech that drew from the nurse an exclamation audible above the combined dins. "What on earth was *that*?"

I raised my head without turning it and mumbled something inarticulate again, at the same time shrugging to profess total ignorance of what she was talking about — even disassociating myself from the proceedings going forward under her charge. Then I lowered my head onto my arm again.

The obstruction, as far as I could infer, was bypassed with a roundabout incision by which she also circumvented other objects encountered in her downward passage, which became increasingly gingerly and tentative. However, that side of the cast was slit in due course, and I turned over for the other side, which was slashed without incident, though the nurse continued with a caution born of experience. Once she said something to Marion that I didn't get, but the gist of which seemed to have to do with the extraordinary articles sometimes recovered from children's casts. Marion nodded and smiled, watching with no change in her posture and none in her expression, except perhaps for a slight tightening of her lips. Her arms were folded over a white and blue peasant blouse, with a scoop neck and drawstring, like that of a purse with precious contents. Such is the metaphorical line of thought set going in me by sight of girls so dressed.

When the cast had been split down both sides and two short transverse incisions made in the foot, the nurse shut off the power saw, laid it by, and picked up a large pair of pincers with which she pried the halves apart. The cast cracked open noisily, like a nut. As she separated the two portions, the contents began raining to the floor. First the knife fell with a clatter, followed by the spoon, ruler and fork. I joined the women in glancing down curiously at these articles, as though I had never seen them before.

"Would you like these?" the nurse asked, after stooping to

pick them up. I shook my head, closing my eyes. She disposed of them, along with the fragments of the cast, in a large waste container.

"Now then, sit up. Up we go."

My broken leg, dangling down over the side of the table, was surprisingly weak and frail. What was more unnerving, it quivered uncontrollably, and also, exposed to the air for the first time, began to itch unbearably. The ants were as nothing compared with this. I sat for fully five minutes scratching with both hands in an ecstasy almost orgiastic. Marion averted her eyes from my face, the expression on which must have been distasteful, even obscene. The nurse, apparently used to this phenomenon, ignored it except for the humoring smile common to her kind. Dead skin, clawed free, fell to the floor like snow.

I was given a tunic in which to hobble across the passage to another room, where the leg was x-rayed and found to be knitting beautifully. "You've got the bones of a three-year-old," the doctor said. Then I was led back to the room I had been in previously, where a fresh cast was put on, this one reaching only below the knee. Thus at last sufficient mobility for getting up and down stairs was restored to me.

"How do you feel now?" Marion asked, as we drove off.

"I can dance as well as ever," I answered from the back, where I sat with my leg stretched out on the seat.

"Now you'll be able to resume your classes."

"Has Hodges! gone?"

"Yes, he's in Rome. Where would you like to eat?"

"How about the Blue Lantern. If the school office is still open you might run in and pick up my salary check."

The Blue Lantern was a country restaurant halfway to the

Illinois border. We drank wine by candlelight, at a corner window over an illuminated waterfall. Nothing was said about the flatware that had fallen out of the cast, or what I had yelled in chapel, or what was thought of these and other matters connected with the basic train of events, though I could sense Marion turning them all over in her mind as she appraised me with the speculative compassion peculiar to her. The veil of silence having best fallen, I did not discuss Norm Littlefield's reactions either, or the turn in my own fortunes brought about by his unexpected misconstruction of my behavior. I began to suspect that everybody knew Littlefield had been the intended butt of the remark except Littlefield himself. It seems likely now that Marion had not been sitting *with* him in chapel, as I had originally thought, only next to him; that they had never been in one another's company and had gone their separate ways when chapel was over, and so had never discussed the incident. I now wisely saw that all these sleeping dogs must be let lie, but there was one unfortunate feature about that. It was a pity that I could not share with her Norm Littlefield's misapprehension, because masculine folly seemed to magnetize her. That gave me my first uneasy inkling of what I had in common with Hodges! It was plain that she was not a woman to be "won," swept off her feet, mastered or overpowered, or anything of that sort. She rather required an object for salvation.

All this was of a piece with her formal adherence to Christianity, which in turn informed and even dictated the substance of her teaching. As we drove home we were soon again deep in one of those discussions of human fundamentals that occupied so many hours of our courtship. I sat in back again, my leg out on the seat.

"The emotions a given religion itself inspires are a yardstick of its worth, I think," she said over the wheel, and again I had the feeling that I was being treated to a set of classroom notes. "Historically speaking, Christianity speaks for itself. It not only civilized the Western world, it gave rise to a wealth of art unparalleled in any other place and time. What I feel when I look at a painting by El Greco or listen to Bach's Mass in B Minor or Handel's *Messiah* makes it impossible for me not to *believe* what they say. El Greco doesn't paint religious subjects, he paints religion. Bach and Handel don't simply 'take' Christian themes, or embody them — they embody Christianity. When I listen to them, I believe the God they glorify. I have to."

"By that logic, the emotion inspired by *The Nibelungen Ring* is reason to worship the Norse gods," I said, "while the *Rubáiyát* proves that there are none at all, my dear Marion. I think you'd best take me home."

fifteen

PEOPLE WHO FEAR ridicule seem most to attract it. Or perhaps this is nothing more than an illusory reversal of the truth that those who provoke it develop an understandable fear of it. I was back in harness again, settled down to normal after the first constraints and embarrassments attendant on my return had been survived, stomping busily from class to class between my crutches, when a fresh complication arose, of an emotional order that made it a sort of "relapse" in my fortunes.

184

I had completely forgotten the letter I had entered in the contest, on the theme of why the movie starlet Angela Ravage had failed to find happiness, until one afternoon in early March I received a telegram saying that I had won. It was signed by a studio representative named Lapchick, and assured me that Miss Ravage was on her way from the Coast for the date with me that was part of the first prize.

This was appalling. When I had written the letter, of course, I had supposed my days at Polycarp numbered, and had only been casting about for any extra money I could lay my hands on. A thousand dollars had seemed a fortune at the time. I had never really imagined I would win, proud as I was of the entry I had finally turned out (or ashamed, depending on how one looked at it). Now that I had regained what I had jeopardized by my first folly, and more, thanks to Norm Littlefield's confused grasp of my heckle, it was twice as imperative that I nip this thing in the bud and not make a fool of myself on an even larger scale, at least without allowing a longer interval of time to elapse than this.

Lapchick was apparently head of the Chicago office. At any rate the wire had been sent from that branch. So I put in a telephone call to him there and told him that the award was quite out of the question, that I must decline the prize, and that he must consider my entry withdrawn from the contest as of now.

"It's too late for that," said a voice evoking a man sitting in a bowler hat with his feet on the desk.

"Now look, pal," I said, in a tone that figuratively clutched him by the lapels and threatened to give him a couple across the chops, "this whole thing is a mistake. I want it to go no further, under pain of suit. I cannot afford it at this time

185

for professional reasons. Am I making myself quite clear?"

"You're a professor, ain't you?"

"How did you find that out?"

"Then you should be proud to win a prize for writing a letter dat was well written. Like I say, it's too late anyway. We released it for publication in all the papers — including the one in your home town there."

"My *letter?* In the *Blade?*"

"Didn't you see it?"

Physically ill, I rushed out and bought a newspaper. I opened and read it on the street. There was the whole hideous thing on page three. "Polycarp professor wins movie letter contest. Local educator defines happiness." The story was run with a picture of the actress, a soft blonde girl with full lips and creamy shoulders. I had forgotten precisely what I had written, but its opening lines refreshed my memory: "A member of the Polycarp faculty has won first prize of a thousand dollars and an evening on the town with the actress Angela Ravage for a letter undertaking to explain why she, the actress, has been unable to find happiness. The author of the letter, a graduate of the college who at present teaches English there, defines happiness as 'like a puppy dog. If we try to catch it, it will run away from us. But if we walk along paying no attention to it, it will follow us home . . .'"

I crushed the newspaper with a gasp of horror and thrust it deep into a convenient litter bin. I entered the nearest bar, where, nursing a whiskey, I tried alternately to recall the rest of what I had written and to keep it at mental arm's length. Scalded by the memory of specific phrases, I would writhe on the stool and wonder how I had become caught in such a network of absurdity. I had again the tormenting round of imagined campus figures laughing in groups over what I had said and done. Without trying to explain the course of events to which I now fell victim, or pausing to elucidate them in any way, I will simply state in bald detail what happened, in the order in which it did.

A string of telephone messages awaited me at Mrs. Duncan's. Things were humming there. My mother had called, obviously to congratulate me, and to add a word of regret that I had neglected to include religious faith as among the ingredients essential to human felicity. There were calls from Marion Wellington, the editors of both the town *Blade* and the *Polycarper*, as well as from Norm Littlefield and Dr. Bagley, the college president. That was marked "urgent," as was another from the dreadful Lapchick, in Chicago. We had rung off with the understanding that he would get in touch with me later about the order of events from the studio point of view. In a burst of courage born of the adrenalin released by the very thought of Lapchick, I phoned President Bagley back and agreed to see him in his office immediately and "explain."

Among those waiting to cluster about me on the steps of the Administration Building was a reporter from the *Polycarper*, pad in hand. "No comment," I said tersely, toiling up the stairs between my crutches. He trailed me to the door, asking in a whining tone I remembered from a chapel speech he had made on the subject of school spirit, "Well, could you expand a little on the distinction you made between a lady and a woman? That the ideal female is half of each?"

Certainly I hadn't said that! Was I to be spared nothing? "Read your Shakespeare," I said, and vanished through the door.

President Bagley was in a state. Pacing behind his desk, he raked his gray hair with a thin hand. The public embarrassment I was causing the college certainly did not justify the degree of agitation he now displayed, it seemed to me. I learned later that it was merely the last of a train of unsettling incidents that had marked his day, but I had to cope with him as he was now, at the climax of the series.

"This will make us the laughingstock of the country," he said. "Just when I'm about to set out on an important fundraising swing. What shall I tell James Hill when he asks me if this is typical of the writing turned out by our English teachers? What shall I tell Josiah Bean, or Mr. Hodges! — a new prospect since we have had his son here in residence? I don't understand you, Waltz. I really don't. You sit with the students in chapel instead of with the faculty, horsing around with them and having to be called to order, just like one of them. You cause a public disturbance in general assembly, and now you enter a screen magazine publicity contest that should be beneath the dignity of a grade-school graduate, let alone a college instructor," he said, flourishing a copy of the afternoon paper, "and *then win* the damned thing into the bargain with a sample of balderdash just about perfect for the mental level of the average moviegoer. It's things like this, seemingly little things you know, that lose colleges their accreditation. Ours is in danger, did you know that? This could be our finish."

Norm Littlefield had slipped into the office just in time to hear this last, admitted so quietly by the secretary that I saw him before I heard him. He was as white as Bagley. Being my apparent sponsor, who had just recommended me for promotion, he naturally took this matter more to heart than the president even. I felt a little sorry for him.

"Yes, Tom," he said, dropping into an armchair, Dr. Bagley having by now managed to compose himself enough to sit down. There was an unmistakable change in Littlefield's attitude toward me since last seen. Instead of acknowledging me, even proclaiming me, as an ally in the faculty politics forever swirling about our heads, he now pointedly identified himself with the president's disapproval, even the semi-disciplinary policy that seemed to be crystallizing here in dealing with me, at least tentatively. In the circumstances this was quite understandable, even justifiable; I could not reasonably blame them. "I must say this doesn't set much of an example to our students. I'm really puzzled by your motive. Certainly it couldn't be for the money. Why would you drag the principles for which we stand — culture, intelligence, a certain civilized taste perhaps hard to define but nonetheless there — through such a — such a travesty?"

In his charge I suddenly found my defense. I grasped at it eagerly.

"You mean, gentlemen," I said, looking from one to the other with a tolerant but somewhat disappointed smile, and speaking in a low tone of general incredulity, "gentlemen, am I to understand it hasn't occurred to anybody that that *is* why? That I was deliberately travestying the contest itself, indeed all such contests, and in so doing satirizing the publicity standards prevailing in this country?" I regarded them in absolute, if feigned, amazement. "Has my spoof misfired that badly?"

Their expressions of wistful surmise were a sight to behold. Norm Littlefield's pasty face even took on a little color, and a sparkle of hope came into his eyes. "Is that what you were doing, Tom?"

"Of course. I mean it never occurred to me that anybody would fail to see I was aiming it over their heads, and in so doing striking a blow for literacy."

"We must make an official announcement to that effect," said the president, rising. "There must be an immediate statement."

"Leave it to me. I'll be glad to talk to the reporters," I said, so relieved that I was apparently going to have another narrow squeak that I was eager to make concessions — even amends. "It's a sad day when you have to explain you're joking, but I won't say that. It sets people's backs up to be called idiots. And it's the perpetrator's fault, really, if a burlesque doesn't come off. He should make it clear. I'll say it was ill-advised and so on, and offer some kind of apology, as I do now to you gentlemen both. I hope that will show my true feelings for Polycarp," I continued, in gratitude for Bagley's visibly diminished hysteria. "I'm terribly sorry about the whole thing. Not just the letter, but being stuck with the continuing publicity, which I suppose I'll just have to go through with. That bird-brained actress and all. So if there's nothing more, I think I'd best get busy and straighten this muddle out."

We left it that way. I hurried out to make my statement to reporters and now even photographers waiting in front of the Administration Building.

"You can say," I began, hunched between my crutches as I weighed my words in the attempted balance between explanation and apology, "that my entering the contest was a jape aimed at seeing just how far you can go in satirizing such publicity devices, and I never doubted this would be obvious to any intelligent person. However, it backfired, for which I express keen regrets. I apologize to the college authorities for the risk I thus took with the school's good name. It was ill-advised. I had no right to do it."

This statement appeared on the front page of next day's *Blade* side by side with Norm Littlefield's statement: "He had every right to do it." In our confusion, or rather our haste, we had got our stories mixed. The fool had come to the defense of behavior I had just admitted to be indefensible. He was now left holding the bag — or as they say with egg on his face — in a skimble-skamble making the college twice the laughingstock it had been before. What had begun as a comedy had degenerated into a farce, into which the school was now up to its neck. The president was apoplectic when next I heard his voice, on the telephone.

"I have never," he said in a mounting squeal, as though unseen hands were closing round his throat and attempting to throttle him from behind, "in all my years as head of this institution seen or had to cope with anything so preposterous. Now we really are a joke. There was something about it on the AP."

"I realize how you feel, Dr. Bagley," I said. "I'm sorry now I apologized. That was hasty."

"You're sorry *what?*" he piped, as though gorging himself on the outrage of seeing just how finely calibrated the absurdity of which he was the victim could become.

"I'm sorry I apologized. That I shouldn't have done. I see now I shouldn't have gone quite that far. But how was I to know Norm, Dr. Littlefield, was going to — "

"How were you to *know?* Why, I presume by simply inquiring. By a moment of simple, elementary consultation. Is that too much to ask of my staff? The least you could do is get your stories straight before rushing out on another impulse as ill-advised as the first. Now I am beginning to doubt that your explanation was true. I'm not at all sure you entered this contest for the reason you gave. It strikes me that you're a highly unstable character, Waltz."

"Well, you see, I thought — "

"You couldn't have thought anything, or we wouldn't be in this muddle. What we apparently need is a press relations department here, to coordinate public statements, to establish some sort of liaison among departments here, so nobody will go off half-cocked. This is a long felt need in this school." I had the image fatally evoked by this cliché of a need long and slender, made of felt, and had to cover the mouthpiece with my hand to keep my laugh from being heard at the other end. But the gravity of the president's state continued to foster an alarm quickly stanching such threats of levity. "To make sure that things are checked, intradepartmentally as well as interdepartmentally, before somebody opens his . . . We need lots of things here. We need better screening of applicants. I now learn that you who assign atheistic reading to your courses, and are known personally to spout godless infidelity in class, are also seen in church lustily singing hymns and devoutly kneeling in prayer. Is all that true?"

"I would like to recall Emerson's remark about consistency and the hobgoblin of little minds."

"Well, we haven't time for that now. We've got another hobgoblin on our hands, believe you me. I'm going to reorganize this college from stem to stern, I'm . . ."

I let him discharge what was an apparently dangerous head

of steam before even attempting further to express my regrets at the pass things had come to, let alone submit my suggestions as to what course of action might be taken with a view to salvaging at least a little of the school's self-respect. But when he had finished blowing his top, at least to all intents and appearances, I did suggest two or three alternatives that might be profitably pursued.

"I can withdraw my retraction, and say it was headstrong. I can accuse the press of garbling my statement. Or I can issue another statement saying that Dr. Littlefield was merely acting out of chivalry, perhaps misguided, but for which I am personally — "

"Oh, for the love of heaven! What will that do but worsen the mess. Let's forget our public image for the moment and *think* of Dr. Littlefield. He's taken to his bed with mortification. He refuses to talk on the telephone . . ." Here President Bagley's voice became again an indistinct squeal, as though the assailant, momentarily fended off, was renewing the attempted strangulation. "I think that in the circumstances you should by all means try your luck at getting through to him. And tell him, if you do, for heaven's sake not to issue any more public statements *until we all get together and agree on what's to be said.*"

"Right. And if I may sum up, sir, here's the way matters seem to stand at this juncture. I saw a certain thing my way. Then I changed my mind and no longer did, being persuaded by cooler heads to see it their way. Meanwhile these cooler heads ceased to see it their way in the attempt to see it my — "

But he had hung up, with a last splutter of rage.

I had an appointment at the doctor's to have my second cast removed and a walking cast, with a metal heel plate, put on, which enabled me to throw away my crutches. I did not immediately do so, however, deciding to retain as long as possible the sympathy that accrued from their use in a situation still highly critical to myself. I needed more than ever the immunity of the invalid. I winced frequently as I moved about in public, as though physical pain might have deranged my faculties and clouded my judgment in recent events.

The instant I left the doctor's office I called Littlefield's home from the nearest booth. He refused to come to the phone. He *could* not, his wife told me, on learning my identity. She was hostile, and there was an edge to her voice that left no doubt she considered me responsible for his "nervous collapse," as she freely termed it. I thought this rather dramatic of her. Still, the fact remained that Norm had "taken to his bed," as Dr. Bagley put it, a fact disquieting in itself, and unpredictable as to its duration or outcome, as resorts of that kind always are. Mrs. Littlefield's attitude must meanwhile be taken as measure of its gravity. It was on my account, she said, that he had made a fool of himself publicly, and neither for this, nor for the betrayal of his faith in me as a responsible underling, could she forgive me.

These were hard words. But whether just or unjust, needing to be digested. All in all, it looked like a rough weekend, and I was glad to see five o'clock of the next day, Saturday, roll around: time to catch the evening train to Chicago for my date with Angela Ravage.

sixteen

I WAS MET at the La Salle Street Station by Lapchick and a studio press agent named Quincy. These two helped me down the train steps in the walking cast to which I must now become accustomed, and by which I had told my tormentors they might identify me.

Lapchick was a ruddy, bony-nosed man with cheeks that looked as though they had been scoured with a cleansing powder rather than washed with conventional bath soap. He wore a shirt with wide stripes and a white-on-white necktie secured with a gold clasp, and flourished a cigar in a hand on which gleamed a large signet ring, as though he, too, were engaged in the dangerous business of parody and must use a broad brush in order to leave no doubt that he was offering a popular caricature of his type. His speech, however, revealed no such special intention. He was manager of the studio's Chicago office, as surmised. Quincy I liked on sight, though at the same time somehow doubting that he would wear well. There was a mirthless humor about him, that of someone basically wretched. Thirty, to all first appearances intelligent, he was very possibly the kind of public relations man President Bagley said the school needed — to avoid in the future such conjunctions as this.

I move in a fantasy through the station, like a prisoner between these men. Neither makes any secret of viewing this whole thing as a stunt, nor any bones about assuming I do too. Neither intrinsically good nor bad, just a stunt. If I encounter the same attitude in Miss Ravage, then I shall be so taken aback by prevailing cynicism that I shall be tempted to defend my letter on the subject of happiness as containing some sentiments that might be legitimately espoused. But I must be careful. I must not let people know that I am a square. At bottom. That is the secret I must carry to my grave. I once defended a line in a poem about "seeing rainbows in our tears" (the tears acting as a prism through which light is broken into its component parts) to my social detriment for that evening. I must try to let my sob ballads as a hobby smuggle sentimentalism over the borders of human relations humorously for me. I must conceal the fact that I am the End. With luck I may get through this life without its being discovered.

In the cab going toward the hotel where Miss Ravage awaits me, Quincy is openly bitter about his employment, on extremely short notice. He is a fleshmonger. Pure and simple. He would like to publicize something besides another Miss Twin Peaks. "Just once, somebody who can act." Every time the West Coast sends him another picture to place in the Midwestern papers, he knows before he opens the envelope what it will be. "Another moocow." Yet he is required to get the word around not only that the subject can act, but that she has a mind, and even a soul. She wants really to direct, she reads Camus, she is thinking of going into a monastery. Oops, convent. "But they can all only act with their neckline," he says. "Wait till you see this one. A pail and a milking stool and you're in business. I don't know half the time whether I'm running an office or a dairy."

"He wants to go out with them," says Lapchick, with what seems like nothing more than good-natured banter, but which turns out to go directly to the heart of the matter.

"Don't pay any attention to him, Professor Waltz." I sit between them, and as Lapchick turns to grin in my direction he releases a further cloud of the shaving cologne with which the cab is already permeated. Leaning forward, he says past me to Quincy, "You did take that one out who came through last week, didn't you, Pete?"

"Yes, I did."

"You cop her biscuits?"

"It's a question of arranging interviews for them," Quincy explains to me. "When an actress stops overnight on her way to or from the Coast it means she wants to be interviewed. You can fly through. So you have to rustle up the reporters and columnists." He asks abruptly, proof again that people divine one another's thoughts without dreaming it, "Do they ever use a press relations man at your college? What's the name of it again?"

"Polycarp," I say, having to think a moment myself. I am so far removed from my customary habitat that it seems like another time as well as another place.

"The way I hear it, anybody can cop her biscuits but you can't get the silk down," says the dreadful Lapchick. "A real teaserino." I trust he is talking about the moocow who came through last week, not the one with whom I have an engagement, and toward whom, on this formal ground alone, chivalry forbids my brooking any such familiarity.

"It's named after a second-century saint," I say. "The college. Polycarp was Bishop of Smyrna and a Christian martyr. Very little is known of his life."

"Right! Pete here will fix that."

Whether he is engaging again in idle irony or seriously accommodating the possibility of losing another employe in a

field with an understandably rapid turnover is hard to say —
and impossible at the moment to explore. We have stopped
in front of my hotel, where Lapchick himself springs out to
drop my Gladstone bag off for me, my condition being an
added complication in a tight schedule allowing no time to
"freshen up or anything." I move over to the corner of the
cab he's been occupying and, in the few moments while we
wait for his return, take Pete Quincy in a little more closely.

He has light red hair and the pale pink skin that often accompanies it. His features are neat and symmetrical, at present outlined in profile against a broth of neon light from
State Street storefronts, but despite its regularity and the obscurity in which it is viewed his face clearly betrays the queru-
lousness behind his humor. I guess him to be quite lonely.
His mood, my predicament, and a kind of despair diffused by
the anonymous swarms of pedestrians combine to infect the
hour. How many of these people are hurrying to rendezvous
of any intrinsic joy? Most of them may be no happier than
Quincy. He wants to date this Twin Peaks while I wish I
were flying through the Indiana dunes in Marion Wellington's open car.

"Walk, moocow, walk. See the moocow walk. Tom watches
the moocow walk," Quincy mutters to himself. After a few
sentences of this routine I gather that it is a way of declaring
the plane on which he works to be that of a grade-school
primer, and of implying that that is also the level on which
my own evening will be pitched. Only a profound personal
bitterness can account for such behavior on such short notice.
He is biting down on an aching tooth. The pit into which I
have let myself be drawn yawns at my feet. How did I ever
get into such a muddle?

"The moocow turns. She sees Tom watch her walk. Watch her walk, Tom, see the moocow walk. Now the man with the camera takes the moocow's picture. Does the moocow like to have her picture taken? Yes, she likes to have her picture taken." It seems to me we have had enough of this — far too much in fact. A stop ought to be put to it, and that instantly. But Quincy continues. "The man now has enough pictures of the moocow, and he tells Tom to go over and stand with her. They stand together while the man takes their picture."

"Do you mean," I say, deciding to put an end to the performance, "that there will be photographers here tonight?"

"Yes," Quincy answers, smiling for the first time. "They will be there. See the man with the box. The box is called a camera. Stand over there, moocow, stand with Tom. The moocow stands next to Tom. Tom stands next to the moocow. A light flashes. It flashes over and over. That is enough that way, moocow. Now dance with Tom, so the man can take some pictures that way too. Then we will have them to put in the papers tomorrow, and in the magazines. The kind that the moocow can read . . ."

His ragging must be borne as good-naturedly as possible. It is no good asking whether he has been hurt as a child. Some other method must be employed if the best is to be made of this, and further untoward results be kept to an absolute minimum. Perhaps some good may even come of it. After a moment of silent thought, I say:

"Look. I don't know whether you were serious about what you said a minute ago, about a press relations man at the college. But I could arrange for an interview if you had any such thing actually in mind. You seem discontent with your present work. I can't promise anything of course, but it's the sort of thing schools often talk about the need for, and occasionally even get around to. I don't know myself how good you are, but my own test for a press agent would be *how well he can keep stuff out of the paper*. Especially in a man's home town. We could discuss it later. Here comes Lapchick. Shh."

The instant Angela Ravage opens the door of her hotel suite to admit us I see what a misrepresentation Quincy's account is, and that it must serve as some kind of protective mechanism. She dresses precisely so as not to dramatize the famous prow, in a soft green evening gown with a straight neckline that displays rather her white shoulders. Perhaps it is a stratagem, but it also reveals an instinctive good taste. Her hair is gathered in a cluster of curls at the nape of her neck. The petulant smile of the "hoyden" roles results mainly from a pinched, slightly tilted upper lip which in real life, especially in unguarded moments, gives her a somewhat vulnerable look. Since due to this faint malformation her lips are always slightly parted, there is a vaguely wondering air about her, as of the dew still on her. It is easy to see how much of her true spirit is vitiated by all the silly smoldering and emoting she is instructed to do before the cameras. Nor does it call for any speculative acumen to sense that Quincy is smitten, and requires the safeguard of his sour-grapes caricature. When she extends her hand I remember to press it with the warmth, and retain it for the interval, regarded by experts as signifying neither extreme of introvert nor extrovert, but a mature blend of both.

Flashbulbs pop in our faces and continue to explode as we become acquainted. There are two photographers, who kneel on the floor and crouch on the furniture in the contortions common to their trade for the procurement of interesting angles. We are shot "getting to know one another": leaning forward in earnest conversation, smoking cigarettes, drinking champagne. There is general laughter when the cork I pry from the bottle flies across the room, narrowly missing Lapchick. It is then that I catch an accidental glimpse of Quincy, watching from the sidelines. He isn't joining in the mirth, but taking Miss Ravage in with a tense, almost hopeless expression. He gives the impression that his eyeballs are sweating. I am glad to see the photographers assemble their gear at last preparatory to departure, but dismayed to hear that they will "see us down in the dining room," as will Lapchick and Quincy.

Miss Ravage and I are left alone for a moment to finish our champagne cocktails. I have noticed a book lying on a table, *Existentialism and the Theatre*. "Are you interested in that?" I ask.

"Which? Existentialism or the theatre?"

"Either. It makes no difference."

"Well, both. I'm an Existentialist, I think." This kind of remark is either a silly affectation or the expression of an honestly thoughtful nature. It is a little disquieting to find it more the latter; the need for Quincy-like insulation becomes understandable. "Well so," she says, composing herself with a smile. "I wish we weren't stuck with the others, so we could really get acquainted. Sort of reminds me of Sartre's definition of hell. You probably remember it."

"No, I don't believe I . . ."

"Hell is other people. One of the characters in *No Exit* says it."

Talk, moocow, talk. Talk to Tom. Cite authors, make literary allusions. Show Tom that you know big words and the titles of plays. Tom listens. Tom sees that the moocow knows big words and the titles of plays. Make Tom see that you are not a sexpot, moocow, so that Tom will be twice as captivated by you.

Tom helps the moocow into her wrap and they go down the elevator. The elevator makes your stomach feel funny when it stops quickly. The others are waiting on the mezzanine and together we enter the dining room, where the headwaiter bows us to our tables. Miss Ravage and I share a choice one near the window, next to one from which our sponsors watch and supervise the proceedings. We are photographed making selections from menus the size of pup tents, then eating what we have ordered, roast duck and a vintage Burgundy. By the time we reach our baked Alaska the orchestra is in full swing, and couples are walking out onto the floor.

"Would you care to dance?" I ask with a laugh. "Dance with one of the others if you'd like, moo — I mean Miss Ravage. Dance with Quincy."

"I don't like him."

"So dance with him. You believe in the Absurd. He's unhappy. I know he'd love it."

She acquiesces, and I crook a finger at Quincy over my shoulder. "Miss Ravage would like to dance and I can't. Can we throw you into the breach?"

Lapchick frowns on this development. After consultation they have decided to omit my broken leg from the publicity releases and the pictures, but they do want one of us dancing. So I hobble out to the floor, where I hold Miss Ravage in my arms a moment, then clomp back to the table, leaving her to Quincy. His eyeballs are still sweating, and he seems to have difficulty swallowing. As I cross the room this time I stumble into a man who has as much trouble walking as I, though not with his leg. He holds a rubber cushion under one arm, and he brings up the rear of a party the captain is showing to a table while at the same time trying to ignore their existence. The captain manages to get them well out of sight, though one does catch a glimpse of the little old man placing the air pillow on his chair preparatory to sitting down on it. For some reason this pleases me enormously. I derive a certain perverse satisfaction from it, and only wish the man would at some point blow air into the valve before returning it to its place under him. That would make my evening complete, especially if it occurred in full view of the captain, perhaps even while he was pouring their wine. The cushion is circular with a hole in the middle, like a doughnut. Most refreshing.

"You dance divinely," I tell Miss Ravage as Quincy wafts her past my table. She sticks her tongue out at me over Quincy's shoulder. How well the evening is going. After dinner our supervisors want only a shot or two of us chatting between the acts at the theatre, before a last one saying good night at Miss Ravage's hotel room door again.

Now it is much too late for the theatre, and neither of us wants to go in any case, but a lobby shot is faked against a wall outside the mezzanine entrance of the restaurant. Lapchick holds Miss Ravage's wrap while she stands, elbow in palm, a cigarette burning in her fingers, listening to an intelligent comment I am making on the play we are seeing. Then the good night, shaking hands at the door of her room while she thanks me for a wonderful evening — though in actual fact she has secretly asked me in for a nightcap. The others disappear into the elevator, Quincy throwing a last haunted glance over his shoulder while I close the door of the room.

"Thank God that's over. Now can I give you a brandy, Professor Waltz? Hell, Tom. Order yourself a drink while I change into something comfortable. I think I'd like a beer."

I telephone room service for two bottles of Löwenbräu and stand at the window looking out across the lake front, the lamps along the drive and the moving lights of cars against a dark backdrop of water offering their unfailing nocturnal magic. I cannot get the little man with the air cushion under his arm out of my mind. I want him to go from restaurant to restaurant of this rotten world, deflating them all with his pneumatic doughnut.

Miss Ravage emerges from the bedroom at last in red lounging pajamas made precisely for what she said — comfort. She curls up in bed against a wad of pillows and without either affectation or any particular egotism rambles on about herself.

"I can't act. Not really. They spotted me for a gamin type — America's answer to the European ones? — but it didn't work, and the gamin vogue's about over now anyway. This contest was a last gasp. I kicked at first, but then figured what have I got to lose. Same as you probably. Actually that guck you deliberately turned out has a truth you can give a respectable statement, like corn usually can. Don't you think? Fitzgerald says somewhere how we look back on periods when we thought we were only waiting for the pleasure, to find they were the pleasure itself. I'm sure you feel deeply about things. I think I do. But then who the hell doesn't? We're all a mess of quivering, fearing — I mean inside — pulp, which is why we need the protection reason tries to give. Philosophy. The enamel around the naked nerve. The heart is a muscle — my father just had a heart attack — and people say, 'It's just a torn muscle. It'll heal.' But I think it's more like a tooth, with this nerve inside, ready to quiver any time a cavity shows up. That must be our beer."

I pay for the beers and pour them. I sit on a chair beside her bed, like someone visiting a friend in a hospital. She resumes her jabbering.

"I tried mysticism once, but that's no good. That's just cotton batting stuffed into the cavity, with a little medication on it maybe. You've got to seal the cavity over with cement — the good hard cement of reason. Face facts. Life is neither good nor evil, it just is. It has no meaning, no point, so just forget about that. Religious faith — " She interrupts herself with a swallow of beer, still gesturing with the free hand. "I hear it means nothing to people on their deathbeds. A survey was made once."

"You mean they actually interviewed dying people to ask whether their faith meant anything to them now?"

"Well, not that blunt. But something. I forget where I read it. But I asked a doctor that once too, and he confirmed it. Not that people *reject* it or anything — they just don't *think* about it. He said. What's of value I suppose is what it means to people in their lives. Mortality comes down in the end to just an organic matter. If you do believe in the fiction about God — " Here she smiles, and says, "You remember what Heine said about whether he thought God would forgive him."

"At the moment I can't seem to . . ."

" 'C'est son métier.' That's his trade."

Quote for Tom, moocow, quote some more famous men. The moocow sits on the bed talking. Tom listens to the moocow. She tells him what the man Heine said, and then translates it for him too. She translates it into English so Tom will understand. They smile at each other. There is a silence, and they drink from their glasses at the same time.

"I'd like to go back to school."

"You would?"

"I'm twenty-two. I only had two years of college when some character 'discovered' me in a play there. It was Skidmore. I wasn't too happy there, or then. I'd like to try some place else. How's Polycarp?"

"I don't think it would be to your taste. The head of the philosophy department is a Platonist, an idealist. He'd be dishing out a point of view you wouldn't care for."

"All the same I'd like to take a look at the place, now that I'm this close. I'm staying in the Midwest for a few days. I'd like to go back with you."

"There was a man in the restaurant, I don't know whether you noticed, who took an air pillow in with him? The captain's face was a sight to behold. Tickled me pink. I hate snobbishness, and I like to see it brought low."

"You've got something in your craw. What is it?"

"May the Lord smite all those who put on airs, all those who upstage another. May he dash them to pieces with a rod of iron."

"Waltz. What kind of a name is that anyway?"

"I have no idea."

"You mean you don't know what nationality you are?"

"We lived in a neighborhood where there's a dense Polish

population. At least they seem dense to me." Father forgive! Mother forget! Heed not the crowing cock again!

"You say you teach Shakespeare. Do you take any position about all these theories? Who do you think wrote the plays?"

"I lean to the group theory. Anybody can write the stuff who puts his mind to it. You even get so you think that way. Even find yourself extemporizing it."

"Extemporize some. Say something to me in Shakespeare."

"To celebrate thee suitably a contradiction were, for best to do thee homage would be to show how thou hast stopped me dumb. For thou hast so infested my commuting blood, which to the suburbs of my feet doth flow and back again, that something something further heats my somethinged brain. Fevered brain. Till in mid-flight the pinions of articulation falter, and my tongue palsies at its sweetly hopeless task."

She smiles watchfully at me across the top of her glass. I see that I am making far too much headway.

We drove down with Quincy in his car the next afternoon, as it turned out.

Since I expected to be fired anyway, I could see nothing to lose by showing Miss Ravage around the school. She would certainly make a hit with the students, especially the boys, and might just charm the faculty if generally put on view. Quincy's motivation for the trip was twofold: continued closeness to Angela Ravage, and the interview for a possible job as press relations man for the college which I had promised him. He took a camera along, a device not far short of blackmail. There would be no more pictures in local newspapers provided I made good my promise. He insisted first that the interview be accompanied by my personal recommendation, but I convinced him that in the present pass this would be a liability rather than an asset. He packed in the camera just in case — and of course there remained the possibility of our getting a shot of Miss Ravage winning over the student body, or Miss Ravage thinking about enrolling at Polycarp: publicity of a kind that would make people forget all about my letter and might even prove advantageous to President Bagley on his fund-raising tour. I arranged by telephone for Marion Wellington to join us on a double date, a stratagem by which I hoped further to appease Quincy by throwing him Miss Ravage in the resulting foursome. Marion herself proved entirely sympathetic on the phone. "How can anyone go on making such a fool of himself?" she said.

All in all, I felt a good deal better about things as we left the main highway from Chicago, that afternoon, and turned into Slow Rapids, climbing the long street that mounted toward the college. My dismay at what awaited me, therefore, can be imagined. As we wound along the driveway leading into the campus proper, I saw that the flag above the Administration Building was flying at half mast. We had not heard the news in some hours, and wondered if a governmental official or other national figure had died. Quincy stopped the car, and I sprang out to make inquiries of several students who were walking by. It was then that I learned the news that Norm Littlefield had passed away.

A word of comment which anticipates the story somewhat is not, I think, amiss here. It will put certain facts otherwise open to misinterpretation, and even now still often garbled in the telling, into some kind of badly needed perspective.

Norm carried too much insurance. There was no doubt

about that. And who knows how many a demise is not has-
tened by the burdens unwisely shouldered by being too heavily written up. The thing becomes a kind of vicious circle, a
self-defeating paradox in which an outcome feared is brought
on by the means intended to provide against it. Among people familiar with the facts of Norm's private life, this was his
besetting folly. The strain of meeting unrealistic premiums
was only the last straw among other fiscal imprudences. Wisdom had dictated a life far more moderate than Norm actually lived, one free of the stress he so recklessly invited by the
many administrative chores he also needlessly took on, not to
mention the pace a socially ambitious wife led him. That the
amount of coverage with which he humored her was out-
rageously more than he could afford was in due course reflected by the scale on which his widow was presently able
to live — far more splendidly than she had on a poor professor's pay! But I do not wish to indulge in personalities here,
or criticize the woman unduly. Anybody's life is his own to
live as he wishes, or as he must, which was perhaps the case
here. I am only revealing facts which came to light, and assurances with which people very kindly came forward.

The Administration Building was open, though it was Sunday, and I suspected President Bagley was in his office seeing
to "arrangements" and attending to other matters relating to
the misfortune. As I stood uncertainly in the driveway, his
secretary appeared in the doorway and urgently beckoned me
over. "President Bagley has been trying to get you," she said.
"I think you'd better go and see him now."

I dismissed my frieinds, giving them directions to a tavern
where they might get a drink and possibly stay on for dinner,
as well as await word from me, though there was little likeli-

hood that I would join them. I explained to Quincy that an interview with the president was now out of the question, as was showing Miss Ravage around the campus. They drove off as I made my reluctant way once again into the president's office.

"Well, you've killed the head of the English Department."

This was what I had been hoping he would say. I wanted him to blurt out an excess from which he would in all conscience have to retreat, owing me an apology. The result was that the grievance rather dramatically changed hands.

"I'm sorry. I shouldn't have said that."

"It's quite all right. We all say things we don't mean in circumstances like these when everyone's upset. The thing to do is pull ourselves together and decide what is best."

The best thing to do when someone dies is bury him — that was the thought brought readily to mind by this way of putting things. But President Bagley knew I was thinking beyond the immediate tragedy to the larger aspects of the problem from the school's point of view. Making a visible effort to control himself, he said:

"Unfortunately we can't always have what is best. The blow of Norm Littlefield's loss turns out to be all the more bitter because neither Blodgett nor McGeese plans to return next year. Both have just told me they have taken jobs at other colleges. It's as though everyone is running out on me. This is very serious as far as I'm concerned."

"I too. They're both bangup men, and I'm sorry to hear they're leaving."

"Yes. That means that neither of the two men logically next in line, both in terms of seniority and general merit, can be counted on to step into Norm Littlefield's shoes. Everything seems to be unraveling here like an old sock. Jowett is a brilliant but erratic young man. His reviews have won him a following and given the faculty a dash of the avant garde that's all to the good, but he wouldn't set well with our more conservative supporters." He paused and, darting a quick glance at me before rearranging the blotter pad on his desk, said, "We shall have to make you acting head of the English Department."

Needless to say I was stunned by this announcement. I had not expected anything of the sort. I recovered myself long enough to reply, very nearly choking up, "Dr. Bagley, it is unnecessary for me to say that I hardly consider myself worthy of this honor, this trust — "

"At least we are in agreement on that point."

" — but I shall do my best — my absolute dedicated best — for Polycarp."

"It's only temporary of course, until we find someone who . . ." He tried by a vague gesture to indicate the general concept of adequacy lacking in the present patchwork. "We're in correspondence now with a couple of people. This is an emergency measure, and I emphasize that you're *acting* head. Seeing to it purely that administrative processes go on. Nothing more. In fact, one of your first duties will be to help us find somebody better — as well as replacements for Blodgett and McGeese."

He pushed across the desk to me a sheet of paper on which were the names of three or four possibilities for the post in question, all teachers at Midwestern colleges and universities, only one of whom I recognized, as the author of some treatise Norm Littlefield had made me read. Teachers must keep up with their homework as well as students. This was followed by the files on these prospects, including correspondence and notes, as well as folders on possible new English teachers as such, irrespective of their likelihood as executive timber. The president must have extracted some of the latter material from Littlefield's desk.

"I'd like you to take it home with you and study it. Especially the dossiers, which aren't by any means complete. Do what you can about filling them out and keeping them up to date. Find out what you can about everybody. Read what they've written. That's important."

"I'll drop everything but my classes for it. My own research certainly."

"What's that?"

" 'The Clowns in Shakespeare.' It was a field Norm wanted me to devote myself to."

"Oh, yes, I remember. Well, do your best for everyone's sake. Pitch in. Now I've got to get busy over the arrangements. There'll be a service in the Episcopal Church, in which the school will participate. I'll deliver a brief eulogy myself. So if you'll excuse me. God bless you."

"God bless you, sir."

As I shuffled humbly out the door and down the front steps, clutching the folders, my eyes to the ground, I felt that my pants were baggy, my shoes several sizes too large, and the tears were coursing down either side of a huge putty nose.

seventeen

I WISH I could say that this marked the end of the string of maladventures so far related. Such, however, is not the case. We are all from time to time subject to one of those runs of bad luck that have an almost mystic reality about them, as Maeterlinck noted — sequences we call jinxes that yet strike us as being organically related in some kind of cause-and-effect chain reaction. The most dismal episode of all occurred, unfortunately, at Norm Littlefield's funeral.

The service itself was quite a nice one. All were agreed on that. The sole exception was the somewhat stilted eulogy delivered by the rector of the church, which Norm of course attended. He kept referring to "the deceased," and the like. The deceased! Norm had never been that to me, or to any of us who had known and loved him in life. He had always been just good old Norm Littlefield, the pipe-chewing, pleasantly professorial friend to all. I noticed Marion Wellington sitting three pews forward of me with her head bowed during this oratory, for embarrassment I was sure, because she sat erect enough throughout Dr. Bagley's much more human and touching tribute, and when the college choir sang a Bach chorale. The church was quite full. Burial was said to be at a local cemetery, Norm having lived here long enough to feel Slow Rapids was his home. It was during this part of it that the difficulty arose.

I was driving Quincy's car. Both he and Angela Ravage had stayed on, the one in hopes of still obtaining an interview with the head office, the other out of some vague sense of partial responsibility for all this, however indirect or unintentional. With Marion we had all gone out to dinner the night before, a rather subdued occasion in the course of which the women got off together for a bit and Angela pumped Marion about everything, including the dramatic antecedents of this mess of which we were all victims. The two had hit it off beautifully, while any rapport between Quincy and myself had rapidly dwindled to nothing. He sulked while I brooded. At any rate, having gotten an earful of what was what, Angela wanted to stay till the funeral was over, even though she didn't attend it. So I borrowed Quincy's car. I could drive perfectly well since it was an automatic shift requiring nothing of my bad left leg. That was how the following rather harrowing incident came about.

I did not plan to go to the cemetery. Far too much work, of the kind I was carrying on in Littlefield's stead, remained undone, and I felt it my duty to get back to it as soon as possible. I slipped out of the funeral cortege, therefore, at what seemed to me the most discreet possible moment — at a street intersection a hundred yards or so from the front of the church where we were all lined up along the curb. I turned right up Simon Street and, settling down behind the wheel, headed for home in anticipation of the afternoon's work I might still get in. I had gone about half a block when I glanced into my rear-view mirror and saw to my horror that the entire procession had followed my lead and were turning off with me.

Frantically, I tried to get hold of myself and decide what was best to do in what was an appalling emergency. I seemed to remember that I had been very close behind the flower car — only two or three cars ahead of me as I recalled — and so

214

I had indeed deflected very nearly the bulk of the cortege, and was now leading them through town in a direction exactly opposite from where the Fairmount Cemetery lay. In my panic, all I could do was try to shake them. Detached from me, they would presently see their mistake and rectify it with no harm done, or very little. Merely a few minutes' delay. That was my reasoning.

But it was impossible to give them the slip. I stepped on it. So did they. I turned right and shot up Willoughby Avenue. So did they. I was soon doing a decidedly undignified forty-five miles an hour on this boulevard, the entire train rocking in my wake. Or at least the few cars visible to me remained there — perhaps behind them the whole cortege was disintegrating. This was becoming a nightmare. I saw a double-decker, or piggyback, truck carrying new automobiles up ahead, and conceived the stratagem of whipping in ahead of it in a burst of speed and in so doing detaching myself from the blundering hordes at my rear. Which I accordingly did, getting into position there just in time for a red light. The light changed almost instantly, a stroke of good luck, and I was off again in a quick getaway. I kept watch in the rear-view mirror to check the success of this maneuver, which seemed sure. But then after another block or so I saw the next car in my retinue nudging round the truck, which slowed respectfully as the driver of the truck apparently saw it was a funeral. There were stickers to that effect on all our windshields, pasted on by someone during the services. I tried to scratch mine off, without success. The mourners by now must have been doing fifty-five or sixty at least, and managed again to close the gap behind me.

My faculties were now in full rout. I had no idea what I

was doing except that I must make my escape. Every moment made that more imperative. The need to do so became an obsession, frenzied in its intensity. Yet timing, and a certain subtlety, were at the same time required. I slowed down in order to approach the next traffic light just as it was turning from green to red, guaranteeing that my pursuers would be caught by it just as I myself shot free across the intersection. At the same time I made an abrupt left turn, going hell-for-leather into something called Ashland Avenue. For some moments my rear-view mirror remained blessedly blank. I held my breath. Then I saw the entire damnable file turn into the street with me as traffic on the one I had just abandoned dutifully stopped to let it pass through the red light. What other motorists and pedestrians thought of the speed with which we rocketed through town God alone knew. My next turn was the last possible. I had headed into a vermiform appendix, a blind alley. The street was Edgeworth Court, an obscure lane in a part of town I had certainly never been in before. It seemed to peter out into some sort of private drive, up which, however, I turned in a last desperate measure. There was nothing else to do. I bumped through a few hundred yards or so of sandy rut, and came to a stop in a lumber yard. I bowed my head on the steering wheel and waited for them to come.

I heard, rather than saw, the cars draw to a stop behind me, anger in the very motors. Doors opened and slammed. There were footsteps, then several people looking in my window. One of them was President Bagley.

"Waltz." His voice sounded as it had over the telephone a few days before, high and strained. His face was the color of eggplant, and his hands worked spasmodically. "Waltz, if I could understand what you were up to just once, I would go to my grave a happy man."

"And very soon too," I thought to myself in alarm, genuinely concerned by his appearance. I wanted to tell him that, warn the man. There were rumors that Dr. Bagley had a cardiac condition warranting prudence as to his own way of life, as well as the avoidance of unnecessary agitation such as this. I murmured apologies in as soothing a tone as I could as I opened the door and climbed out to join the now considerable party. "I was just . . . All a ghastly . . . How it ever . . ." I began by way of explanation, gesturing in the direction we had come and revolving one palm against the other in a motion intended to convey the idea of highly complex maneuvers. There was a crowd of at least twenty people, all talking and giving advice at once. Three or four stood to one side and simply shook their heads. The rest of us tried to figure out what was best to do.

The main objective was of course to get on the right road to Fairmount as fast as possible, but before that outcome could be brought within reach we had to figure out a way of even retracing the *wrong* track. We were in a dead end that seemingly allowed of no convenient swing around the lumber piles and then back out onto Edgeworth Court, because we were so many that the first car (mine of course) would have come around and met one of the last before they were off the lumber yard drive, which was too narrow for two cars to pass. So that the procession would have been like a snake encountering its own tail. The yard itself was a *cul-de-sac* which admitted of no turning around at any point, car for car, so as to reverse the procession.

As we were analyzing matters in that light, the back door

of the yard office opened and a man in a mackinaw emerged, donning a bright plaid cap as he did so. He thought we were customers come to buy lumber, or perhaps cordwood, which was also copiously on sale here. When he learned we were a funeral procession that had lost its way he became sympathetic and then, immediately, very helpful.

His theory was that it would be best by far if we backed out one by one from Edgeworth Court onto Ashland Avenue again, beginning, of course, with our last car. We could then re-form on that thoroughfare — which, though busy, was broad — with the entire expedition about-faced.

This plan was instantly put into effect. Two of the mourners ran out onto Ashland Avenue to supervise the maneuvers, one directing traffic, the other guiding each motorist as his turn came to back around.

While this was being done, I tried to keep President Bagley, whose face was still suffused a dangerous shade of purple, engaged in as relaxing a conversation as possible.

"That was a splendid eulogy you gave," I said.

"Thank you," he said, looking away.

I hitched a foot up onto my bumper as we watched the operations going forward. It would be a few minutes before they got to his car, which was the second behind mine.

"I see you have Mrs. Bagley out with you again." She had been ailing for some few months. "Tell me, how is she?"

"Oh, my God," he said, threatening to become agitated again. "We'd best get back into our cars."

A fresh element in our problem had by now occurred to me. I was by no means sure that we would know what we were doing after our procession had become reorganized on the lines agreed on — that is to say, that we knew the quickest way to Fairmount from here. I would now bring up the rear (for which I was thankful) but the question of whether our new leader could guide us to our destination did not seem to me to have been sufficiently aired. So I strolled over to the lumberman and said, "Can you tell us the best way to Fairmount from here?"

Fortunately this anxiety turned out to be needless. Someone with even more presence of mind than myself had used the office telephone to call the police for an escort, and before we were ready to resume a squad car had been summoned by shortwave radio from an adjacent neighborhood and posted itself in our van. We were led away in a steadily flowing train of which, as I say, I now gratefully formed the rear. In the circumstances I was completely free to detach myself from the retinue at any time, but I had decided that in view of all that had happened it might be best if I went along to the graveyard after all, if only for appearances' sake.

The burial party were waiting for us when we arrived at last, about fifteen or twenty minutes late. The ceremony was brief and to the point, and conducted without further incident (though when the cleric stepped forward to deposit the traditional clod of earth on the remains his foot slipped on a crumbling mound of soil and very nearly pitched him forward into the opening, giving us all a bad turn). He was known as rather a bumbler.

Marion was not there, but she learned within hours what had happened, and was quick to express her sympathies. Others came forward as well with assurances that they considered it rottener luck than any man deserved. Among these was Angela Ravage, now filled in on the cycle of misfortunes up to that point. I must say up to that point because it appeared still not to have run its course, as the evening was to disclose.

We made rather a cheerless foursome again at the Green Lantern. Openly unhappy about the course of events to which she was now privy, Angela kept saying she felt it somehow "all her fault." "Please don't blame yourself," I said. "You didn't mean it." Quincy was glummest of all. His cause was now well-nigh hopeless with Angela, whose constant company, nevertheless, stoked his futile ardor anew. I did not feel too sorry for him, imagining he probably did well enough on other romantic fronts. I thought he cut quite a figure, taken all in all. He was decently enough groomed, danced suitably, and talked well in the presence of women (giving no evidence that he considered anyone a moocow now, though that would return in doubled force when his rejection was final). None of this seemed to cut any ice, at least here. Both women were too busy showering their attentions on me to respond to his. They seemed to vie with one another in consoling one whose contretemps were piling up at a rate faster than could be humanly absorbed. Huck Shenstone, the athletic coach, was destined to be narrator of the latest installment. He was dining with a party in the same restaurant, and he came over to our table when we were drinking brandies to say, "I suppose you've heard?"

"No, what?"

"President Bagley's had a heart attack."

Again I anticipate the story to give an accurate account of events totally garbled in the telling, and related with considerable prejudice to myself, as most neutral observers will admit — even insist. The facts are briefly these.

I hurried to Dr. Bagley's side the very first instant I could — the moment he was permitted visitors in the hospital —

and congratulated him on having had his coronary at such an early age (he was only forty-five). The sooner one has it the better one's chances of a quick and complete recovery, apparently; in some cases the heart is the stronger for the rehabilitation. "It's only a torn muscle," I told him. "Remember that."

I explained what I had been unable to explain at sufficient length at the time, that I had attempted to leave the funeral cortege only to attend to the press of administrative work lately devolved upon me, and then passed quickly on to more cheerful matters relative to that. I was able to report some considerable success in pulling the department together. Two new instructors had been engaged, and I had signed my own contract for next year as well, he would be glad to know. Things were looking up. I now offered my services for any expansion of the chores recently laid upon me, anything in which I might help him out in his own work, even. Dean Shaftoe was for the time being serving as acting president.

"If you mean you think you're executive timber and might want to run the college one day, Waltz," Dr. Bagley said, regarding me ironically from the hill of pillows on which he lay propped, "you could get your wish. At the rate you're killing us off there'll soon be only you left."

I could not think of an adequate reply to this, and remained silently sitting in my chair near the foot of his bed. He scrutinized me a moment with his small, bright blue eyes.

"There are people who don't like you, Waltz. No, I shouldn't say that. Who don't think much of you, even though they may like you. Put it that way. They say you're adolescent. But I differ with that judgment."

"You do, sir?"

"Yes. I don't think you're adolescent at all. I think you're infantile. You've got a long way to go to be adolescent. That doesn't mean you're to be dismissed out of hand. Completely written off. In fact you fascinate me. I don't see how anybody can get to be twenty-three and still remain two years old."

"That cheers me enormously."

"I'm interested enough in your case to have you around for a bit out of sheer curiosity, before I die, and at the same time give you more work in hopes of helping you develop a little responsibility. How does that strike you, Waltz?"

"Why, sir —"

"So since Dean Shaftoe has to get a paper ready for an important upcoming conference of college deans," he went on, his color deepening and his voice taking on a dangerous ring again, "I think I'll appoint you acting president of the college." His tone was now definitely sardonic, even abusive. He laughed oddly. "Don't be misled by the title. Because what I'm going to dump on you is dirty work — mountains and mountains of it that have piled up *thanks* to you. It means that now you'll really have to buckle down. It means that you'll be stuck here all summer — for the summer session. I believe you chaps call it Siberia?"

Heartening as all this advancement was, it seemed to me not all as flattering as on the surface it appeared, but contained some ulterior and even perverse elements. First, the honorary title was only honorary, and hollowly so at that. A mass of drudgery indeed awaited me. I knew that. Second, I am now reasonably certain that Bagley rather malevolently wanted somebody filling in for him who would be less than sensational, as a means of making himself look good by contrast — even indispensable. This kind of thing is true of many egotists. It is undoubtedly the sort of vanity behind the business tycoon's familiar "I haven't had a vacation in fourteen years." Such men fear, not that things will go to hell at the office in their absence, but that they will run as smoothly as ever without them. I did not think Bagley would have been cheered by any such outcome; it might have retarded his recovery, while rumors of ineptitude would speed it. Thirdly, it had come to light that Mr. Hill, our chief donor, had taken rather a shine to me after seeing me around at divine worship. He was a very devout man, whose moneys the school was having increasing difficulty luring away from the pious causes uppermost in his heart. My religious side appealed to him — a factor not to be underestimated in the school's constant need of funds. In fact, Bagley might deliberately be trying to give the impression that I was being groomed for his successor, or at least for a position of eminence in the school. I would not put it past him. Nevertheless, all this *arrière-pensée* on Bagley's part aside, it was enormously gratifying to think that one would walk into the office of the president one morning and sit down at his desk.

But Dr. Bagley was not yet through with me.

"One administrative decision that must be made soon is this. What's your opinion of these handwriting analyses the new guidance counselor, Miss Holroyd, is recommending for all students and for all applicants for jobs. She's rather keen on that sort of thing as one way of getting a slant on people's personality. Not hipped on it, but she regards it as useful in supplementing other tests. Limited but valid. What's your opinion?"

"Why, I'd go along with that moderate approval. It can do no harm, and may be useful. Obviously any handwriting is a kind of graph of the individual's nervous system, much as a cardiogram of his vascular. Of course the problem is to read it back. How can you go about that in a way you're sure is scientifically accurate? That's the question. Still, it may give us some clues to the person's makeup, some leads, at least in the case of extreme disturbances."

"I'm glad to hear you put in a good word for it. I think it's snake oil, but I may be wrong. It so happens a specimen of yours was turned over to Miss Holroyd — anonymously, of course, like all the rest — and it's come back with a report."

"Oh? Do you mind telling me what they found?"

"Not at all. It showed latent criminal sexual tendencies."

"Penmanship was never one of my strong subjects. 'Hen tracks!' my teachers used to say, laughing like anything. I can still remember Miss Weems. I was her despair. But I'm working constantly to improve my script — ironing out things that are wrong with it, and in general trying to develop a much more legible hand."

"The analysis only says 'latent,' so perhaps these potentialities will never come to flower." At intervals Bagley would pause and make a growling sound in his throat. He was only clearing it, but the way he did it was rather disturbing, and often accompanied by a habit of wringing his hands in his lap in a repressed manner, as though he was impatient to be off and attend to all the matters in the world in need of rectifying. But in this instance he emitted also again the sudden odd laugh, while the unhealthy glitter in his eyes deepened as he took me in. It was as though for the moment he contemplated with secret relish the prospect of an associate running amok and giving vent to fiendish impulses. Perhaps he was himself at bottom slightly warped? His conduct in this interview certainly suggested a personality not in all respects stable. He now rapidly concluded, "I think all this sort of stuff ranks with phrenology, so perhaps we will all be feeling the bumps in one another's heads around here one day. *Mmbahaha!*"

"I'm glad to hear you say that, because I happen to think it's a lot of malarkey myself. Snake oil! Well, I'm glad to see you on the mend, sir, and I hope we'll have you back with us in jigtime. I know what it is to be laid up." I hurried out.

The other important element in my life, the romantic, gave similar promise of expanding without stabilizing. Marion's first fascination with my family had worn off as a source of interest in myself, but we still remained "more than friends." A good deal more. The affair had its familiar ups and downs, its ebbs and flows. Not the least of the complications was the fact that my acquaintance with Angela blossomed into something rather more than friendship too. She returned to the Coast to make a picture, the last scheduled on her contract. There was a general air of gloom about it at the studio, quite prescient, as it turned out, for it failed both financially and artistically. Well before that happened, however, Angela was confirmed in her decision to quit acting, at least for the time being, and resume her interrupted education. The stage to which we had brought our relationship was a factor in making her consider Polycarp, and so on a trip East in her own car she swung off at Chicago to see me. This was toward the end of the summer, when the press of administrative duties made it impossible for me to pop off to Chicago to see her. We had dinner at the Green Lantern, then drove back and parked by the river. I drew back at last from a long, searching kiss, and said: "I mustn't get involved with you, Angela."

"Why not?"

"There's the problem of outlooks, always more important than people seem to realize in courtship. Approaches to life, the fundamental problems. You consider Christianity a fairy tale for grownups. Those are your exact words. In that case, you have to dismiss all the art the Christian Church has inspired. All the glories of Bach, El Greco, the poetry of John Donne and Gerard Manley Hopkins. All nothing. I suppose you're prepared to do this?"

"But pagan religions have given rise to great art too. Do you embrace them for that reason? Do the glories of Homer make you believe in Zeus?"

This reply is so uncannily like mine to Marion when the reverse positions in this question were taken that a kind of affinity seems to me to be shown as existing between Angela and me, against which it behooves us both to be on guard. The need to keep her at arm's length intensifies with each embrace, so to speak, in order that a rash mistake not be made, something rushed into we would later regret. "The fact remains you're a skeptic, an unbeliever, even a scoffer, judging from some things I've heard you say, and your ideas would clash with something deeply ingrained within me. You've heard Catholics say they can never get it out of their system, try as they might to overlay things with an intellectual approach and give reason its day in court. It's just as intense with me. No, there would always be this gulf between us, Angela."

This exchange came to the ears of Marion, veteran of many another herself, of course. Now she seemed more determined

226

than ever that I get to the bottom of my problems, and try for some satisfactory resolution of them.

"It's that same old business of these two backgrounds you're in revolt against. Don't you think you ought to see somebody?"

"I don't know what good it would do. Psychiatrists can't even straighten people around with one childhood, let alone two."

"Miss Holroyd doesn't have much training as a psychiatrist, actually. Maybe she can all the better talk your problem over in a human, informal way."

"The guidance counselor!" My first reaction was one of vehement protest, modifying itself quickly into one of quiet amusement. "I'm not a student any more, you know."

"What difference does that make? It isn't as if you were very long out of school anyway. The point is a mere quibble. Besides, teachers do sometimes come to her. And we've no one else around. She's intelligent, and quite a pleasant person. Besides, I'm now getting to be genuinely worried about you. Oh, don't think I don't know that's what you want. Like all men. You feed yourself on the compassion and solicitude we're always there to give. Even Don Juan admits it in Shaw. He goes to woman for comfort. And indeed we want you to. Any wife is always half mother. It's in the nature of things. I suppose it's part of sex."

"I love you," I say not unkindly, angling tenderly in her blouse. "Come lean your breast upon this head . . ."

"Only if you promise to see Miss Holroyd."

"Oh, all right."

What could I lose? And one was naturally curious to inspect at closer range someone who had detected in oneself

latent criminal sexual tendencies. One could imagine the type
she was!

eighteen

"I HAVE these two childhoods."

Miss Holroyd draws her skirt down over her knees, at the
same time pressing her lips inward till they are fleshless, in an
expression indicating extreme concentration. She says she has
heard a lot about me, and has been dying to meet me. I do
not like the sound of this at all. She is, at thirty-eight or forty,
not unattractive. A slender woman in a tailored suit, and one
likes slender women in tailored suits, does one not, just as one
does rounded ones in flowing skirts, and short ones in neat
silk scarves. She is brunette — just one's type, like blondes and
those with auburn hair and red as well, they are all one's
type. She has those small hard breasts one so greatly prefers
to the large dramatic ones, and vice versa. Has she ever been
possessed? She reminds me, in a flash of isolated memory, of
a woman seen at a church bazaar when I was a boy, years
ago, not thought of since. The woman was piling her pur-
chases on her chauffeur's arm with such style that several of us
watched in awe. She's the mistress of Hollingworth they told
me, and I says who's he, and dey says it's not a he, it's a estate
jist outside a town. So she's a mistress but of a house, some
hacks.

Miss Holroyd asks a few introductory questions about my
problem, using no jargon and drawing me out with rather

heavy subtlety, unaware that as we speak her flesh is being systematically consumed. I take up the long and very elegant shears lying on her desk and slit her clothing deftly from neck to hem, peel away the remaining silks and ravish her on the spot. "There, I guess that'll teach you to go around calling people latent sex criminals." I stand over her a moment before dismembering her, breathing heavily. The scene is enacted in detail more vivid than the childhood incidents I am recounting, which though they seem to absorb her have begun suddenly to bore me — so abysmally that I resort to fabrication to hold my own interest. "My mother used to tie me to the kitchen stove." She strikes me as remarkably cool and self-assured for one hacked into sections and stowed into a steamer trunk and left uncalled for at Pier Sixteen. Suddenly I resent the disclosures I have been making and decide to "resist" this whole line of interrogation with gibberish. That is claimed to be as revelatory as fact to the trained listener, so let her go to work on it then. Too, I recall my status as acting president of the college, which should make me immune from this sort of thing. Let her think this is all a trick to catch her off guard and put her on her mettle as an employe. When she asks whether I prefer either parent to the other I reply:

"That depends what you mean by fascism. If you mean mechanical outward conformity to a totalitarian regime, that's one thing. If actual party affiliation, that's quite another. With the additional difficulty of determining how much outward loyalty is voluntary and how much dictated by prudence in the face of an existing police state, the problem becomes almost hopeless."

Q. Would you say your parents merely differed, or that there was open hostility between them? Did they just quarrel or did they fight?

A. It's very simple if you just remember the following rule. Both stalactite and ceiling have a "c" in them, so stalactites are those that hang down from above, while stalagmites point upward from the ground.

Q. Are your parents both still alive?

A. Yes and no. When we say that women are worse gossips than men we really mean that they are better ones. They engage in it more constantly, but they are not necessarily on that account more malicious or more vicious than men, who merely spend less time at it. I would like to dwell on this point a moment if I may. Gossip is the satisfaction of curiosity, and woman is more omnivorously curious about life because she is its custodian. She is meant by nature to be a talebearer, having an instinctive stake in What Goes On.

Q. Did they argue or fight in front of you?

A. Edna St. Vincent Millay. Because she has both intensity and control. She is one of the few modern poets who are frankly and openly lyrical, and that's why I would probably pick her as my favorite, as I would Chagall among the painters, for the same reason. I think most of us miss the unabashed romantic element. The drying up of permissible emotion in the name of discipline and restraint is one of the curses of our time. Painters like Mondrian give me the horrors. It's time we got back to nice fat girls sitting naked on the grass out in the country. I mean awaaay out.

Q. Whom among the musicians do you like?

A. Shibboleth. The word derives from an incident in the Old Testament. It was a Hebrew word used by Jephthah for

distinguishing the fleeing Ephraimites (who could not pro-
nounce the "sh") from his own troops, the Gileadites. Hence
a test word, or standard for sorting out people.

Q. Do you shed tears when you listen to music, or read
a book or watch a movie?

A. Hair.

Q. How would you describe your relations with the opposite sex?

A. 1066.

Q. Have you been drinking? I don't ask it critically by any
means. I often wish people coming to see me would do so
beforehand. It would help them open up.

A. There's been a study made about what makes people
become actors. Actors are apparently either people whose
parents have never allowed them to express themselves, or
whose parents have allowed them to. There are statistics seriously compiled on the subject, on money given by some
foundation. There is no doubt about it. Easy money! While
you're up get me a Grant!

Q. Do you sleep well?

A. (Here a successful attempt is made to resist emphasiz-
ing the point by tearing up the blotter on her desk and eating
the fragments.) Why, the custom of standing up during the
Hallelujah Chorus of Handel's *Messiah* dates back to the time
when King George I spontaneously rose during its performance, as a sign of its effect on him. Since then it has been
traditional for audiences to rise to their feet when it begins,
though there are some cynics who regard it as little more
than the equivalent of the seventh inning stretch with which
we relieve a numb bum at a baseball game.

Q. Do you like to get up?

A. If that's what she wants.

Q. Do you dream a great deal?

A. Why, on that, Dow Chemical has developed a pill that produces a low-grade infection when swallowed, not enough to harm the dog but enough to kill the ticks, which are then theoretically supposed to fall off. But it has never been successful to my knowledge. You still have to pick them off one by one, that's all there's to that.

She was not in the least impressed. The hash I strove to make of the interview was a perfectly understandable safeguard against exposure of my secret — which she was perfectly confident she divined anyway from the surface facts themselves: that I hated my parents. "The mature thing is to *recognize* this for what it is, not let it fester within us. All of our personal relations are full of these hostilities, which we must simply face up to and somehow absorb into the give-and-take of civilized realities."

Hated my parents! This was such old stuff that the very assumption that she was telling me something new redoubled my irritation. She said nothing the previous guidance counselor hadn't, when I was a student, and I half expected her to draw the framed diagonal cross he did (like a voting mark in a square) to illustrate the intersecting oppositions that comprised my personality. I wished she charged a fee so I could refuse to pay it. Still, I reflected as I thanked her and walked home, the session did one thing. It precipitated the riot I had felt myself building up to for some weeks now. Periodically, I had to plunge into one or the other — often both — of the conflicting emotional seapools of my life, to appease impulses or desires deeply buried or long denied. These were like emotional sprees, of the sort to which we are all subject,

232

sops to the private furies by which we are all driven in varying directions. They serve the function of getting things out of our system, of clearing our spirit, for the time being at least.

For me these bouts have always involved the revisitation of old haunts. Sometimes they are stimulated by sight or thought of them. It was early evening when I headed toward the center of town, and, after a few drinks at a bar long associated with my boyhood as a hangout of my father's, I wandered into the Gospel Mission, still the same old rented store as always. There were folding chairs set in two sections, an aisle between. It was Wednesday, and the midweek meeting was in session. A middle-aged woman usher thrust a hymnal into my hand and led me to an empty seat. The danger that my mother might be here occurred to me as I sat down, but a quick glance around the half-filled hall revealed this not to be the case. The congregation was singing "Shall We Gather at the River?," in only a chorus of which I was able to join before the hymnals were shut and the minister rose and approached the pulpit.

He was a revivalistic spellbinder of the old school, with a shock of gray hair which he kept flinging out of his eye, and the brassy, nasal voice for some reason characteristic of the breed, either naturally or developed as a result of years of service as one of God's barkers. He was soon going strong, waving his Bible and thumping the pulpit as he shouted out the exhortations that would rededicate believers and bring converts to the front. He was new here, at least new in the year or so since I had last dropped in. I had not seen him before, but he had not spoken ten words before I knew here was a prize specimen. He had the strong, gamey vulgarity I have always found bracing, and I gave myself wholeheartedly to an experience that was as much a kind of intellectual wallowing as it was a dramatized nostalgia for faith. Thus my experience was the reverse of that of my co-worshipers. They were being saved, while I was backsliding. I was, aesthetically speaking, going to hell, and I abandoned myself to it like a drunkard to his drink. The man was so supremely awful that I was soon under his spell.

"Are you starving your soul within reach of the banquet table of God's grace? There is the board of his divine sufficiency, groaning with the riches intended for your spirit's sustenance. Reach out, eat. Oh, brothers and sisters, reach out and eat! Are you thirsting in the desert of reprobation while beside you flows, crystal-clear and cool, the quenching stream of his eternal love? Turn and drink, brethren, drink and slake your parched tongues forevermore! And let me tell you one thing. Don't go for that mirage, the illusory satisfactions of this world that recede forever before us as we stumble on in our hallucination, but quaff the water of life which flows freely at your feet."

As his oratory mounted in hysteria, it became increasingly punctuated with "Amens" and "Glory be's" from the audience. These swelled in a steady crescendo, at their peaks drowning out the preacher's words. All his hearers were worked up into a lather. I joined in these outcries, furtively at first, then more boldly, till I found myself shouting "Amen!" and "Christ be praised!" at the top of my voice. It was an exhilarating experience.

Whipped into the greatest frenzy was the speaker himself. Pulpit banging and foot stamping were at last not enough. He tore off his coat and began beating the floor with it to emphasize a point. All this was in a sense relative; the entire speech was climax. Crouching on his knees as he flailed the platform with his jacket, he shouted: "Art thou weary, art thou languid? Dost thou sometimes long for the final deliverance promised to all who will heed his call?" Here he dropped his coat, and, facing the audience squarely on his knees, he flung his arms wide to them, like the everlasting arms themselves. The chills ran up my spine. I could scarcely breathe, I became so choked by the ecstasy in which, together with the congregation shouting "Yes!", I found myself caught up. "Oh, don't you sometimes long for that haven to which God's children shall be called, while those who have ignored him shall be flung into everlasting hell, there to burn in flames through all eternity? Well, I do! I long for it sometimes, and I know you do too. I long to be rocked on Jesus's breast. I wish the trumpet would sound and the dead be raised up tomorrow! Tonight! This minute! Because I know where I'll be when it's over, and where you'll be too if you heed his call tonight. Have you ever thought about what an atomic cloud looks like? Well, both Isaiah and Revelation say the heavens shall be rolled together like a scroll. Take heed, make the connection. The time is not long now, the day is at hand, history is drawing to its close. And when it does, when that great day of the Lord comes, I know where I'll be. I won't be deep-frying in the pit of eternal Crisco. No, sir! I'll be — " Here he rose dramatically, and pointed an arm straight through the ceiling. "I'll be up yonder, inside the pearly gates, kickin' up the gold dust on Hallelujah Avenue!"

It was pouring rain when Waltz sank to his knees and accepted the Lord Jesus Christ as his personal savior. I shuffled to the front with six or seven other limp, bemused and battered converts. We kneeled while the evangelist said a special prayer over us, passing along the line and laying his hand on each of our heads in turn. After we had been given his blessing we returned to our seats for the final hymn, chosen and sung for those who had been saved tonight. It was, by coincidence, the one that had come to mind in my recent crisis, one long familiar to me from childhood hours spent in this mission, and I raised my voice in its strains as lustily as anyone there:

> At the cross, at the cross, where I first saw the light,
> And the burden of my heart rolled away,
> It was there by faith I received my sight,
> And now I am happy all the day.

I groped my way out into the street, slightly dazed by the experience. It was a little like awakening from a dream, one of those dreams, not nightmares, that are somehow more vivid than nightmares. The rain had stopped but the pavements glistened in the light of the lamps and there were pools in the gutters, so hard had the brief downpour been. I trudged along reviewing the occurrence, which left me rather shaken. I had never gone that far before. I had thrown myself into the orgies, but I had never been saved. As reality struck me again in the form of fresh air and the sight of people hurrying on normal rounds, a kind of reaction set in. I felt strongly the need of some counterbalance.

I walked into a bar, a very cheerful place, and after three or four drinks found myself fraternizing with two men who had been drinking for a somewhat longer time. They were both truck drivers, I learned from their conversation, both loud laughing fellows who liked a good joke and a ribald song. After a few choruses in which we all joined with the dubious harmony common to such groups, I said, "Ever heard the one that goes, 'At the bar, at the bar'? Ever sing that when you were a kid?"

"Yes, I did, come to think of it," one said. "I haven't thought about that one for years. How does it go again?"

I let go for them in a parody of the hymn with which the revival meeting had just been concluded:

> At the bar, at the bar, where I smoked my first cigar,
> And the buttons on my vest rolled away,
> It was there by chance that I tore my Sunday pants,
> And now I wear them every day.

"And of course you know the 'Nightgown Song,'" I said. "Love lifted me."

"Right. And then there's this one." I led off another mock hymn, my arms slung around my companions' shoulders. "Nero my dog has fleas, Nero has fleas . . ."

Here the bartender, who had been watching us uneasily, or rather uneasily watching a more conventional-looking party of middle-aged couples in a booth, said, "I think you boys better throttle down now. It's getting a little rough. And you look to me to've had enough," he added personally for my benefit. It was notice that he would not serve me any more, which I took as intended. I bade my friends good night and made, mellowly but a little unsteadily, for another bar, where I drank till that bartender declined to pour me another.

Managing somehow to disguise my true condition from the sales clerk, I bought half a pint of whiskey at a liquor store, and took it to the riverside. I sat on the bank for an hour or more, watching the water and tipping the bottle to my lips.

237

The bottle empty, I lay back on the cool grass, gazing at the swarm of stars above and listening to the steady stream of lovers driving in and out of the nearby picnic parking ground. At last I fell asleep.

Sometime after midnight I felt the sharp sting of a club on my foot and a policeman's voice said, "Come on, buddy, get up. We'll take you home — if you can tell us where you live."

A prowl car throbbed nearby, toward which I was led babbling about Leibniz's windowless monads and Kant's categorical imperative. A second policeman waited noncommittally at the wheel till I got in. I was bundled into the back seat by the first officer, in whose lap I tried to climb while asking him whether he knew the hymn, "Gladly the cross-eyed bear." He rather sharply asked again where I lived, and I gave him the address of the dormitory, now rebuilt after the fire which had driven me to Mrs. Duncan's, and where I was once again staying. I remained in an expansive mood as we made for it, calling out greetings to the occasional night pedestrians, and at one point giving a football cheer I had composed some years before as a student, in the blasphemous stage of another such cycle as the one from which I was emerging:

> *Hidy didy!*
> *Christ almighty!*
> *Bim bam!*
> *God damn!*
> *Polycarp, Polycarp, yeah!*

In this way some kind of sanity was maintained, some kind of balance and integration. The cops helped me into the foyer of the dormitory. I was able to pick my way without incident to the second floor room I occupied, and dropped onto the bed with my clothes on.

To say that I awoke filled with remorse is to say nothing unless remorse be taken to mean a sort of psychic gorge rising in endless, unresolvable waves for which the word nausea likewise does not begin to suffice. The room was revolving in two simultaneous directions, its contents swirling and tumbling about like the clothes in a wash machine.

By noon I had not yet been able to set foot out of bed, nor yet by evening, or morning of the next day. Sheer organic existence was possible only by dint of maintaining a fixed point of reference, usually a corner angle of the ceiling, and keeping my head absolutely motionless on the pillow. Any slightest disturbance was pure horror. "This is hell, nor am I out of it," I thought, from *Faustus*. The dormitory matron, Mrs. Willis, looked in on me the third day to ask if anything was wrong. I told her I was sick with the flu, and declined her kind offer of "soup or something." Neither did I want a doctor, I told her, but I would appreciate her telephoning Marion Wellington for me. I had a phone, but it was at the other end of the room, impossible for me to use. I gave Mrs. Willis the number, and she sat down and called, watching me, I felt sure, while she waited for an answer. There was none at the apartment, and I gave her Marion's school office number. She was out there too, but a message was left for her to please come and call on me during visiting hours that evening. "It's urgent," Mrs. Willis added at my request. I had at some point pulled my clothes off and thrown them on a chair. She hung them up before going, also laying out fresh pajamas on the bed.

I was still in a state of rigor mortis when Marion entered. I had had to call "Come in" twice in response to her knock. Speaking in anything above a whisper was like a hammerblow to my head. The vibrations set up by speech killed me; even moving my jaw was an ordeal, so that I lay with my mouth open and kind of breathed my end of the conversation in fragments of words.

"What's the matter?"

"Ango."

"Hangover? You must have tied on a real one."

"Ongona die."

"Have you had anything to eat?"

I replied with a wincing twitch of my face and a recoiling gesture of my hand which said "Please!"

"Nonsense. I think you're giving in to it. When did you go on this bat?"

"Ens."

"Wednesday? This is Saturday. Of course you're giving in to it. Nobody's hung over that long."

"No?"

She turned away, as from the thought that must have struck her too, and drew a chair up to the bed. She sat down and said, "Did anything in particular happen? To send you off on one this size? Because it was obviously a lulu. You look green. But of course that's partly you haven't had anything to eat. Isn't there something I can fix for you? Never mind that," she said when I clapped my hand over my mouth with the seafarer's groan. "You've got to get something into you, obviously. You can't go on indefinitely without nourishment. It's hunger that's probably taken hold now, and you can't tell the two apart. You've got to pull yourself together. Now what'll it be? Soup, little cereal, warm milk? Well, if you're going to lie there and make dying noises I'll just have to take matters into my own hands. I heard of a good hangover remedy the other day and I'm going down in the kitchen and mix it for you. I won't tell you what's in it, because that'd be fatal. I'll be back in two jerks. O.K.?"

As she rose, smiling down, she laid a hand on my forehead. It felt so blessedly cool that I seized and kissed it. I wondered then why the idea of an icebag had not occurred to me. It was rather curious. Perhaps I had simply been too miserable for my mind to function along even the most primitive lines. I asked Marion to try to scare one up for me now, and if she was unable to do so, at least bring some ice back with her.

She returned in about ten minutes with a glass of blood, or what looked like it to me, and a bowl of ice cubes. "I couldn't get a bag," she said cheerfully, "but I'll go get one at the drugstore. But first drink this."

Somehow we got my head propped up, and with her steadying me I managed to gulp down the plasm she had mixed. As a veteran concocter of many another such potion, I thought I recognized some of its ingredients, but did not bother to taste it — being mainly concerned with curbing my revulsion enough to get it down as fast as possible and resume a lying postion. Marion then knotted several of the ice cubes into a handkerchief and set it on my head. It was like a benediction. She chatted with me for a few minutes longer, then slipped out to the drugstore for the promised icebag, which she filled with the announcement that she had some work to do at home, but would return for lunch tomorrow. There was to be no nonsense. If I had not taken nourishment by then, she would see to it that I did. "And afterward," she said, getting her coat and bag from a chair, "we'll go for a ride."

She made good on what were, in effect, ultimatums. My resistance to the tray of light lunch she brought was met with cajolery, persuasion, and then a firm hand. But when I boggled at a ride in the car her manner became almost vehement.

"Now look." She stood over me with folded arms. "It's now or never. If you don't make an effort to get up, dressed and out, don't ever expect to see me again. I mean that. You're not going to parlay this into a nervous breakdown. You're not going to keep this state of mind, or state of body or whatever you want to call it, going indefinitely as a way of running away from whatever you're running away from. Life, you, me, us or what have you. Now it's nice weather. The sun is shining. We can go for a ride with the top down. And then you can tell me what Miss Holroyd said."

Somehow, God knows how, I got out of bed, dressed, and down the stairs. I moved slowly, in gravitational chaos. The stairs seemed escalators moving upward while I descended them or vice versa. The floors swam up to meet me or dropped like trapdoors, with consequent illusory elongation or shrinkage of my legs. Sometimes they seemed stubs, sometimes stilts. I believe there is a medical distinction made between vertigo and dizziness, the one being objective, the other subjective. That is to say, in vertigo external objects seem to whirl about, in dizziness one's own head. Perhaps it is the other way around. Both, at any rate, contributed heavily to my sensations. I took the distances to be traversed in visual gulps, opening my eyes long enough to see where I would be going for the next ten or a dozen steps before closing them again and thus temporarily shutting all this confusion from view.

Marion helped steady me out of the building and into the car, clapping the door shut and springing in behind the wheel with a cheerful "There, that wasn't so bad, was it?" I nearly answered by hanging my head over the side of the door, like an ocean-goer again, but the crisis passed. I closed my eyes and off we went, slowly at first, like two figures floating away in a Ferris wheel.

For it is that sensation by which the ride was characterized in my mind. The conviction that we were describing wide vertical rotations through space was so vivid that I was sure that if I opened my eyes I could look down over the side of the open convertible and see the houses and streets below in that faintly delirious perspective in which fairground rides put things.

"Now then, tell me about your binge. Where did you go? What did you do?"

It was a story soon enough told, and I told it without either omissions or embellishments. It was one of those sacred-and-profane cycles with which Marion was familiar as typical of me, though hitherto embracing much longer intervals (like those of a manic-depressive), and not compressed into so brief a span as this. That was the alarming part of it. It was indeed like a disease of which the time pendulums were shortening.

"If there were only some reasonable middle ground combining both sides in some kind of synthesis. Like the Existentialist Christians of today, or the atheist Catholics Robert Frost said there are. Maybe he was twitting, maybe not. You never know. Maybe we know some ourselves without knowing it. Anyhow, some kind of synthesis where you could be reasonably happy. But no. With me it's in-again-out-again-Finnegan. Because, as Miss Holroyd — and everybody else — says, I have this unresolved hatred of both my parents."

Marion was curiously quiet for some time. I sensed the car making two turns, then slowing to a stop. When I opened my eyes we were parked at the river's edge.

"*Hatred* of your parents? Is that what they tell you? Is that what you think? Why hatred? Why not affection?"

"I never thought of that."

"You never thought of it. Nobody ever does any more. But why does it always have to be hostility at the bottom of everything? Why does that always have to be the explanation, for Christ's sweet sake?"

There is such fire in her voice, even for one given to controversial outbursts at the drop of a hat, that I turn to look at her. Her flashing eyes convey the same sense of moral anger.

"We know too much. We've gotten so used to assuming that the cynical interpretation is necessarily the right one that we automatically think the worst of everybody and everything in order not to be considered naïve. But the analytical clichés get to be naïve too. So you go to the mission and sing hymns to hit back at your father, and get drunk and blaspheme as an outlet for the same antipathy toward your mother. Why not the other way around — the *simple* explanation? That you do each to satisfy some basic affection for them? And why do I have to pussyfoot with a word like affection? Why not come out and say love?"

I embrace her without any nausea whatsoever. These epiphanies are so simple. The obvious is always under our nose, and therefore often unseen, but the minute it is pointed out we knew it was there all the time. It becomes our property, appropriated like a good joke we could never have thought of ourselves but ours to repeat as though we have; or a good melody, inevitable once somebody has composed it, and ours to whistle at will.

Now for the third time I sing that the burden of my heart has rolled away, but this time I know it is true. It will stick.

"This bind we've gotten ourselves into," I say. "Thinking that the less we think of one another, and ourselves, the more acute we're being. This rotten age!"

"Sure we hate. Sure there's hostility, open and buried, everywhere. But that's not the whole story, and I doubt it's as much as half of it. That's the point. I think people love each other a little more than they hate each other, and that's why we can go on. In pairs and in families and in multitudes. Love has a slim hold on the human corporation, like fifty-one per cent, but it's enough. Enough for human beings to stay in business with one another."

"Then marry me. After all, you owe me something. You saved my life, and the least you can do is help me live it."

"Maybe. Why not? It's as good a beginning as any."

"I'm an ass," I remind her. "But we could fight that together."

"You're so absurd a person can't help liking you. I suppose there's some challenge in any hookup any woman makes with any man, and vice versa. Taking it on makes a woman a woman."

"And a man a man."

"How do you think we could stand you if compassion and humor weren't in us? Our feminine job. Only a woman would marry you! Of course we have our own piece of the human

245

folly. You'll learn that in time. But we're not asses. You're asses. We're something else."

"What?"

"You'll find out. But, Tom, you'll simply have to. Stop. Behaving. The way you do. No running off to church one day and spouting Nietzsche the next. Praying and scoffing till they run together till you can't tell which is which. And joining different organizations and talking out of both sides of your mouth. You've got to stop taking both sides of every question."

"I will. That's all a thing of the past. I know why I've been doing it now, and it's no longer necessary. I'm free. I'm cured."

"Because I can't live with a man who's blowing hot and cold on basic issues. You know what I believe, what I have to believe to live. I'm not bigoted, but it's my faith. I belong to the Episcopal Church, and you have to let me go, without any of these endless and inconclusive arguments."

"I'll even go with you, some of the time."

The whole thing was like a transfiguration, a resurrection. I rested up that day, and the next evening we drove to Chicago for dinner. It was one of those dim restaurants, vaguely Oriental in feeling, of which the walls are covered with floor matting, and where brands of beer one has never heard of before and never hears of again are available. A hint of incense hangs in the air.

Afterward we go to a party given by a young North Shore couple Marion knows. The woman is a classmate of hers from days at Mrs. Drew's. He's a young stockbroker on the rise. I have one highball, two, but that's enough. No need now for the cup that inebriates but never cheers. I'm drunk enough with happiness. In such raptures I can hardly contain myself. My mood expands, and I find myself speaking well to a group collecting in the kitchen, holding forth fluently in a friendly argument that develops on the subject of the Church. I tell them all that Christianity is a mass of plagiarisms from pagan cults anyone with half a mind can see through, and that anyone who believes in God believes in Santa Claus — proudly recalling my father in his prime when I do so. Oh, how different it all is now! What a change there's going to be. Later I will get down on my knees and thank God for the gift of reason that makes such thinking possible. Perhaps next Sunday I will remember my well-meaning mother and go to church. Yes, that Presbyterian limestone on the north end of town nobody goes to any more. Literally nobody. The minister reputedly preaches to empty pews. He is said to mount the pulpit nonetheless and stoutly declare the Gospel to empty air. I will be the entire congregation, and he will proclaim the message of salvation to me alone. If a hymn is announced, I will rise and sing a solo. After the service the man of God will hurry out ahead of me to a squall of organ music and be standing on the porch steps, waiting to shake hands with me as I pour out of church . . .

These are some of the things I will do in the days ahead, which I secretly hoard and ecstatically think about, on this night that I wish would never end.

nineteen

WHEN THE DORMITORY had been rebuilt, a three-room apartment had been provided for a married housemaster. Into this Marion and I now moved. I was trying to return by degrees to something like my previous schedule, no easy matter. President Bagley had been, as feared at the time he had designated me acting head of the school, suffering from nervous disorder. When he was removed to Nestle Down for an indefinite rest, colleagues who had openly regarded his deputization of myself as proof positive that he was certifiable claimed to find something odd in my occupying his chair more firmly than ever as a result. Some went so far as to say I had sent him round the bend. I thus conceivably had a grudge, which, however, I did not bear them. I had no wish to occupy the chair. Far from it. But I pretended that I intended to remain there — and could not be dislodged except by forcible measures highly embarrassing to the college — only long enough to relish a bit the discomfiture of my enemies, before plunging wholeheartedly into the effort to find a successor. We had by now found one for Norm Littlefield, a fortunate catch we all thought. The new head of the English Department was a thirty-five-year-old-man named Inskip, who had taught at Middlebury. Harvard was his alma mater. A Matthew Arnold man, a much-needed exponent of criticism as it was just prior to the reign of Eliot and Company. Then suddenly we had a president too, a dean of admissions at an Eastern college who agreed to come on at Polycarp at the end of the first semester of the new year. Until then, in addition to teaching one class, I discharged the routine affairs of the president's office, more or less under Dean Shaftoe's guidance. He made the speeches for which I had no stomach in any event, while I "did the dirty work," as poor dear Bagley had accurately warned.

Since this consisted in little more than writing letters beginning "Pursuant to our conversation of the fifteenth," I spent most of the day behind a dictaphone. I continued very conscious of the signature I put to these letters, developing at last one that seemed to me a happy blend of feeling and intellect, imagination and discipline. What do we strive for but these? My t-bars were streaks of bird flight, far above the main body of the letter, which itself, however, indicated both feet on the ground. These marks of a model adult were evident also in the way I sprang to my feet to greet callers of whatever rank, and in the warmth and duration of my handshake, calculated to the point held by most experts to express also this harmonious balance of opposites; likewise borne in mind in matters of posture and bearing and socks. When I had nothing else to do I practiced my script, devoting particular attention to the "z," a slimy cipher at best, letting slip all sort of secrets if not watched, especially those relating to irregularities in the downward loops indicative of disturbance on the animal level.

So matters sorted themselves out, for the time being at least. Hodges! appeared to be out of our lives for good, though one can never tell about such things. All I knew was that Marion seemed to have him out of her system. Quincy had kept his promise not to send any pictures to the local papers, despite the impossibility of my delivering my end of the bargain. Where else they might have appeared I never knew. I certainly never went out of my way to find them. The prize-winning check I endorsed to a charity — Norm's favorite, as I went to some effort to find out. Angela had presumably enrolled in a college somewhere else.

Next to my marriage, the happiest development by far in those days was the apparent emergence of my father. He rose phoenix-like from the ashes of that hangover. He refused to come to the wedding, a small reception at the Chicago North Shore home of Marion's parents, and tried to keep my mother away too (unsuccessfully), but the instant we were settled down he came out of his shell. My mother then at last hinted that his years of burial alive were the result of something he had done, long ago, that he feared would cast a shadow over my life. She refused to say what, and I never learned. But now that I had married "a nice cultured girl" he considered me safe from harm on that score, and snapped out of it. I took him out for his first ride. He dressed slowly, in his best suit, appraising himself in a bureau mirror tilted so as to behead himself, so he wouldn't see his face but only the old brown suit encasing the muscles in which he had once taken such pride, grown flabby with disuse now. So he went out of the house, and eventually back to the office, but never again back on the truck. He visited my office once, just to see what it looked like, before "skedaddling" in fear that his presence would embarrass me — as indeed it did. The turmoil of emotions prompted by this experience were destined to precipitate the next crisis in my own life.

His visit, or rather his uncontested flight, had reminded me of the sob ballad in my record collection, "Just Plain Folks," and as I walked across campus for a cup of tea in Hamley

Hall, my dormitory, I found myself ruefully humming and then singing the words:

> *We are just plain folks, your mother and me,*
> *We are just plain folks like our own folks used to be.*
> *As our presence seems to grieve you,*
> *We will go away and leave you,*
> *For we're sadly out of place here,*
> *'Cause we're just plain folks.*

Inskip was sitting at a table in the lounge with Pilbeam, who taught in the Philosophy Department, and Fangle, a resident composer. All Harvard alumni, they were known as the Harvard Group, or, my me at least, the Three Little Prigs. They roused the divided feelings always generated in the breast of the bohunk by the presence of worldly company: that of wanting to belong while simultaneously resenting such a group. There are people who eternally feel themselves the butt of snobbery, real or imagined. I sometimes think this kind of exile worse than sexual rejection, for that can be repaired by "the next girl." In the case of myself and the Three Little Prigs, at any rate, I was sure the snobbery was real. Inskip, the suavest of the lot, and now, of course, my departmental head, glanced at the empty fourth chair at their table, in apprehension I was sure, but there was nothing in the circumstances for him to do but convert this expression into one of invitation. So I sat down.

"How are you, Waltz?"

"Beginning to take a little nourishment."

I found myself affecting Inskip's dry tone when I talked to them, for which I hated him, and myself too, of course. I was convinced that they secretly regarded me as a square. I did nothing that afternoon to offset the estimate. They had been talking about Picasso, in tones which assumed him to be the world's greatest without question, etc. No one would dream of not taking that for granted — such was the implication. I felt my hackles rise. A certain stiffening resistance to all this caused me to make the remark I did, and with more heat than I had intended. "He lacks one thing," I said.

"What's that?"

"Heart."

I saw Inskip look at Fangle and Pilbeam, and they all raised their teacups to their faces, no doubt to conceal or stifle smiles otherwise irrepressible. They had perhaps never heard such talk — certainly such language. The silence piqued me further.

"He hasn't got it here," I said, and laid a hand on my breast.

They were appalled. I had gone too far — I knew that. But there had been nowhere else to go from the original point (which I certainly had no intention of abandoning) but ahead. One is, in such cases, lured across the borders of tolerability by the sheer necessity of increased emphasis which the defense of a position entails. I had been driven to it.

The rather constrained silences into which conversation petered from then on left a fairly clear idea of the subject into which they broke after I left. I encountered them a day or two later, walking together across the common toward lunch in Hamley Hall. They smiled a little too broadly at my approach, and when I stepped behind a tree to watch them after I had passed, their amused exchanges left no doubt as to their content. My secret was out. They had discovered that I was the End.

My festering resentment led to the chain of events to which I am now coming.

I had recently had sent over on one of my father's trucks a chest of things stored for some years in my old room at home. Odds and ends including a couple of tennis rackets, fishing tackle and the like. Mainly things left over from boyhood days on Sparrow Street. Going through them late one afternoon when I was alone, I saw that they included an old air rifle I had completely forgotten about. There was some buckshot in it still. Idly, I pointed it out the open window, and as I did so I noticed the Three Little Prigs approaching across the common on their way to tea again in Hamley. The door to the dining hall and lounge lay under my second-story window and to the left. They were cutting diagonally along the walk on my right, in more or less three-quarter profile, and some fifty feet off, sauntering along with that familiar air of being something special. I was seized with an urge to pepper their shins with BB's. Why not? It was darkening into dusk, my light was out, and the chapel carillon was booming out its regular vesper round — in effect the call to tea. So they would not have been able to hear where the shots were coming from any more than see. The lamps were not yet on in the quad.

Fangle was the first to get it. I caught him smartly on the ankle, causing him to stop short with a little yelp and raise his foot to nurse it. The other two gathered sympathetically round, and between the peals of the chimes I thought I caught the word bee. They were evidently debating the question whether bees might still be about at this time of year, late October. I was on my knees on the floor. Now, propping the rifle carefully on the sill, I drew a bead on Inskip. He jumped too, and, hopping about with his hand on his instep, became in turn the center of interest. My aim was still as deadly as ever it had been as a lad, potting away at bottles and birds. I began firing briskly, working the hand pump which cocked the rifle and pressing the trigger alternately, as fast as I could. They were a sight to behold. "Come on dance, boys," I said to myself. "Little more action, shall we? There, that's better. Heart not important, eh? Well, we'll see about that. Little livelier there, hop to it. Now we're in business."

At last they had sense enough to put an end to this polka and run for cover. Led by Pilbeam, they ducked into a side door, a service entrance, and vanished into the basement.

I thrust the rifle into the corner of a closet, put on a coat, and rushed downstairs to the lounge. I was sitting alone at a table sipping tea and reading a book when they came in. I lifted my cup without raising my eyes from the page, but my position enabled me to take them in on the edge of my vision. They set up a hubbub among two or three occupied tables at the other end of the lounge, relating what had just happened. I saw that my pretended immersion in the book would, beyond a certain point, cast suspicion on me rather than divert it, so I rose at last and went over to the group they had agitated.

"What's all the excitement about?"

"Well, it's the damnedest thing," Pilbeam said. His face was flushed and his long thin hair hung in disordered strands. In a way he was the most satisfactory of the lot. "We've been shot at."

"Oh, come now."

"No, really. Right out there. As we were coming across the quad."

"You mean with a gun?"

"That's one of the points. It seemed like it — a shotgun — scattershot you know — but there was no sound. Look it here."

He put one foot on a chair and pulled up his trouser leg and lowered his sock, displaying several red welts.

"This is extraordinary," I said. "Let's have a look at you chaps."

Inskip and Fangle each hoisted a foot up and exhibited their wounds, in their case unhooking garters in order to drop their socks. We all bent to examine the collective damage more closely.

"That's not shot," said Bromley, a newly acquired young history teacher. "Obviously you wouldn't be here to tell it. That's BB's. Buckshot."

"Well, we'll soon find out," I said, and led the way outdoors. I was after all housemaster.

Friends have said that it is impossible for me to lie, or put on an act, owing to a foxface all too ready to grin. In real emergencies, however, I have found myself perfectly able to dissemble. Nevertheless, I was glad for the relative obscurity of the twilight. Which, however, at the same time added to the difficulties of instituting a search for signs of ammunition at the spot where the trio said they had been ambushed. Somebody ran back for a flashlight, but a few of us meanwhile struck matches, by the light of which we found two or three of what Bromley had predicted.

"It's buckshot all right," I said, holding them in my palm.

"Yes," Inskip said, bending his heavy, black head to look. "Now who would want to do a thing like that, and what for?"

255

"Some nut," Pilbeam put in. "The first thought that came to mind, I confess, was 'a madman amok with a shotgun.' With a silencer on it. But somebody amok with an air rifle is just as nuts. And dangerous. We've got to find him."

"Where do you think the shots were fired from?" I asked, resolved to set a brisk initiative in this search before it was seized by the student governing board with which the resident housemaster divided the responsibility for law and order.

I was glad to see some confusion on this score. They all seemed to think the pellets had come from different directions, depending on where precisely they had been nipped. And once they had begun dancing, of course, chaos was complete. They could not agree on a coherent reconstruction of the crime — typically. A fake incident, involving someone rushing into a classroom firing blanks from a pistol, etc., is often staged by law teachers to demonstrate from the students' later conflicting reports the unreliability of eyewitness testimony. All the three could agree on was that the shots had been fired from somewhere in Hamley Hall. I promised a prompt and thorough investigation.

"Now you chaps have your tea, and then go back to your digs. You've had a rough time."

When I got back to my own quarters, Marion was just returning home from a late afternoon class. I related what had happened. She did not seem very interested, regarding it as merely a prank on the part of some student. She laughed at the thought of the unctuous trio doing their jig, and went to take a bath I had drawn for her. I fixed us something a little stronger than tea, and we settled down to chat about her day.

Needless to say no arms were uncovered as a result of such

inquiries as I launched, and the matter began to drop from public attention. Once Fangle nailed me as I was hurrying across the quad and rather impatiently demanded to know what progress I had made. I said impressively, "None. It's a complete mystery. We're up against a blank wall." I faced him like a thoroughgoing inspector, narrowing an eye. "There's always the question of motive. Why would anyone want to take a pot at you? Have you chaps been doing anything lately?"

"Oh, my God," he said, and popped away into the dusk.

The air rifle I stowed in the backmost depths of a storage closet where it would never be found, with the uneasy suspicion that I might very well avail myself of it another day when the factors leading to its original use again combined to send the trio into their predestined rhythms. Meanwhile the war on the Three Little Prigs proceeded on other fronts.

The one I disliked most was Fangle. Inskip and Pilbeam, however competent as teachers, had easily his degree of smug superiority; they were as great snobs. But Fangle I took a special scunner to. He was one of your "intellectual converts," in the familiar latter-day line I tend to find rather distasteful. Sophisticated embrace of the Nazarene, especially when combined with a tendency to upstage the general run of mankind, has always stuck me as more than a little odious. Fangle's musical compositions likewise lacked all bowels, in that fine Pauline sense of the term. Part of his arrangements with the school required the production of a new symphonic score while we boarded and fed him. That this was going forward as prescribed was evident from the disagreeable sounds regularly issuing from the auditorium, where the college orchestra was rehearsing for the premiere also specified in the terms. This would be another of those brilliant technical exercises without — heart. Yes, I would nail my flag to that mast. All of this became involved in my mind, focalized in it, by the thought of this stiffish, buttoned-up figure saying he was a Christian. Well, if he was a Christian why did he not behave like one? A dash of footwash fundamentalism was what he needed, and that right early. I slipped into the cloakroom one day at teatime and pinned to the lapel of his overcoat one of the Jesus Saves buttons I had got from the mission.

When he discovered it I don't know. It was still there when he exited from the lounge between his two companions, talking of Cocteau. What its effects might have been on others while it remained in view I could likewise only try to imagine, for I obviously couldn't take the risk of following him to see. It must certainly have been disposed of with alacrity the instant it was discovered. But I soon had a substitute. This was in the form of a Jesus Saves bumper sticker for his car. The mission also gave those out. I pasted it very tightly down on his rear bumper in the parking lot where he had been assigned a personal slot with his name on it among the places reserved for faculty members and important office personnel, and this time I had a fine view of the show.

It was from a window of my apartment I stood watch to await his emergence, some hundred yards away, from a building where I knew he had a class in modern harmony during an hour when I myself was free. He usually came out the back, of which there was an unobstructed view. It was noon. The clock in the tower boomed the dismissal hour and, five minutes later, sure enough he came mincing out the door and across a short space of lawn to the lot.

258

The sight was again something to behold. When he saw the evangelical legend blazoned in large phosphorescent red letters across the back of his Buick, he did a double take that would have done credit to a movie ham. He looked around him in angry bewilderment, then began to scratch furiously at the offending banner with his bare nails. It wouldn't come off. A good soaking in hot water, and then possibly a sharp razor blade, would be needed. "It's what you believe, man, isn't it?" I said. "Then why don't you say so? Tell the world. Spread the news. Gospel means good tidings."

By now he had hurled some books he was carrying into his car, slammed the door shut and marched back into the building. He must have gone straight through it to the Administration Building, because he returned in a minute with the new president, Smadbeck, now well in the saddle. He pointed to the bumper, all the while talking agitatedly. President Smadbeck, a tall man with smooth gray hair, shook his head sympathetically at what must have been a full account of what must by now have become borne in on Fangle as a full-scale operation. More was to be expected.

When the car reappeared in due course with the streamer removed, except for untidy scraps still adhering to the chromium, other wholesome propaganda swiftly replaced it. GOD IS LOVE, CAREFUL — CHILDREN R BACK IN SCHOOL, and BROTHERHOOD WEEK were among those that followed. At the same time the war on the Harvard Group was pressed on every sector. Lines of poetry of a romantic or otherwise unacceptable turn were left in the trio's mail pigeonholes or thumbtacked to the doors of their rooms, like theses. "I hid my heart in a nest of roses," "Give smiles to those who love you less, but keep your tears for me," "A heart once broken is a heart no more," suggest the general tone of these. Sometimes a traditional wall motto supplanted the poetic fare — EARTH HAS NO SORROW HEAVEN CANNOT HEAL, KEEP ON KEEPIN' ON! and the like. Then suddenly the technique would shift violently in the other direction and a more cerebral author be invoked to lend justification to the prevailing rain of treacle. A line from Henry James about intellect without emotion being like a bedspring without the mattress greeted Inskip on his return to his dormitory room one afternoon. But mostly the broadsides were kept in a key calculated to sicken and outrage — "heartfelt" sentiments would be the term for them. Pilbeam and Inskip lodged in Creighton Hall. The one was a bachelor, the other divorced. Fangle, whose wife was a voice teacher confined by her practice to their home in Boston, was given a furnished apartment off campus for the two semesters of his residence. He received a steady flow of inspirational matter through the mail when the bumper strips were discontinued for reasons of prudence as well as lack of supply. One day he was edified by the quatrains of Francis William Bourdillon's about the mind having a thousand eyes and the heart but one, yet the light of a whole life dying when love is done. This occurred on a day when I was also interested to read in the paper that a dog in Minnesota had saved a child from drowning by jumping into the water and dragging it out of a pond into which it had fallen. I felt this to be another blow struck at the Harvard Group. Indeed, I clipped it out and sent it to Pilbeam. Life is in the end a soap opera. It is not Hamlet writhing in a skein of verse, nor the *View of Toledo*, nor even the *Eroica*. It is Beethoven going deaf, Joyce blind. It is the newlyweds in New Jersey colliding with another car ten minutes after the marriage and the bride wailing over the body of her groom, "Oh, my God! I'm a wife and a widow in one day!"

The mood in which these activities kept me immersed naturally revived interest in some of my own compositions. I got out the uncompleted "Christmas at the Whorehouse" and glanced over what I had written so far:

> 'Twas Christmas at the whorehouse,
>   And round that festive board
> More gay than at the poorhouse
>   The mirth and laughter soared.
>
> Save in the case of gentle Peg,
>   Who deemed it rather rough
> The way the girls did loll about
>   Stuffed with stuffing and stuff.

I deleted the last line as unworthy of the rest, and set to work rebuilding the stanza around a change in the second line running "deemed it unbecoming." Perhaps the madam in charge could then rudely scatter her brood with the announcement, "The Mayor will be coming!" The Mayor might turn out to be Peg's father, in keeping with the intended dramatic plan of the whole, with its tragic implication of incest narrowly averted.

Anyone with a nostalgia for hogwash will have a taste for the old chromos. I came across a worn print of Watts's *Hope*, the painting of the bowed female figure plucking the last string remaining on her lyre, and took it upstairs to the second floor of Creighton Hall where Pilbeam's room was. I had darted my usual glances in either direction to make sure I was alone in the passage, and had stooped to slip the print under the door, when it opened and a short fat man with a jolly red face smiled at me.

"Looking for George?"

"Why, no," I stammered. "I guess I must have the wrong room."

"I'm Mr. Pilbeam. George's father."

He extended his hand with a cordial expansion of his grin. I mumbled apologetically that the room I wanted was one flight up, and hurried toward the stairway accordingly. Mr. Pilbeam, who was evidently visiting his son, had been "on my way out for some cigars." I hung over the stairwell to watch till he was safely out of sight before leaving the building with my mission undischarged. I decided to suspend the campaign — the emotional current behind which was not, however, checked. It was diverted into another channel.

The subtle duality present in most remarkable natures may take different forms. In my own case, the vital polarity resulted from a conflict that was sometimes between faith and reason, sometimes between intellect and emotion — or "head and heart." But the two are really in the last analysis one. Faith puts the requirements of the emotions first, skepticism the claims of the intellect. I have described my debaucheries as sins of the intellect, a *nostalgie pour la boue* that periodically set me to wallowing in bad standards like a pig in the mud. It was as simple as that. The Harvard Group could by contrast be thought of as bluenoses of the mind. There is a species of aesthetic puritan, with principles as rigidly intolerant of intellectual and artistic shortcomings as their New England forebears were of moral. When prudence decreed a truce in my war on them, the cycle in question had by no means run its course, as I say. The need to do something substandard still ran high. Temptation presently offered itself in another contest, to which I again succumbed. This was a competition run by the sponsor of a television program, a manufacturer of a line of breakfast cereals. It was shortly after Thanksgiving, the holidays were approaching, and a prize of twenty-five hundred dollars was offered for the best letter from a listener, of fifty words or less, on the subject, "What Christmas means to me."

Something that would make the Three Little Prigs gag was how I defined the problem to myself. It was my criterion. I finally wrote: "To me, Christmas is the one day of the year when we show ourselves what the other three hundred and sixty-four could be like too if we wanted to make them."

Needless to say, my letter won first prize. I was again called on the carpet. President Smadbeck asked me to come in and see him. He exemplified the tendency among many gray-haired men to dress all in gray as well: gray flannel suits, gray shirts, ties, socks. Perhaps some kind of protective coloring is the object behind such grooming. In any case, Smadbeck was very well groomed in this mode.

"I see you've won another contest, Waltz."

"I'm sorry, sir."

"I've heard about the last one, of course, as well as — all the other things. I should have thought that would have cured you."

"I guess it hasn't."

"You know this will reflect on the school." There was no longer any question of hushing it up since it had already appeared in a story in the local *Blade*, which recalled that the member of the Polycarp faculty who was victor had also won the movie-magazine contest. The sponsors had announced on their program the plans for my appearing on the show Christmas Eve to receive the check.

"I suppose you do it to pick up a little extra money."

"There is always that problem." This seemed the best way to pass the matter off with Smadbeck, an unexcitable, eminently sane man who tended to take a practical view of things. Certainly a full explanation, with all the emotional and psychological complexities and ramifications gone into, would be very difficult, as well as take up more time than either of us had. Not that I was at all confident of my ability to make a satisfactory elucidation, if it came to that. Better by far to take Smadbeck's line. Too, the economic motive might again point up the inadequate salaries paid teachers, their need to supplement their incomes from less dignified sources. Another round of agitation in the press, lamenting our plight, might well result. This would be all to the good.

"Well, we shall have to think about it. I haven't taken the case up with Inskip, who is your department superior of course, or the faculty. Certainly he should have a say in the matter, don't you think?"

"By all means."

"Meanwhile, pull yourself together, for God's sake! And try not to enter any more contests."

"I'll do my very best, sir. You may bank on that. You've been most understanding."

And he had. I was genuinely impressed. This seemed the best handling of me to date. By far. Smadbeck's own example might well be the turning point by providing the corrective that I needed: some way of finding a stable balance between the two extremes within which I so wildly oscillated, as though each excess must purge the other, each must cast out

264

the devil of the other. The golden mean, that was the ideal to strive for. The thing was to be warm and human, but not offensively so.

This vow being as strong as it was, I had occasion to wonder again, as we so often do in our passage through life, why a firm resolve is so long in taking hold. I tried to put this into Shakespearean claptrap:

> As one who, amply though he slept, upon arising
> Stagger'th worse than had he not lain down,
> Till the refreshment he hath ta'en hath ta'en effect,
> So this revival to the spirit delayeth oft
> To yield her dividend until the mind
> Its fullest consequence doth 'sorb.

My good intentions were in any case abruptly routed by the poor example set by Inskip himself.

I encountered him crossing the campus not five minutes after I had left Smadbeck's office, or nearly did, I should say. Because when he saw me approach he stopped short some twenty feet away, turned pale, and fled in another direction. I shook my head. If he so shrank from human contact of any intensity as to be rendered paralyzed by the sight of an underling who had embarrassed him, then what in heaven's name was he doing as head of a department? What was he doing as head of an English department in any case, since he had dropped Matthew Arnold and to all intents and appearances become a Proust nut? He was lecturing and writing articles on the man for a fare-thee-well. I wanted to turn him around by the collar and, pinning him to the wall with a knee in his groin, say, "Don't you realize the technical fallacy running through Proust? A narrator describing in infinite detail scenes at which he could not possibly have been present?"

That afternoon I spoke with my mother on the phone about something, and was seized with the familiar affectionate desire to say something strictly from hunger. She spoke of a man we both knew, a local parvenu, who had now built a thirty-room house on the outskirts of town. I said, "What good does it do you? You can only sleep in one bed, eat three meals a day, bathe in one tub . . ." The need to talk crud arose from a feeling that I was probably a snob about my parents, especially my stupid and ignorant mother; a guilt in part appeased by sinking to her level on occasion and saying things that "pleased her," or would have pleased her if she could have heard them; which were automatically things that would have galled or sickened the Harvard Group — hostilities on whom were now reopened with a bang.

I got Inskip on the phone after dinner and whispered with a handkerchief over the mouthpiece, "Fra Angelico always knelt when painting the sky," and then to Pilbeam, "Heathcliff, fill my arms with heather!" Swept along on the tide of romanticism in which I was now irresistibly caught, I peppered their shins with buckshot once again when the factors conducive to this measure in the first instance were once more combined. I was alone in my apartment, feeling sentimental, as dusk deepened along the old quad and the chapel bells boomed out a vesper anthem calling the faithful to tea. I got the air rifle out of the closet where I had hidden it and knelt at the window with the lights out, to await the appearance of the Harvard Group. At last with their usual punctuality they came sauntering three abreast along the walk, with that superior air so in need of chastening.

I thrust the barrel of the BB gun cautiously out between the sill and the window sash, raised an inch or two. Emotion not important, eh? Well, we'll see about that. We'll just defrost this tight little, right little group and see what we've got here, shall we? *Pffwang*. The first one catches Inskip, who executes a fine caper indeed. *Pffwang*. That one must have ricocheted off Pilbeam's shoe and pinked our Fangle in the shin, for they both join the jig. Under the covering thunder of the bells the sniping continues. All dancing nicely now. Hopping mad and glancing about in all directions are we? That's better. Little more human, don't you know. That's the stuff. Coming along fine there, soon we'll be real people. Come a long way from the position that feeling is nothing, haven't we? Need lots of work yet though. Plenty of heat there but no warmth. The whole trouble. Why a chap has to do this. Show you. Not ordained of God or any such nut notion, just know it's our duty to crack that infernal poise and let in a little *spritz*. For our own best to throw a fit now and again. Enriches us.

I did not turn up for tea myself this time or await developments, setting out immediately for a walk instead. There was an early, full moon. That evening Fangle was rung up and anonymously treated to several phonograph measures of a composer he had publicly termed saccharine, Delius. Long a favorite of mine. Through the heartrending choral and orchestral strains of *Sea Drift* could be discerned Fangle's own more piercing cry at the other end, "Waltz! Damn it, Waltz, we know very well it's you who are — all this damned — " I clapped the phone into its cradle (a mistake) and stood a moment frozen in that position. Had I heard right? Or was my imagination playing tricks on me? It had been hard to be sure through the bittersweet crescendo into which the music was now steadily mounting.

267

My abandonment to the mood of the Delius work, based on Whitman's despairing poem about irremediable loss, was unfortunately apt in the present circumstance, having domestic relevance. All, all too much so.

Marion had gone off to spend the weekend with her parents after a quarrel about this latest contest. She had not taken it at all well. One's wife is not Smadbeck, of course — just as she is no longer one's sweetheart, alas. That is the difficulty of marriage. We fall in love with a personality, but we must live with a character. That is all too often like living within walls from which paper and even plaster have been stripped, leaving the pipes and wiring exposed, along with glimpses of some ugly lath-work. There was no reason for my wife to show the degree of tolerance and forbearance in this case that she had in the first, when we were still single. Frailties that may lend a suitor charm will be found unacceptable in a husband. Still, even allowing for those realities of the human relation, I thought the disapproval with which she greeted my latest epistolary triumph a little extreme. The rigidity of principle that I have tried to show as always more than half commingled with her girlish humanitarianism, her "youthful idealism," had rapidly taken over in the business of daily life. I might almost say that the honeymoon being "over" took, in our case, this form. I saw gradually crystallize in Marion a kind of integrity, severity even, that reminded me more than a little of the Three Little Prigs. I must grow up. I must develop more sense of responsibility — this was openly the theme of the dressing down I received at home promptly after having found a far more understanding attitude on the official carpet. I could not help thinking that Smadbeck would have handled this whole situation differently. But then one is not married to Smadbeck, as I say.

"You're not the girl I married."

"Well, you're the boy I did, and that's the trouble. Won't anything? Make you? Mature?"

Seated on the studio couch, her head back against the wall and a drink in her hand, she watched me pace the living room. "You've got the emotional development of a five-year-old, you know."

I completed a lap about the room, circling toward a window. I stood looking out of it. I said at last: "A five-year-old what?"

And now I am alone, slumped on the couch reading the lines of the Whitman poem reproduced on the back of the envelope in which the Thomas Beecham recording has come. The copy on the backs of record envelopes seems to me on the whole excellent. Much of my musical education is derived from it. *Sea Drift* is an unabashedly emotional dirge, slopping over the way such things ought to, get it over with and on with it, lay it on with the old trowel and maybe we'll feel better after a bit. Two birds nest on the Paumanok seashore. One vanishes, and the carols pouring from the throat of the survivor become the symbol of eternal heartbreak. The lovelorn songster on the desolate bough sings for us all:

> *O throat! O throbbing heart!*
> *And I sing uselessly, uselessly all the night.*
> *O past! O happy life! O songs of joy!*
> *In the air, in the woods, over fields,*
> *Loved! loved! loved! loved! loved!*
> *But my mate no more, no more with me!*
> *We two together no more.*

269

I put on my coat and went downtown, crossing the bridge over the river, then the tracks, and headed for a bar near the Gospel tabernacle. At last I was beginning to understand how Hegel felt at the end of his life. "Only one man understood me," he said, "and he didn't understand me."

twenty

BY THE TIME I was standing at the bar, my hand locked securely around a glass, detachment was well back in the ascendant again. I observed from my post of vantage one of those quarrels so frequently overheard in such places. The public ventilation of personal problems is almost a ritual with some people, feminine tears often as not its climax. So it was in this case. They were a young pair, obviously unmarried from the nature of the exchanges. The girl had rather a pale, wistful face, framed in long straight hair perhaps a shade too yellow.

At last she exclaimed, "Oh, go on, get," and he did, rising from the table where this had been enacted and snapping up his cigarettes with a truculent gesture, perhaps in compensation for being sent packing. He marched out, zipping his leather jacket up to his chin before disappearing into the light swirls of snow that had been falling since dusk.

I remained at the bar, not watching the girl directly but taking her in out of the tail of my eye. She tidied herself with a will, then sat looking straight ahead with her chin tilted, as though determined to regard herself as well rid of him. When she had finished her beer and consulted the check preparatory to settling the account her banished hero had left behind, she began to poke about in her bag, apparently fruitlessly, and with fresh accesses of anger.

I sauntered over and asked whether I might be of service.

"My mother told me never to talk to strange men," she said without raising her eyes from the task of prospecting in her purse.

"What's strange about me? I should think familiar would rather be the term to describe me," I said, laughing sociably. "You knew *him* well enough and all the good it did you," I added with a jerk of my head in the direction her youth had gone. "May I sit down?"

"Punk. If I never see him again it'll be too soon. I've been going with him for six months and all we did was fight. Some people do it for a lifetime. How can they and still want to be together?"

"Love is not love that alters when it altercation finds," I said, drawing a chair out and sitting down.

"What?"

"Why don't you have a drink with me? It's all I'll ask in return for cleaning up your debts. So you see, some of us are not as unscrupulous as others."

"I can see that. One thing. You married?"

"I'm not a loyal husband, my dear, so much as a cad *manqué*."

"Well, as long as you're not married it's O.K. You're kind of cute at that, with that silly grin."

She scrutinized me thoughtfully, feature by feature, as though totting up a column of figures. I surveyed her in the same manner, although not to arrive at an estimate of her trustworthiness. Someone, I think one of those Frenchmen who have written on the arts of love, has said that women take in a man's face *en bloc*, that is as a whole, while a man savors a woman's individual features — a sensuous mouth, suggestive eyes, etc. It's perhaps another of those plausible aphorisms that sound valid without much basis in actual fact. I did in this instance, however, live up to its masculine half. The girl's moist, pulpy lips were parted, showing a row of pretty white teeth flecked with lipstick. Various conflicting schools of makeup were represented cosmetically in her face. There was the white mask of the skin itself, the mouth altogether too bright for it, and the livid blue eye liner which was unsuited to both — or so it seemed to me. The effect was agreeably touching rather than not; perhaps a little childish. There was also something childlike in the way she rose halfway out of her chair, after declining my offer of another beer, and pointed to a liqueur among those racked on the back bar, identifying what she wanted by the shape of the bottle. It was the tall conical bottle in which the Italian cordial Galliano comes. I told the bartender to bring us two.

Corners could be cut by declaring straight out that I "picked her up," not a very edifying phrase. In this case not strictly true either. At least the girl, whose name was Marjorie Wilkins, went to some lengths to make her favors appear not obtainable without some effort and even struggle on the part of the applicant — though freely given when that test had been surmounted. Not that ceremonial resistance was the only obstacle to an evening's incidental triumph. About twenty-one or twenty-two, she lived with her parents, and though we had the dark cottage parlor on Finch Street to ourselves, there was always the uneasy specter of elders asleep in quarters overhead, if not that of a father appearing nightgowned on the stairway, in keeping with the stereotypes of the cartoon strip, to inquire if "that young man is ever going home." But the next night, Saturday, they were in Chicago for a lodge dinner, and we had the house to ourselves for a good three hours. She led me by the hand toward her bedroom.

"You're quite a rascal," she said, when we were chatting together once again, cigarettes in hand, against propped up pillows.

"If you're going to fall into a category it might as well be head first."

"And so smooth." She laughed, running a palm over my arms and shoulders. "Like your skin. Which is probably hard to get under. Never like anybody I've known before." It was apparent that she had now reverted to her original meaning. "Not just educated. Lots of fellows who've been through college come out not knowing anything, and some know it all. Which is just as bad. You're in between. But you play it all so cool. Nothing does get under your skin, does it? Does it?" she inquired, peering at me in the dark. "What have you got to say for yourself?"

"Life, liberty, and the happiness of pursuit."

"So cool and rat fink. What college did you go to? That made you so cultured and rat fink."

"I can never remember the name of it. It was somewhere in Colorado."

This was part of the identity I had rapidly assembled for myself on hearing her say, and give as justification for her "surrender," that she guessed she was "ready to switch boy friends." That was a rather ominous note, not to be underestimated. I had told her my first name but had cooked up a last name. I said I lived in Chicago but traveled much in my work, which was selling office equipment. I had completed my regular canvass of Slow Rapids and was returning to Chicago tomorrow, from where I promised I would call her the minute I got in. The absence of a car I explained by saying it was in the shop for repairs. "Well, you're a fast worker," she had said, towing me into the bedroom.

The mountain of falsehoods made me feel guiltier than the misdemeanor they were erected to conceal. The girl had been, after all, willing enough, and in any case the term "seduced and abandoned" seems hopelessly inapplicable to any relationship conceivable under today's broadened standards. Nevertheless, I did feel a sense of regret, vague but corroding, as I made my way home — sharply intensified at the sight of Marion standing there unpacking her suitcase.

"I didn't expect you back till tomorrow."

"I can see that."

The remark had an all too specific point. Not having expected to see her, I had taken no precautions of checking my appearance before entering the apartment. I noticed her glancing at my cheek as we exchanged these greetings, and hurried into the bathroom at the first possible opportunity, to find to my horror a scarlet smudge staring back at me in the glass. I made the even greater mistake of rubbing it off. So that when I returned to the bedroom where Marion had continued silently unloading her bag, she said after another look, "I see you got rid of it."

"It certainly wasn't yours," I said, referring to the cool welcome I had received — as cool as her departure the day before.

Frozen silences are more than I can bear. Words of any sort are better. I kept talking in hopes of bringing some about,

274

any state of mind but this, under which we might retire. Anything would do, heated retort, bitter rebuke, any storm to clear this sky. My sentences ground doggedly away, like an icebreaker through solid glacier.

"If you knew how casually these things come about, you'd realize how little they mean."

She put into a bureau drawer the last garment from her grip and snapped it shut. I reached to relieve her of it so as to stow it in the closet myself. She swung it clear of my grasp and walked around me. I followed her and stood in the hallway as she put it away.

"This is the ill-wind department, but you learn what somebody means to you when you've wronged them. That's the fastest way. Thank God you get the idea from a trivial peccadillo. A stumble may prevent a fall."

She bathed and went to bed, settling down there with a book. I said with sudden spirit, "You ran out on me, you know!"

She slammed the book shut and looked at me with her eyes flashing. "Which is why I came back early. Guilt! Oh, my God. All the good it did me. This is what I hurry home to."

I was on my knees at her side, traversing the last steps in that position.

"Oh, darling, don't blame yourself. I won't let you. You didn't know what you were doing. All of us do rash things, things we'll later regret because in so doing we've wronged others. So don't reproach yourself."

"Oh, Tom, how could you," she said with her hands to her face.

"Don't ask me, darling. Because I'll never know myself. I just. Don't. Know. I'm a thorn in my own flesh!"

After an hour of this we lay back in a state of emotional exhaustion, glad enough to have it so, our hearts hollow and our minds emptied. Not in one another's arms certainly, but not at one another's throats either. A kind of nervous calm had settled upon us, that was very nearly peace, or at least a truce. One more touch was needed to restore us at any rate to the tolerable. The right fond word, perhaps one of our private jokes.

I smiled tremulously over at her as I climbed into bed and said, before pulling the lamp cord to extinguish the scene, "Know what my mother used to say? She used to say — you'll love this, ducks — she used to say, 'There ought to be a law against all these illicit relations.'"

On that note we managed at last to drop off into a little troubled sleep.

Remaining yet to be confronted were the Three Little Prigs. For that jig was up too.

Smadbeck called late the following Monday afternoon and asked if I would step into his office. When I arrived, the trio were there, looking like anything but plaintiffs with a grievance to air. In fact they all looked guilty as hell, with the possible exception of the prickly Fangle. Inskip was the worst. He was evidently shattered by any kind of run-in, any sort of direct human collision. He sat with his elbow on the arm of his chair, his head bowed in his hand. From time to time he rubbed his forehead with his fingers, offering glimpses of a face white as a sheet. Pilbeam had too high a color ever to be called pale, but in his embarrassment the blood drained from his cheeks, too, leaving them mottled, like an overripe apple. Under his thinning blond hair his brow was beaded. He sat slumped back, his mouth open as though gasping for air, with one arm hooked dangling over the back of his chair. Fangle alone, as I say, looked anything like the part of an accuser. Yet even his belligerent manner, with which by contrast he glared at me as I entered the president's office, did nothing to offset or mitigate my opening impression: that they were curious champions of the principle of detachment.

Smadbeck came directly to the point.

"These men claim they have been consistently annoyed by mail, telephone and other means of communication for some time," he said, "and that the nature of the intrusions and assaults points to a single perpetrator — you."

"Me?" I spoke with a smile modestly disclaiming the talent for an undertanking of such large-scale ingenuity, rather than protesting innocence.

"It would be best not to hedge or diddle about, Waltz." Another gasp from the wretched Pilbeam and an uncomfortable fidget from Inskip in his chair suggsted that mercy for the accusers was the aim in bringing these proceedings to as rapid a close as possible. "How do we know? Comparison with a, well, legitimate document from your typewriter, a departmental memo to Inskip's office as a matter of fact, hint strongly that those were typed out on your machine too."

Smadbeck indicated a jumble of inspirational matter on his desk, everything that had in recent weeks been dispatched by post, tacked to doors or slipped under them, pasted to car bumpers or affixed to coat lapels. It was rather an impressive pile. Add to these the telephone calls by night, and other devices, and my war on the Harvard Group was seen to have been an operation of considerable scope and diligence.

"Why would I do anything like that?"

"And those phone calls," Smadbeck said, ignoring this. "They say they have been even more troublesome."

There was a note in Smadbeck's voice and manner, as of ill-concealed sardonic amusement, not with me so much as the three, that indicated he might be as much ally as judge. From North Dakota, he could be considered even more an outlander than myself, with a name even more onerous than mine. Perhaps honyock origins of his own linked him in spirit with me far more than with exemplars of eastern urbanity. Certainly the fragility of that under fire did little to impress him in its favor now. I thought he was smiling a little behind the hand bunched at his mouth. That was one thing that made me decide to come clean. The other was the evidence itself. The Three Little Prigs must early have suspected who the tormentor was from the cardiac theme uppermost in the sentiments rained upon them, following so closely upon my statement about the importance of heart in matters of artistic expression, in the argument about Picasso. My sensed hostility toward them offered an even stronger, if less tangible, clue.

Smadbeck leaned suddenly forward over his desk and said, "And the buckshot business. We happen to know there is an air rifle in your room, Waltz. It's been searched."

This was so transparent I nearly laughed. It was the familiar trick by which the detective tries to trap the suspect into confession by pretending they have got the goods on him anyway. Almost as banal as my thoughts for the day. But Smadbeck had so won my respect and confidence that I wanted him to look as good as he deserved in this affair.

"Well sir, you're a hard man to fool, so I won't try to fool you," I said. "Not that I made any particular effort to do so with these chaps. I mean surely they must have known I as-

278

sumed all along they realized who was having the fun with them," I continued, turning to the trio. "Surely none of us thought the anonymity act was anything more than part of the prank."

"Prank," said Fangle, the one member of the coterie who had reason to feel the shafts not altogether unbarbed, in an intellectual, or controversial, sense. "*Prank*. When a man comes out of his class in Harmony and finds on the bumper of his car — "

"All right," said Smadbeck, rising. "That's not what we're here for. We're here to confront somebody with the evidence and extract an admission. That we've done. The rest, the — " He seemed to be groping for a word other than "punishment." "The final disposition of the matter is my province and that of the discipline committee. I'll excuse you gentlemen with the assurance that I shall deal firmly with the matter now that the culprit has been brought to heel. Waltz, I'd like a word with you."

The three rose and filed out, looking rather hangdog as they closed the door behind them. When they were gone, Smadbeck extended an open humidor to me, which I declined, then helped himself to a large cigar. He dressed and punctured it, and reached for a box of matches which he shook briefly before opening.

"Why did you do all that?"

"They make me sick."

He turned this motivation over in his mind as he set fire to his cigar, seeming to revolve it seriously as something far more cogent than complex rationalization would have been — certainly more healthily direct and easier to grasp for someone hailing from the robust heartlands of this country.

"That may be. But it is no reason to — " Here he gave again the impression of awaiting a substitute for the term springing most naturally to mind, but in this case deciding to settle for the original rather than waste time on euphemisms. "To take the law into our own hands."

"I know. But sometimes the law is slow, and, in this case, leaves no provision whatever for dealing with the offense."

"Ignore them."

"I can't."

"That's your problem. Mine is, how to handle you. I have to do something, you know, and something drastic." He regarded me through clouds of smoke from the cigar he was now contentedly puffing in his chair. The air became rather pleasantly tainted with tobacco, as a room will from the first few relatively benign fumes of a good cigar. "I cannot let this pass."

"I understand."

"I see you've got quite a backlog of difficulties here, all more or less in the same general vein, or mental level. I'm going to have to get rid of you."

"Is it that bad?"

"Not permanently. For a while. Because I don't think you're a very stable character. I mean you're not responsible. I use the word on two levels. You're irresponsible, but for reasons for which you may not be entirely responsible. If you get what I mean. I think you're going through a phase, but how long it will be, who knows? By the time you're mature you may be ready to leave this earth. Shaw bemoans that somewhere, I think in *Back to Methuselah*. That it takes seventy years to make a grownup, by which time he's got to go. Your dossier is appalling," he said, gesturing to a

Manila file I had seen before, now fattened perceptibly. "You need help, and I think you should have a leave of absence until you get it."

"How long were you thinking of? And while I'm out will I be . . . I mean those things cost money."

Here Smadbeck rose and walked to the window, where he adjusted a blind to admit what little sunlight there was.

"That's the thing. You see, according to our scale for faculty members, which gets to be damned complicated, no provisions like this are made for ordinary instructors. I mean leave privileges and other 'mercy' considerations on the scale you'll need them. Only those with professorial standing. So we're going to have to promote you to associate professor."

"That's quite all right."

"Just cutting somebody off who's — " Here Smadbeck made a vague gesture which came precariously close to describing circles in the air near his temple. "Who obviously needs rest and so on wouldn't be humane. And you *are* in the Humanities Department. Naturally I shall have to take this matter up with the faculty, but they'll probably take my recommendations for the action to be decided on. And it will have to be looked into. It may be that not even associate professorships provide for financial considerations on the scope your case needs. In that case we'd have to make you a full professor, with tenure."

"Please don't worry about it. And you may be sure I'll use whatever means are decided on to the fullest. I may even take a trip. Much as I dislike travel, they say a change of scene often does wonders."

"You've got to get yourself straightened around, Waltz. That much is certain."

We shook hands on that note, and as I closed the door and walked down the hall to the front of the building, whose stairs I seemed so frequently to have descended in moments of strain before, I again felt tears of genuine emotion welling to my eyes.

The understanding, presently confirmed, was that I would leave at the end of the winter term. The solution of one problem is rarely unattended by the appearance of fresh ones in its wake. What about Marion? She, of course, had another full semester to go before summer vacation would release her for a bit of a holiday. I delayed bringing the matter up because I could not do so without revealing why it had come about; I wanted to spare her the news that I had become again the object of disciplinary measures. Yet I knew my silence only postponed the inevitable. And meanwhile there was the risk that she might learn from other sources of the jam I was in. Only full professors constituted the portion of the faculty which dealt with its own members in the fashion required by my circumstances, so Marion had not sat in review of my case; but it was unlikely that she could go on indefinitely without its being brought to her attention by some gossip. I was on tenterhooks all that period up to the holidays — when the trouble was swallowed up in another far worse.

I had to run into Chicago on Christmas Eve to collect the twenty-five hundred dollars on the television broadcast for which I had written the prize-winning letter. The president of the corporation manufacturing the sponsoring product presented the check to me with a few words, if possible even more heartfelt than mine, and a congratulatory handshake.

282

The show was at seven, and I was back home by half-past nine. I knew instantly from Marion's face that something was wrong.

"Your friend called," she said, stonily.

"Who?"

"The one you were out with."

"What are you talking about?"

The crisis was all too quickly clarified. The girl I had picked up in the bar had been sitting in front of her television set that evening and seen me. She had also learned from the formalities my right name, as well as my address and true occupation, and had lost no time in telephoning.

"She was surprised to hear a woman's voice, and to learn her Lothario was married. Needless to say, I don't feel much like celebrating Christmas, but your folks are expecting us tonight and mine are tomorrow. So let's get through the holidays, and then that'll be that."

I did not understand. "What'll be what?"

"I think I'm speaking in plain English."

"But we've been through all this before," I said, puzzled. "I thought we thrashed it out and it was behind us. That incident. I mean — what did you find out tonight that you didn't already know?"

"What kind of girl she is."

"Now look, Marion, if you're implying she was just some cheap — "

"That's exactly what I'm not implying! Won't you ever learn anything? That's what I might have thought then, and bad as that would be, I could forgive it. I know now she isn't. From just a few words on the telephone I could tell what she is, that she's been hurt. She's not fair game, Tom.

283

You can't ride roughshod over a creature like that. A physical fling such as you said may not be anything more than you said — if you want to stick to your odd principle that the casual use of sex justifies it — but seducing the little match girl, really! Don't you understand that people really can have their hearts broken?"

I dropped into a chair as though I had been clubbed into it. I was still in my overcoat. Amazing, I reflected, how little we know of one another. The woman I was married to did not know that what she had just said was what I firmly believed. It was one of my cherished principles. "Hearts are so easily broken, let us be tender awhile . . ."

"That's been my whole point, what I've been trying to tell you from the start. I think we even talked about it the night I visited you in the hospital with Arthur. That you *can't* separate sex from love. That it's indecent and that you pay for it. That it's even against nature, as our grandparents would say, try as we will with all this Dionysian stuff that's going around these days. Musical beds! You called your little lark a peccadillo. That's exactly what's wrong with it. A real love affair with another woman I might forgive. But your ability to be so casual with somebody you should have seen was innocent, could be easily hurt — no, I don't want a man like that for a husband. I couldn't live with a man like that. Come on, your folks will be waiting. The presents are all wrapped and in the bedroom."

I drove the few miles to Sparrow Street in something of a daze, even a trance. When we stopped in front of the old white cottage my mother was standing behind the lace curtains, watching for us. Marion had the presents in her lap. She started to open the car door.

"Wait," I said. "I'm trying to get this straight. You wouldn't leave me for hurting you. But you would for hurting the other woman."

"That's about it, I suppose."

"Jesus Christ," I said softly, more to myself, "you *are* a Christian at that, aren't you?"

Again Marion started to get out, and again I detained her. I spoke in a rush.

"The school's giving me a semester off. Something like sick leave. Maybe I am sick. I'll go away. I'll leave you for a while, get me off your neck and try to come to some sort of terms with myself. And do you know what I'm going to do? I'm going to take my father with me. He's always wanted to visit Poland. So do I. And do you know where I'll stop on the way? I was reading your notes for the lecture on James's *Varieties of Religious Experience*. The business about faith healing is very impressive, and what you said to me about the history of Lourdes the other day. I didn't realize so many tourists went there on pilgrimages. I think I'd like to stop off at Lourdes."

"Whatever for?"

"Well, a whole psychoanalysis is pretty involved. It takes years, and it's pretty expensive."

"Oh, my God." She put her hands to her face, her elbows resting on the mound of brightly wrapped packages in her lap. She shook her head, uttering some further muffled ejaculation I did not catch. I didn't know whether she was laughing or crying.

"The place has always held a certain fascination for me. Sixty miracle cures have been attested, did you realize that? One has to recognize facts, whatever your definition or explanation of 'miracle' may be. But what's often occurred to me — why don't neurotics go there? I mean if the waters can cure physical symptoms psychologically induced, why not the psychological condition itself? Why can't it be reversed?"

She removed her hands from her face and turned to look at me in the dark. Again she gave a shake of her head.

"Let's go in, shall we? Your folks will think we're fighting. And we don't want to spoil their Christmas, do we? So let's try to behave as though that's what it is. For their sakes."

STAN

twenty-one

THERE'S NO REASON for me to take up the thread of the story again on my account. I do it on Tom's. And only because he won't. He "doesn't want to talk about it," as people frequently don't about some out-of-the-ordinary happening they've been through. Soldiers home from the wars say it. Divorced people sometimes do. Religious experiences affect others the same way. So I'll have to wind the story up in my own words. I'll be brief.

Before I am, however, I ought to say something about the changes underwent in my own attitude toward things in general in the course of my doz. or so years in limbo. That's what I believe they use to call the suburb of hell where you laid around waiting for orders to proceed one way or the other.

You can see I still mock. But with a difference. I ridicule only outmoded theological conceps, *not the human realities behind them conceps.* Certainly not the human need for belief as such. What happened to Tom at Lourdes is his own to think about in his own way, to make his own head nor tail out of, and in his own good time. I still say there's some rational explanation *if we knew it.* But we don't, so let it stand as it is for him to make what he wishes out of it for his own lifetime. After which will be the curtain, is my firm opinion still. Firm but not bigoted. There's a difference. A bigot is a spigot whether of the right or left, always ready to turn hisself on full force whether anybody asked him or not. I use to be that way — notice my new attitude? I been through enough hell to know we don't need no more in the form of any eternal P.S. We make it all here and it will have to suffice, ditto any heaven we're going to have too. Now that I've come back to life I been trying to behave toward others according to the above ideal. The golden rule, me; that knock you over with a feather? The golden rule — beginning with my wife.

Like a fool, I should never of given her all that argument. That only stiffens the other party's determination, like young people to get married when you oppose them. Say down with the match and up goes the ladder under the old bedroom window. Same with discussions of politics. Criticize a man's candidate and he'll pull the lever twice as hard. My narrowness helped make Elsie more narrow, etc., a vicious circle making it a throwup who will prevail in the end. In those days I regarded myself as an intellectual though my actions bellied my words — a statement you would not make about me now. At all events its not the formal beliefs themselves that are important. Its the human relationships behind the fussade of all our religion and philosophy that count. I was so grateful that my wrong didn't damage my son's life in the end, like I feared, that I have become a much better person. I'm decent to my wife. I take her out to dinner much oftener than I did. I help around the house the way she does at the office, and more than at the office too if it comes to that. I let her go out estimating the way she likes to, to meet people, even though I know full well she's leaving her tracks everywhere. A pamphlet with every figure she hands out. Sometimes she even likes to pitch in and help unload the truck at the elevator. Many's the job we unload together. I've even been to church to humor her. Not the Gospel tabernacle to be sure, she knows thats too rich for my blood, too primitive. But once in a while I'll look in on the liberal community church to see what the intellectuals are up to. Its made up of several of the more modern congregations going in cahoots with one another, and the services "follow no fixed denominational pattern," as the ads say.

The first time I dropped in there was a Sunday evening about a year ago. The pews were pretty sparsely populated for a combined congregation, but the minister was a very good speaker, very well educated. He opened on a modern enough note, but then references to an after life began to creep into his sermon — and even to some kind of heaven, where we will continue our existence on a whole nother plane where all memories of this earthly life will gradually disappear, like the railroads. I turned my head to rubber a little and see how my coworshippers were taking this. Near me sat a young mother who was very rapt up in what was being said to all appearances. She *wanted* to go on. She had a little boy who was reading a comic in his lap, just like in orthodox churches. Behind me was an old man the sandman had got, and a young couple holding hands, and even necking it seemed. This was apparently what was meant by the services not following any fixed denominational pattern. For a hymn we sang "The Spanish Cavalier" and then let go with a couple choruses of "Aura Lee." In a weird way, I

291

didn't mind. The last time I went back was Good Friday, again more or less out of curiosity. I think they should call it *Pretty* Good Friday, what with all the doubts they have to work out a compromise with.

I made a similar attempt to make some sense out of my sex life. I mean I made a concerted effort to get that on a sounder and more satisfactory basis, investing in one of them manuals for married couples with all sorts of tips on cohabitative harmony and conjugal synchronization and what not. Things that are easier done than said if you ask me, but anyway. Not that swarming all over your mate to my unfailing delight was the sole outlet I give her. Not by any manner of means. Hitherto I hadn't paid enough attention to the little things around the house that women harp on because its their domain for God's sake! Lets get that through our craws, shall we boys? Her big crotchet use to be throwing chairs and sofas out and replacing them down to Pete Potmesil's borax store, the local hdqtrs. for obtaining things worse than you have at home. I saw that she needs other releases — little drives into the country, spins into Chi to call on old relatives or track down new ones. She seems to need such stimuluses more and more as the years go by. Bad furniture is no longer enough. Then like I say I even humor her about attending divine worship.

We're here to use our intelligence, yes, but that ain't everything. It's our duty to see through things, but also to see things through. Or I'll put it another way. We're not primarily put on this earth to see through one another, but to see one another through. So all this psychology? Great — up to a point. Get too skeptical about everything and you wind up as narrow as the know-nothings. So no more firing at the wife, "Man is a digestive tube pierced at both ends." Whats needed is a little compassion here. I remember once Tom and Marion were having a discussion on a subject and she mentioned that Wilde told Gide when he got out of jail, "The most beautiful thing in the world is pity." "I never realized Gide was in jail," I says, to help move the conversation along literary lines so she wouldn't think we were all a bunch of ignoramuses at 922 Sparrow. I had read the name somewhere, and as to Wilde I suddenly remembered Lena Salerno bringing him into the conversation years ago. It seemed like another lifetime! Anyhow that was what Wilde said. Which he was right. You can't forever:

> Live in your house by the side of the road
> And hurl the cynic's ban.

I quoted that poem in this conversation at our house. I don't remember what Tom murmured exactly, but something, running his finger around the rim of his glass, as though doubting the purity of its circumference.

Notice that last remark? It showed I didn't sit around all them years in limbo doing nothing, but tried to improve myself. I read and I thought, I thought and I read. Not the kind of reading I'd been doing, radical pamphlets only, but books. Literature. That way I began to broaden my horizons, learning to absorb new impressions and think in metaphors that enrich your life. Thus I was able to see that the days were going by with the infinite banality of telephone poles. Things like that. I aim to go on taking in new impressions like that till my intake valve is shot. I use to be awful. Now I cultivate enlarged sensibilities, along with the moral lesson which I'm trying to emphasize: that there are no solutions, that people simply have to rub along, like everybody else. All that has the limpidity of Jell-o to me now. Not till Tom was in the clear did I snap out of it however.

And now before I be brief I want to say a word about that.

How delightful to watch Tom grow up, combining in a mature man the best of both heritages that we give him. My, they must be proud of him over to the school, giving him that much Sabbatical so soon and all, and we're mighty proud of Polycarp's pride in him. They even had him doing some work in the President's office for a while. I know there were those who said he wasn't executive lumber, but that don't hurt. That part is all right. Detractors always arise in the land, putting down their betters. The point is that they liked him enough, and the President thought enough of him to appoint him acting head as his last official act before being judged off his rocker and carted off to the foolish factory. Those things make you feel good.

I can remember him as a little shaver, then as a fine lad, beginning to get pimples from impure thoughts. As for sex education, I figured he knew more than me all ready. Once when he was oh fourteen, fifteen, he asked me about extramarital relations, and I says, "Oh, wait till your married for them!" But I wasn't always serious in my advice — sometimes a joke does it best. Once when he asked me for a shotgun I says, "No, son, I love you too much to give you one of those. Every boy with a shotgun is potentially fatherless, and I don't want that to happen to you." So do it with humor whenever you can, thats a must. Humor sees us through. Tom was always pretty fast with a wisecrack himself. As a shaver he would say, "Pa's a standing joke — or would be if we could get him on his feet." Oh. Incidentally I can drink again — the sure sign of somebody who's not an alcoholic . . . So my thoughts drift in and out of mind, with the random trajectories of snow in windless air. Wow.

The greatest single satisfaction of my life was his marriage. I held my breath when I see who he was hooked up with, hoping to God it wouldn't fall through. I always wanted him to marry somebody sophisticated, but by sophisticated I don't mean one of them women that theyre so brittle if you kissed them you'd bleed. No. I mean a smart outside with substance inside. I was tickled to death to see somebody from the Chicago North Shore and the right families and all that, much as I didn't in the least care about social standing persay. Not the type who can love you for yourself alone as long as you've got money. Not a bit of it. She was one girl who if she gave you the business about love being all, she'd live with you in a tent if need be, you could believe it. Most of them mean by a home today a place a husband can provide that he can get them *out* of, and *fast,* and *often.* This one was all wool and a yard wide. I could spot that at a glance, sick as a dog as I was. And cute as a cricket into the bargain.

So only two generations to climb out of the proletariat into the boorgeoisie. And maybe upper boorgeoisie at that. And like I can't stress enough, all this in a not superficial vane, people sitting on patios nibbling bedeviled eggs and sipping cocktails — but in the genuinely cultured sense. And the beauty part of it all is, Tom never come to think he's too good for us. No forgetting the old folks while he goes out and be's continental.

Life is no easy matter today no more, if it ever was. No

central belief giving cohesion, like in the Middle Ages. No clearly defined purpose or direction. No. Once a relatively simple dirt road with forks where the traveler had a simple choice, life is now a crowded superhighway with bewildering cloverleaf exits on which, after a maize of turns, a man is libel to find himself speeding back in the direction he came. I did somewhat, as per the above shift or anyhow modification in emphasis, and so I think did Tom — not that you were always sure what he had on his mind. But he has had a lot of readjustments to make in his thinking too. The big thing today among young people seems to be identity crisises. You have to have one of them. What we worried about at that age was where our next meal was coming from, but today they have to rack their brains about who they are. Which I think they tend to give theirself airs, intellectuals. Every time I hear an intellectual say, "Oh, who am I?" I want to say, "Oh, who the hell do you think you are?" But Tomasko's I think was a little different. Deeper. Which brings me to Lourdes.

twenty-two

TO PUT IT in a nutshell, Tom got deathly sick at Lourdes. In fact he damn near didn't pull through, to hear him tell it, though I think thats exaggeration. It pleases him to think so, is the point. To think God's hand was laid on him in that offbeat manner so to speak, rather than the more normal method of arriving there sick and getting better. That type of revelation. I must give fair warning: from here on in you

296

are on your own, to draw your own conclusions. "The belief that he was singled out in this way is important to him and probably typical of him" keeps being Marion's estimate of what happened, and that may very well be what we shall have to settle for. But again, don't look at me. You are strictly on your own. "Man has to live by *some* kind of illusion," Marion says. Check. She doesn't take *it* with a grain of salt, she takes *him* with a grain of salt. What every wife has to do with her husband I guess, and with that saving gift of humor or the union is a dead duck before its hatched. She's got his number when she says God can't be obvious with him, no, he, Tom, is different. Special. But the faith he got as he was being rushed to the hospital, making deathbed promises to God all the way and looking like something the cat dragged in, after arriving there in A–1 shape, in fact fine fettle, is just as important to him as the conversion more simple pilgrims get by arriving there sick and getting cured, which as you know is the more normal procedure in that little town at the foot of the Pyrenees. But he was a sight when he got to the hospital, his eyes bloodshot, his face looking like one of them portraits not aiming at verisimilitude. It was a near thing.

Good thing I was with him. He first invited both his parents along but Elsie refused — probably shrewdly enough thinking father and son together would get more out of such a trip, some much-needed friendship and understanding. And who would take care of the office? I bucked too at first, thinking he was only humoring the oldsters by asking them at all, but it was a token resistance, I was only too tickled to go. The plan was to visit Poland after doing some things like the Riviera (the Palm Beach of the old country), Rome and Athens and so on.

Tom never got to Poland. At Lourdes I could see that the place fascinated him more than I had bargained for. Anybody would be fascinated, believer or non. There all carping has to stop. There the complaints of the intellect are mere niggling. We stayed on, watching the ever renewed streams of pilgrims and attending service in the Church of the Rosary and listening to the singing and even, in the case of Tom, joining in the praying. He haunted the Grotto — or vice versa. He liked to stroll around the crowded town and talk to people till he struck one who could talk fluid English, when he would carry on conversations as long as the traffic would bear, asking the victim about the city and picking his brains about his private life and why he was there. Tom knows very little French himself. Marion is the one who can get along in it but she wasn't with us — yet.

Finally one morning Tom broke down and says, "I'm going to bathe in the water. Why don't you come with me?" I kicked at first, but he finally convinced me that it didn't make any difference what you were, tourists all do it the way they kiss the Blarney Stone or mustn't miss Lake Como. And the church certainly isn't hidebound about it. So I agreed and went with him.

It was the next day during the service at the church that he said, "I don't feel so hot."

Not so hot was right. He was burning up with a fever of a 103.4 (translated into our Fahrenheit, for of course the French use Centigrade). I took his temperature at the hotel with a thermometer he made me buy on the way. When he found out what it was he insisted I call a doctor.

Doctors are easy to come by in Lourdes. The town is practically a medical center, as it would be with people flocking

298

to it from all over the continent and even the world. Though Tom reversing the routine as noted.

What I thought was that he had probably just caught his death in the healing waters. Because forget your picture of a natural rustic spring in which pilgrims go to bathe. The water is now piped through the Grotto wall to a row of brass faucets in a bath house, where you queue up and are herded through by attendants passing out loin cloths which you slap around your naked middle prior to being grasped under the armpits by a couple of other devout muscle men and dipped backwards to your mouth and nose in freezing mountain water. You dress again sopping wet — no towels are provided — and leave. No cures are needed to prove supernatural intervention here: just not getting sick is miracle enough. That water sloshing perpetually around on the floor is never disinfected. Yet people not only immerse themselves in it but sometimes for extra measure scoop up a handful and drink it — with no harmful results. Tom changed all that. *If* that was it. We don't know for sure what went on, but anyway it seemed he was to break new ground — or they would soon be breaking it for our poor Tom, judging by the look of him. He was green as well as hot.

"The doctor is on his way," I told him.

"How about a priest?"

"Oh, cut it out. Don't act like a damn fool. Its probably something you ate."

Because not only are the baths modernized — the town itself is commercialized. So that besides the inevitable little shops selling religious articles the way they sell maple sugar in Vermont and alligator lamps in Florida, there are restaurants and wayside stands serving nothing better than the hamburgers and hotdogs you'd get in a similar tourist center in the U.S.A. None of this matters of course. What matters are the attested cures, on which the church itself keeps a strict and scientific eye and no nonsense. My description of the baths you know to be first-hand. You probably want my reaction to it too while I'm at it.

Well, it's an experience quite unlike anything you can imagine anywhere else. The chief sensation is not being submerged in water as such so much as in a terrific unifying emotion shared with a lot of other half-naked strangers you never saw before and will never see again. Its a profound feeling of being *anonymous,* or merging your little ego in a mystery that makes your own identity unimportant — or that elevates it to importance, whichever way you want to look at it. But I don't want to go into all that here. I just want to add that I also experienced with Tom a few of those lousy French hashhouses, so I was relieved to find some digestive symptoms develop that collaborated my theory it was probably something he ate — if it wasn't the water he drank.

The doctor, who could talk a smattering of English, agreed it might be food poisoning, though the high fever and other symptoms pointed to something else, possibly a virus. He dosed Tom with something or other and told him to stay in bed. A caution hardly necessary, he couldn't get up. Four days later he was still there, and getting worse, so I called the doctor back. He took some blood specimens for tests. None of them showed anything. It was very strange. This doctor was something of a gossip, and the story soon got around about a mysterious ailment striking one of the pilgrims, and one evening a priest did show up with the doctor. They were cronies.

This priest was a plump, red-faced man, and the most cheerful and worldly character I ever met. Someone said he was straight out of Balzac. I'm not sure where thats located, but probably a town near by there. Forget what you hear about how you can always find someone who can speak fluid English everywhere you go. Its not true. But thank God this priest could, not that I could follow him much better than if he was talking French.

"It's undoubtedly psychosomatic in origin," he said, kind of playfully poking Tom in the ribs. He sat on the bed kidding him about it. "That would seem to be since none of your symptoms are chemically verifiable. Yes, obviously psychogenic, the product of some deep emotional disturbance."

"Isn't that in itself mysterious?" Tom says from the bed in his weak condition.

"Tush tush. We are not going to canonize you yet. You need something to eat. We will have a little something sent up, the roast chicken perhaps, and a bottle of the white Burgundy they have here. It's quite excellent."

"I'm not hungry."

"Well, your poor father is, and so are the doctor and I. And meanwhile my advice to all you Americans is, stop punishing yourselves. Leave that to God. He's so much better at it."

The fever went down, but most of the other symptoms remained, with the addition of a sore throat and some mouth sores that broke out. Tom got weaker. The doctor came back, with the priest, around lunchtime again. We had some fish sent up and another bottle of the white Burgundy. Tom didn't eat much and neither did the doctor, but the priest and me tied another one on. He carried his glass to the bed and sat down on it to cheer Tom up.

"The Pope is interested in your case," he said, digging him in the ribs. "It's just what the church needs. These cures get to be a little tiresome. What we need is a miraculous affliction. We'll get you on the Calendar yet." Some of them priests sure can be worldly Joes. You have to give them credit.

Still it seemed to me this one wasn't quite as jolly as the last time. He seemed to be trying to hide his anxiety for Tom's sake. It was then that we moved him to the hospital, where he could better be put under observation. X-rays were taken that showed nothing. Other tests drew blanks too. At this point the priest suggested that the local vet be called in.

I gave him a look of mingled incredulity and disbelief. "Is nothing sacred to you, Father?"

"There is a disease of sheep — and goats — called ecthyma," he said. "It has occasionally been known to affect human beings. It is highly contagious. One of the symptoms is a sore mouth. These lesions he has apparently got. I once saw them on a sheep of a parishioner of mine. It is worth giving a try, nest pa?"

We gave it a try, and drew another blank. It turned out the priest was right about the complaint though. I got a little more confidence in him, and let him talk. He was obviously only too eager to get his teeth into the situation.

"With everything organic ruled out, at least to the best of our poor human knowledge, the likelihood persists that he is suffering from some sort of trauma. An emotional upset. You say he's married. Where is his wife? Why is she not traveling with him instead of his father?"

302

I decided to get Marion on the transatlantic telephone. The connection was a poor one, but her consternation came through over the wire clear enough.

"You mean he's taken *sick* at Lourdes?"

"As a dog. They can't explain it. It baffles medical science. There's got to be some other explanation they think. I wish you was here."

I described some of the symptoms. Then there was a silence, except for a long exhale at the other end, as of someone exasperated about something. Then she said, "What about temperature? Does he have any fever?"

"Yes. It keeps coming and going. It's up to a hundred and two and a half now again."

"I'll be out on the first plane I can get."

Marion arrived two days later. I let her go in to see Tom alone. He was as white as he could be, and getting whiter. She was with him a good hour. I had no idea what went on between them. I knew by now something was amiss. On the way over from the hotel, she had let drop that they had had some kind of trouble — a surprise to me I can tell you, as those things often are. Though I should of tumbled that his going off alone on this Sabbatical had its disturbing side. But Marion looked in good enough spirits when she come out of the room. She said she wanted to go out for a bite to eat and to talk.

"Now I want you to tell me everything that happened since you left home, and even before, for that matter," Marion said. "Leave out nothing. I mean nothing. Did he eat pastrami at some delicatessen. Have you been in a room that was painted recently. Sprayed for insects. I once had a classmate with a toxic condition that they finally traced to some cosmetic she was using. Has he cut his finger. Could it be a tick. Anything. But it's got to be *something*. It's got to have some natural explanation. It doesn't seem to be viral, so it's got to be toxic. Now you go ahead and talk. Tell me everything that's happened and leave out nothing, no matter how trivial or ridiculous it may seem."

I rambled on for a good hour. I told her everything we'd done and every place we'd been since climbing into the limousine for the trip to the Chicago airport. Nothing I could recollect suggested anything. Not that that in itself meant anything. If you were bitten by a tick in the south of France how would you know it?

Nothing came of my night thoughts neither. Marion and I had breakfast at which she again picked my brains, then the same kind of session at lunch at a very good restaurant. Eating my food I felt sorry for Tom, and said so. "Wonder what he's having back at the hospital," I said, "and whether he can eat all right with that tooth of his."

"Tooth? What tooth?"

So I related a filling that had fallen out of his molar the night before we sailed, in New York. There was no chance to have a dentist take care of it, and he didn't want to trust a ship's dentist, if any. He remembered a friend who had patched himself up in similar circumstances by going into a Rexall Drug Store and simply buying a bottle of good old plain everyday glue. That did the trick so well that the friend didn't need a dentist till it was time for his regular checkup. The filling stayed right in. Tom decided on the same kind of do-it-yourself.

"What kind of glue did he use?"

"Oh, some kind of model airplane glue he picked up in a store in the hotel arcade."

"The kind it's dangerous even to sniff?"

She got him out of bed and to a local dentist, who took the filling out, cleaned the cavity and refilled it properly. The next day he was feeling a good deal better. But Tom's story was — *he'd been beginning to perk up before he went to the dentist*, or he'd never been able to drag himself out.

So there you have it. The upshot of it is that the issue has remained forever in doubt. Would he of continued to improve if the tooth hadn't been taken care of? And if he had, what would that prove? Was the toxicity wearing off of its own accord, or he beginning to develop a resistance to it? Was toxicity the basic cause? The doctor we had called said it could be, another we asked doubted it, a third shrugged. The priest was completely skeptical. He said the glue probably had something in it that was poisoning him, and that was that as far as he was concerned, a man of faith.

Marion prefers to let Tom think he was singled out for some mysterious affliction "somewhere on the shadowy border between mind and body," as he put it, because it's good for him to think so for a variety of complex reasons she doesn't even want to go into. That he got sick from drinking the curative waters he rejects — that would be a naturalistic explanation. I've heard the word allergy used. To what? Something he ate or something that was eating him? He seemed to me to pick up damn fast at the sight of Marion. But if you then begin fiddling with the idea that his symptoms were concocted to fetch her, you are then faced with having to explain how an organism can behave in such a miraculously complicated fashion — which leaves you back where you started.

My own principle is never to look a gift horse in the mouth. I went on to Poland, but Tom insisted on flying back with Marion. Which was just as well. I didn't know what shape they were in, but it looked good on the surface. And it looked good when I got back home after a tour of parental birthplaces and visits to Warsaw and Cracow. Like I say, Tom prefers not to talk about it, but once in a while the subject comes up and he'll quote something, like Hamlet to the effect that there are more things in heaven and earth than we dream in our philosophies. Or a poet I never heard of named Ezra Pound. The lines from him that Tom likes to quote are:

For God, our God is a gallant foe that playeth behind the veil.
Whom God deigns not to overthrow hath need of triple mail.

Whatever that means. We get two deliveries a day, which seems enough for anybody, and what thats got to do with it I don't know, like I say. Not that those two claim to understand quite what they're talking about half the time either, with all their education. But its better left that way. Open. Maybe the whole thing is neurotic, maybe true faith. Certainly its better than Nothingness. Oh give us the hand of God, if only the back of it. That general idea. But in the end you do get weary of trying to dope things out that you can't. Then we cry with Shakespeare, "For God's sake leave us sit upon the ground and tell sad stories of the death of kings." That'll do it for a while. Then back you come to flogging your brain over matters again.

If you want my final opinion on the mystery of life and all

that, I can give it to you in a nutshell. The universe is like a safe to which there is a combination. But the combination is locked up in the safe.